GARDENING AT NIGHT

Diane Awerbuck lives and writes in Cape Town. This is
her first novel.

Diane Awerbuck

GARDENING AT NIGHT

VINTAGE

Published by Vintage 2004

2 4 6 8 10 9 7 5 3 1

Copyright © Diane Awerbuck 2003

Diane Awerbuck has asserted her right under the Copyright, Designs and Patents Act, 1988 to be identified as the author of this work

This book is sold subject to the condition that it shall not by way of trade or otherwise, be lent, resold, hired out, or otherwise circulated without the publisher's prior consent in any form of binding or cover other than that in which it is published and without a similar condition including this condition being imposed on the subsequent purchaser

Grateful acknowledgement is made to the following for permission to reproduce copyright material: to Hodder & Stoughton for the Stephen King quote on page vi, to Ralph Rabie for the quote on page 171, to André Le Toit for the quote from *Afrikaans My Darling* on page 239, and to Gallo Music Publishers for the REM quote on page 212. All efforts have been made to trace holders of copyright material and any errors or omissions will be gladly rectified in future editions.

First published in Great Britain in 2003 by
Secker & Warburg

Vintage
Random House, 20 Vauxhall Bridge Road,
London SW1V 2SA

Random House Australia (Pty) Limited
20 Alfred Street, Milsons Point, Sydney
New South Wales 2061, Australia

Random House New Zealand Limited
18 Poland Road, Glenfield,
Auckland 10, New Zealand

Random House (Pty) Limited
Endulini, 5A Jubilee Road, Parktown 2193,
South Africa

The Random House Group Limited Reg. No. 954009
www.randomhouse.co.uk

A CIP catalogue record for this book
is available from the British Library

ISBN 0 099 28735 8

Papers used by Random House are natural, recyclable products made from wood grown in sustainable forests. The manufacturing processes conform to the environmental regulations of the country of origin

Printed and bound in Denmark by
Nørhaven Paperback, Viborg

To my father the failure, who never could get
Reader's Digest *to publish his dog stories*

To my mother, near and far

And to Gordon, because he sells she shells
on the see-saw

We count the birds in the sky and will not turn from the window when we hear the footsteps behind us as something comes up the hall; we say yes, I agree that clouds often look like other things – fish and unicorns and men on horseback – but they are really only clouds. Even when the lightning flashes inside them we say they are only clouds and turn our attention to the next meal, the next pain, the next breath, the next page. This is how we go on.

Stephen King, *Bag of Bones*

The poor white here, though he belongs to the soil, has no roots in the soil. He is by nature a wanderer, with none of that conservative love of place which makes to many men one spot on earth beloved above all others.

Pauline Smith, *Desolation*

You don't stare at the sun and you don't stare at your own death either. You do gain something from these dramatic painful experiences but you are also diminished. There's something in you that becomes permanently sad and a little posthumous. And there's something in you that's permanently strengthened or deepened. It's called having a life.

Susan Sontag, interviewed after the
September 11 attacks

Spy on me, baby, you satellite.

Tom Jones with Mousse T, *Sex Bomb*

PART ONE

HEN-AND-CHICKENS

Nor Any Drop to Drink

There is no sea in Kimberley. We make do with drunken every-other-Sundays on the river, frightening small children and trying to waterski barefoot. The water is cold Milo but not fit for human consumption, as the sign says. There is always a capsized hand on its surface, clutching a beer snaffled from the bar. There are no ladies of the lake, or kings to be called, but there are mutant catfish that live on the bottom of the pan, whiskers trawling for white feet in the water. Eating them is a bad idea; they taste of river mud and lost scuba divers with too little oxygen in their tanks.

The river is a place of beginnings and bad behaviour. In Kimberley, these things are difficult to get away with, and everyone aspires to them. It's the desiccation that does it; the fear of being as insubstantial as the dust devils or the duiker. Mostly this ends badly, with mothers crying and saying, We trusted you, and days spent closed up in bedrooms, gated from friends and barefoot café trips and movies – but never school and church and washing up. Sisters look at you with big eyes, and there are Sunday lunches on stilts when everyone at the table sits very still because the phone rings, and an Afrikaans stepfather presides over the mental pleas for it not to be anyone for you. Pass the jammerlappie.

Out here is the quiet passage before we get to the reservoir and the begging fingers of trees over angry ducks. We shoot film like bullets, heads yanking backwards to catch the last flight in the rush above. Drifting with the engine off is a stolen moment from *Apocalypse Now*. I am always grateful to leave alive – no island and

TV crews to survive, but still the sunburn and thick tongue of expeditions. We are always looking for something over our shoulders. Too young to drive cars, they let us control the boats. It's always the moms who come to fetch us, trying not to seem tight-lipped at the hooting and sniggering in the back of the Kombi, asking what the clinking sound is in the tog bag. 'Towels,' says Elias. Snorts, as the ruts in the dust road jolt us out of teenage space, where you can be hit by asteroids but not parents.

We went back once, about three years after school, and the boys remembered where they'd buried a bottle of Tassies, convinced in the stupor of the time that this was the only way it wouldn't be found by the other fox boys, with their noses to the ground and their tails bushy with suspense. It had fermented. Obviously. Now it was brandy. Elias poured a capful on the ground, for the gods. Perhaps being Catholic and Lebanese makes you more conscious of the workings of the infinite. And they drank. When the minister and his family came out later to sail their boat, we said that the boy lying under the tree had food poisoning. I think that he probably didn't believe us. I think that holy men hear an awful lot of bullshit in the line of duty. Especially from boys who had to go to hospital that night to damp down fires and alcohol poisoning.

Over the ground, under the sun, boem tiddy boem

When I was fifteen I stopped waiting for the Second Coming. My mother has never stopped. She believes in love. There have been second comings and second marriages and second chances, but no saviours. I believe in the redeeming power of margheritas, especially two or three margheritas.

4

We settle back now into our separate lounges to await the Apocalypse instead. The Four Horsemen are our friends; we know them well. Their working names are War, Pestilence, Famine and Death. They are always wanted, more wanted than Osama bin Laden and Billy the Kid. Their lives are busy ones, chock-a-block with fulfilling prophecies made by nursery school teachers and filling out prescriptions scrawled by white-coat doctors. It's a tight schedule. No wonder they want to put their feet up, let the blood run back to their mythical hearts. When they knock my mother always answers. They pop by for drinks; they stay to watch the news with their dusty boots on the table, which I am never allowed to do.

This story, then, must be about the foolishness of growing things that can be blasted or stung or struck by lightning and other forces of nature, about green things, growing secretly in the desert. A story of faith in people or at least in gardens, contrary or not.

I en Jy: Young and Tender

The Pan-Pan Café in 1984 may be a garden, but it's one of coins and cement, where you plant your money and harvest white bread that you slice yourself, juddering with the blade on the machine in a way no plough ever did. My mother makes me go and I don't want to, because she only ever wants milk and bread. So much for a Canaan where the shop is on the ground floor under the flats above, with their sheets of steel on the balconies so the babies don't fall. There is always the sound of TV, and sometimes the daughters of the café slink out and stare at the trip-trapping flat-foot below, with their hair like black flags and just as mute.

On top of the café is a huge metal trolley, sliced lengthways so that it emerges from the wall. If it had to go back to its old job it would be useless because the rubble would fall out. They used them at the Big Hole before the century started and all the miners in the world flocked like mean and thirsty ants to the diggings. Army ants, that ate everything they saw because going around it was too much effort. You made the black men with their black monkey-limbs go down the ropes and fill the buckets, which were hauled up and into the pan-pan cars. After that you would sieve the rubble until you hallucinated water or anything else that would trickle and shine and make you a millionaire. The sad thing is that it did make men millionaires; it made my grandfather and his childhood friend rich. Miners had to eat. And there is no saltwater fish in Kimberley.

They caught and dried them on the coast, and trekked back before there were cars to feed the miners dessicated mermaids, to show them how to chew something and spit the bones out, to use the resources around them and leave the rest for scavengers. Fishers of men.

But eventually fish starts to stink, and then they found that they couldn't walk on water, so they made a synagogue, and it was good. There wasn't place to hide in the corners and Kimberley grew around buying and selling, even though the mines gave out and there were always black birds circling overhead and grown men crying in bars over diamonds they had seen and couldn't have, over the name of the bar which mocked them in the day and at night: the Star of the West. And selling themselves, and selling themselves.

The pavement is cracked, so that if you stare up at the daughters of the café and don't watch your toes maybe you'll smash the Coke bottle and then where will you be? Cut hands and wet face on the diamond shards on the pavement, and no treasure toffees from the trade-in. Be very careful, like an explorer going over a map where the seas boil and dragons surface to sneer at you. Be careful as a man sailing from his motherland. I hop from Livingstone stone to paving stone, presuming ballet will save my balance, never caring about breaking my mother's back. If you do it this way you don't have to look up at the Afrikaans boys on the other side of the road either, with their bakore scooping up the fee-fi-fo-fum of English feet on the cement and their voices too big for their bodies, each with a farmer inside him struggling to get out and making bumps on the body to do it. Bicep, calf.

The café's insides smell of damp and spilt things. There are only ever two of each product on the shelves, both past the sell-by date, and this is what it must mean to be a spinster. Canned, so that the air will never get to you, and faded like Fresh Garden Peas; they always look bright on the label but inside they are sweet and mushier than any pudding. Just desserts. They'll rot your teeth as surely as sugar.

The family is Greek and its downstairs daughters are gold, worth their weight at the till where they clink and chime. They are one-armed bandits who will cheat you of change if you're mean to them. Their eyes are chocolate and their skin is honey; every sweet cliché is true, and Damascus is miracles but it's also nougat and this is how we know they are secret princesses. They clearly don't eat the peas. Or sleep with one under the mattress, either.

The milk is at the back of the shop in a steel tank like a rhino, greyly without dents and harder than your soles will ever be even though you try and try each summer to bake them on the tar. You will never get it right because your mother makes you wear shoes. The milk froths out from the metal cow under the hands of the milk meid, white under pink palms, into the container you have to bring yourself. They say it's cheaper this way.

At the till they are talking to each other in Greek, with their haughty nostrils and straining throats; sometimes they have to do the traditional dances at fêtes, and it's only then that you see them human, sweat and swirl. But now they are ignoring me, so I go over to the racks where they will let you flip through the magazines that aren't in plastic covers.

There are old photo-stories about detectives, with Afrikaans titles blaring over the rope-burned girls on the covers, their breasts pushing against their blouses like giants' sweets you want to open. They never die in the stories; the detective with his Magnum moustache and his stovepipe trousers always frees them from the Bad Man in the Black Hat. And for this the girls are always grateful.

Today there is a game ranger story and the hero wears a cheetah-skin hat-band. He carries a revolver and he looks familiar and when he points it at the baddie I know who he is. My mother always says that before he came back to Kimberley and met her, my father lived in Joburg with women who painted his portrait over and over again. One of the paintings sits in our garage, twice as large as life and flaking, making up for his not being there. She painted it on the wrong side of the canvas; she painted him in reverse.

She was not the only one who thought she could keep his soul by sketching it. The hero in the old magazine is my father; in stages he is handsome-and-happy and handsome-and-angry; his face is always smooth. I don't have enough money to buy it. I am the miners in the bar with their one-drink love and their promises to pay. I am the trolley on the building with my insides trickling out.

Blood is Thicker

There are different kinds of madness and this is something we all know. Sometimes it shows on the outside, when our bodies boil up against us and froth out in bubbles of badness between the teeth. Like rabies. Like love spells gone wrong. Double, double, toil and trouble. Sometimes, and more often, it only stays inside, and hurts and hurts; sometimes you have to show people how much this is, as if they don't already know, as if they can't already tell from the nails bitten down to the pink, from the slash marks scratched on the wrist. These are our red boundaries: so far and no further am I prepared to go.

In my family there is a rich and smelly madness that charms our children, a treasure trove of wet red jewels that we pack carefully away for our trousseaus, that we pass on intact like heirlooms. We knew this early on when there were wars, especially ones where germs and Germans abounded in places over the sea our fathers worried about.

In the East London rectory they have salt on their side, and prayers, which don't quite seem to be doing the trick. Or maybe they just aren't in the quantities that would make a difference. A truckload of salt. A deluge of prayers. And a place to stand in the middle of all this, of course, with dry feet and dry eyes.

Being the eldest is hard. Being the eldest on rations is worse, measuring out my mother's and her sisters' adolescence in flat scones and unhappy choices. Would you like butter or jam on your bread? Never both, because we have to think of others. Inside her oldest sister there is a witch as well as a girl in a tower, and she doesn't know which one to free. She makes two plaits of her hair and cuts them off with the kitchen scissors. She is tired of baking, of being careful with the salt, of only being allowed to use the wooden spoon for mixing when her mother uses it to smack naughty children.

And then she's sorry that she's made the wrong choice, and now no prince is going to be able to reach her, so she clips the plaits back on, but they are cold on her shoulders. She goes outside and gets her bicycle, and she free-wheels down the hill with the wind in her hair. This is better but not enough.

When my mother comes home she finds her spike-headed sister pouring salt all over the kitchen floor, to kill the TB germs, she says. When they stare at her she pours faster and then stops. 'I'll never be able to get them all,' she says, and turns to go up to her room with her head like a cactus. The others kneel down with the grains making patterns on their knees, and sweep and sweep, doing penance. They have to throw the salt away, of course, and that is why you can't open your eyes when you swim in the sea near East London. It is too warm and salty and the sharks know to come here. It is full of the tears of sisters, and surely blood must follow.

Trademark

Anne is in the bathroom, in her new bikini, many years before she will ever be my mother. It is not enough that she has a new body to go with it, and breasts that are pressed into dangerous blue torpedo shapes that will break the waves in the East London seas, frightening the sharks. On her left thigh there is a series of birthmarks in a row, descending. They make a velvet Japan, they make her body the old world. And who will ever want to explore that in the dark? Not even Prince Henry the Navigator would be brave enough to go there, to places that are rough instead of smooth, to negotiate this terrain that would require a tank to tame it properly. So she is crying.

There is only one bathroom in the rectory. Her father knocks on the door with his pipe in his mouth and the paper in his hand; there are netherworlds of his own that need discovering behind the door. She sniffs under her torpedoes, thinks about only ever being able to swim on her side, like a lopsided mermaid, like a pearl diver with nothing to bring to the surface through the foam.

He knocks again; he needs to get into where she is for both their sakes. His insides and her sinuses bubble and groan. Each one is quiet, thinking about whose need is greater. 'Annie,' he says. 'What's wrong?' And she opens the door because she always has to him; her mother is scrunched up, sewing elastic into their old panties, or baking cakes for tea, or cleaning the church in stiff strokes that make her arms strong but not flexible enough to hug. Her father's hands are different; they write boarding school letters in calligraphy, they fiddle bits of radios together to send sounds out from his domestic island, they are hands that have antennae. Perhaps because they do not wash up they are not rough, so that when they stroke little girls they are comforting.

'Daddy,' she says, with her wet mouth and her wet eyes, 'I hate my birthmark,' and below her bikini line it flushes darker and rougher because it is angry at what she says, or perhaps because it feeds on unhappiness. He bends down, runs his fingers lightly across the public sandpaper. He looks up at her and says, 'Anne, it makes you special. This is how I would know it was you if I ever had to find you in the dark.' And this makes sense to her. She likes it especially that he would be able to find her if she ever wandered away, like a miner with a light on his hard hat, searching for something precious. It means she will never be lost.

Nature Studies

My mother moves far away, to Grahamstown, because she wants to be a teacher. She wants to leave her closeted heart-attack father and her mother with the hardening arteries behind in the rectory. Every evening they have to go to arrange the cut flowers in the church and then her father closes himself in his study with notes for his sermons and tiny paintbrushes to wash the red and green genitals of plants. She wants to wear beige stockings to lectures in the daytime and smoke cigarettes in the Eastern Cape gardens at night. Everywhere there will be the smell of pineapples, sweet and sharp as razorblades on the tongue, sweet and sharp like the marijuana they hear about but never see. The soil will not grow anything else, not even mustard seeds.

The girls must be careful about their bare legs and self-tan, their lungs and nicotine, because the nuns at the teaching college have the noses of bloodhounds, and the sad eyes too. Bloodshot, hang-dog, they pad on their paws with their nails clicking in the corridors and down the steps into the night gardens, where there are unpleasant interludes with drunk Rhodes University boys, who come to piss on the rosebushes and shout things up to the girls until Sister Virg swirls out with her smell of sanctity and her fingers lisping on the back of the neck. It's a real mood-killer.

Inside the college is more dangerous; there are no watchdogs to growl at the fleshy older girls in their blue eyeshadow and their curlers, each feature on their faces smudged until they bloom like dandelions. Seedy. They take away your first name as part of the initiation; they force the new girls into talent shows and beauty competitions where they point and laugh low in their cigarette throats. They are doing the new girls a favour. They are showing them how easy it is to make yourself smooth and beautiful as soap when underneath you are a pot-scourer, a pineapple, a cactus ride. Some of the older girls drop out before they have their diplomas; the Rhodes boys marry them and take them away from the everlasting smell of pineapples and make the morning plucking and brushing worthwhile and forever. This is the trouble with deception; it must be continued.

The girls who stay behind find other ways to escape. They learn about fermentation, about things sugary and rich that decay when left to themselves too long. They cut up all the pineapples they can buy from the twitchy man at Spuds and leave the chunks in buckets. They add sugar and yeast. They see that it is good. For days they leave the buckets in the closets in the corridor, until there is fizzing. They know that it is time when the nuns sweep like brooms through the corridors and say, 'Girlss, what iss that ssmell?' and they always point and say, in the voices of the faithful, 'It's her new deodorant, sister.'

My mother and her first-year friends drink the pineapple beer. It makes them funny, it makes them wise. They will never have to worry about shaving their legs again. It also makes them brave, so that when they need to find the toilet they wobble out into the afternoon corridor and do not think about dropping their pineapple voices. Their feet are disconnected; they want to stay rooted to the parquet, but their bodies want to move on. They find that they cannot walk down the stairs the way they would like to, the way a Hitchcock heroine would in the first half hour of the film, before things go screamingly wrong in the sky, in the shower. They must bump down instead on the bones of their backsides and my mother goes first, like Pooh approaching the reader behind Christopher Robin, bumpity-bump, right to the bottom of the stairs, bumpity-bump, right down to the feet of the sister standing like a crow on a telephone wire, waiting to peck at Tippi Hedren. 'Miss Doe,' says the crow, 'come and ssee me in my offisse.'

I Want to Hold Your Hand

Let's start with the army, because that is where my mother's-friend-Helen's-boyfriend has gone, far away and full of Bloemfontein and irony because there are neither flowers nor fountains in Tempe, where he has been sent, no dusky maidens with goblets of sherbet and lamps that house genies. But there are boeremeisies who are plenty willing to do some rubbing and requests, so when Helen gets a teaching post in Kimberley to be close to him, Anne does too.

And this is not so bizarre. They have always been together, from their childhoods in halter necks and equally strangling families where it seems that everyone is not loved the same, to the matching Beatles lockets over their black polonecks that come later. Anne loves Paul. Helen loves John. And nobody loves Ringo. When they walk along the East London pier in the safe evenings, the army boys on leave call out to them and sing, 'Oh dear, what can I do? Baby's in black, and I'm feeling blue' and the girls shout back insults and laugh.

Until one day Helen doesn't, and the boy who stops her has the eyes of a magician and a mouth like a sailor, and Anne knows that this one will be around for longer than a kiss – Helen loves Tony – and so she goes home for supper. In the lounge the budgies in their cages flutter; they know there is something coming.

Oh, but nobody told them how hot it would be in Kimberley, how many Ginger Squares they would have to drink at the Halfway House Hotel, where they got past the building regulation of a six-foot wall around any drinking establishment by digging a trench five feet deep and burying all but a foot of it. Men seemed nicer behind this wall, doing tricks with their hands, mimicking trumpets and playing air guitars and smiling all the while so that their teeth seemed less sharp in this celestial band. And even when they were being rude and changed the words to, 'I want to hold your gland', daytime and divorce were things that could only ever happen to ugly sober people. And the girls did not want to exchange these newbrighthot nights for The Beatles and their old lives.

So when a man named Jack leans her against the bar and says, 'I have seen you somewhere before,' Anne lets him guess where. And back then she does not know that he means *in another life*, that he means she is his *soulmate*, that he means to take her home and make her have tense teas with his Jewish parents who had named him Jack to make him fit in, and called him Jock, because maybe sounding Scottish is even better. She, in her English and German heart, does not know this. She does not know that they are about to produce two children, cosmic fruit salads and dimples all round. She looks down at her rope sandals with the daisies between her toes, and she smiles. She lets him hold her hand.

Where he remembers her from, although not in the uppermost layer of his mind, is the newspaper. The *Diamond Fields Advertiser* ran a photograph of these two adventurous women, Miss Doe and Miss du Toit, because they are the first women in South Africa to wear pants suits in the classroom. In the picture their unmarried hands are folded demurely, and under their tight smiles there is a frightened triumph. It's hard to be brave and sober in the daylight. (Although the line had been drawn at the daisy sandals, when the inspectress, snorkelling down at her from a great height, everything about her silver and grey, tarnished hair, spectacles, teeth, a museum of old silver, winking with the knowledge of the correct cutlery and other gems from Mrs Beeton, said, 'Miss Doe, you do have the prettiest toes, but those sandals are *not* appropriate for teaching.')

So in a sense they have met before. And he is no pretty boy

with a dark suit and a fringe and a mouth that makes a perfect O when he sings, ooh ooh, but he is dark and pretty in other ways, in other ways. And when he asks her to drive away with him, she does, because she knows that he will never hurt her on purpose.

He drives her over dirt roads and tarred ones, where the duiker run in front of the Citroën and no policemen stop them. Because they are doing nothing wrong. And when he drives down to the river she is ready to give herself up to him because this, also, is nothing wrong, and she understands that all the fending off of the fumbling hands in movie theatres has only been a way for her to get to this: that even the captain of the swimming team who had tried to get his fingers inside her baby-powdered thirteen-year-old bra had been part of the plan. Even though he was disgusted when she pulled away and ran home, shouting at her that she was green. Even though he showed his fingers to her brother the next day and said to everyone on the playground, 'Anne Doe puts baby powder in her bra.'

As Jack removes the daisies from her toe cleavage he sees that she has the prettiest feet. He thinks that he would like to try and make her some sandals in his secret workshop, where his Business Science parents will not let him spend enough time; he will make her Cinderella. And then he will hold her hand for a long time, in marriage and in awe.

Los My Kind

The passage is tiled in green and grey linoleum. Anne knows this because she has spent a very long time looking at it on her slow way to the Neo-Natal Ward, where she's mixed her DNA with a man who isn't here. Jock got carried away with the cigars and brandy and back-slapping, and his heart is currently thumping away the pattern of midday coma, heavy and familiar as a priest's hug. The woman behind her shuffles just as slowly, slowly as a sleep-walker. Her flesh in the hospital gown is a container of jelly left over at a children's party. Anne speeds her slippers up. She can cover the area faster – all those bum-walking exercises on the afternoon carpet are paying off – and will get to that door first.

The product of this experiment is tiny and topped with black hair. An isosceles nose from the pink cocoon; this is how she can pick out which one is hers in the cabbage patch of babies in bassinets. Eeeny meeny miny mo, matched up with the name bracelet on her wrist. *Mev. Awerbuck*. Plus one. A fresh start, worth the endless drunken grinding at three in the morning when she has school the next day. Worth the rent vanished as surely as if he'd stood at the edge of the Big Hole and thrown the notes up into the air so that they would have floated down like origami gliders. It may even be worth the four stitches from the episiotomy, although she will shudder in her kitchen when she has to chop liver and she will never feel the same way about cutting bacon with the scissors.

The shuffling is louder. For a fat woman this follower can move awfully fast. She is panting. But that is perhaps because she also has something to get to. They both halt, winners tied at the Public Hospital Paralympics. Anne marvels that they are both here. This woman up close has the fat of baked beans and polony on white toast, the grease behind the stove. She smiles at Anne, a grimace of shared womanpain and achievement. It says, I am just like you. Two of her teeth are missing in that wet pink bridge to her gullet; she is a plump slow seagull, circling for scraps. The smell of fish. Anne smiles back politely in her daughter-of-an-Anglican-priest sort of way and thanks her stars that they don't live in Beaconsfield; West End *just* skirts respectable territory, and it's fine if you don't think about the graveyard. Surely goodness and mercy will follow me all my days.

'Seun of meisie?' Oh God. Now she wants to make conversation. Perhaps she will spray spit on Anne and she will endure it in her politeness. They will have something in common beyond their bracelets.

'Meisie. En joune?'

'Myne ook.'

The two take their stitches over to the bassinets, where the curled offspring of about thirty new Kimberley mothers lie tight as fists, genderless. Anne gently reaches over, the pull between them as sure as daylight, as clean as an OMO advert, and slides her motherhands under the bundle with the Cleopatra nose. The resemblance to the father is unmistakable.

She turns and beats her way back down the corridor, the feeding drum starting up between her ears. She is focused only on the thrum of blood and milk. It is then that the thumps start up again behind her, and at first she ignores them, because surely this is only the sound of her new heart with its face to the outside world. But then there is no mistaking the panic and pleading as someone shrieks, 'Los my kind!'

She pivots slowly, carefully, to face this woman who is real and near in the sharp sweat of her exertion. Anne is prepared to stare her down until she dissolves into a puddle that can be stepped over, quick as Christopher Robin on a rainy day or until rubber-soled help comes. Surely there must be some kind of security here; isn't there a mental ward? The passage stays empty. She must make absolutely sure that she is in the right. Even so, there is a slow creeping dread in her spiderfingers that fiddle the Elastoplast wristband to check the name written there in firm nurse ballpoint. *Baba Meiring*.

Acid Gran

My father's mother is crazier than she should be for a Jewish chemist not allowed to practise her trade because babies have more value than compounds. The stories filter down to me, percolated and left too long exposed to oxygen, so that they are too bitter to drink. She hates the physical, the grief and queasy meanderings of menstruation, of sex. She stomps and mutters as she washes out rags or refuses to get up at night to feed her new-borns. She takes to wearing no bra and sitting out on the stoep in the sun, so that it finally takes pity on her and kindly shrivels her out of her old snake face and into a new one, putting her out of the misery of her real features.

My mother has to be introduced to these parents. It can't be avoided, too late for anyone to stop them because she has already traded all her sexual secrets for the engagement ring with its tiny diamond. He is in debt twice over, once to the jewellery shop and once again to her for taking him on, with his grey front tooth where his brother's spade hit him and his Harley-Davidson belt buckle draped over her chair.

In the lounge they all sit, awkwardly watching the exits and praying for bad weather so they will have something in common. When my grandfather goes to the kitchen to fetch more Marie biscuits to pacify the slobbering dogs, Ettie leans forward and says, 'Don't do it. Don't marry him.' My mother rattles her cup. 'Why?' His mother says, 'Because he's a shit. He'll never do anything good with his life.' They leave soon after, Ettie shaking her head and my mother all thin lips and love, ready to make up for everything else he doesn't have.

So you could say that my mother had it coming, that she knew what she was in for when she went round with her own first-born son, to show him off to a grandmother who had long ago disowned him, as she had disinherited her son when he insisted on marrying a Christian. Back again to the house of the father, the trail from her last visit cold. Ettie sits in her shorts in the evening air which is thick and sugary as boarding school jam as it oozes through the fruit trees in the garden, each one her own planting. Trees are better than children; they bear fruit in your own lifetime.

My mother leans over the gate, not daring to unlatch it, clad in Christianity and a maternity frock, calling, 'Don't you want to see your grandson?' and holding him out here where he is an Aztec sacrifice. Ettie rises slowly and comes over, treading deliberately on the flat stones of the path burning her feet, taking her own loon-time, her breasts low in her T-shirt and far from her heart.

Ettie pauses, looks down at the wizened bundle, prune face to prune face, and says, 'He looks like a monkey.' My mother turns tail and rushes back to the car, her hands turned to paws scrabbling at the handle as if the prophecy has come true. She has expected tea and Marie biscuits, at the very least. Ettie turns and limps back down the path, sits down, carries on reading her secret signs of misery in the clouds. She never finds out that her husband sneaks out every Saturday morning in his safari suit and Brylcreem to buy chocolates and visit his grandchildren, not knowing where to look when it's time for breastfeeding.

Ace of Spades

In the garden my sundown mother Anne squats; no hat and no gloves. She likes to feel the dirt under her fingernails. This is dreamtime, where nobody gets skin cancer and the earthworms are your friends. For every new house we move to she makes a garden, lugging sacks of stinging fertiliser and wheeling red soil in the wheelbarrow. Squares of dying grass lie ready to be transplanted. My mother is God, playing with her clay. Other mothers make gingerbread men; she makes Adams and Eves and lays them on the ground. If she could breathe life into them she would, but she settles for saving her lips to tell us not to walk there.

She stands and waters the lawn by hand, mother radar searching out her cats and dogs and children, all the while the smell of the thirsty ground in her nose. Inside all is well and the new baby – to go with the new lawn – is sleeping his dribbly sleep with Sheba the ridgeback guarding the cot. Out in the road Susan comes walking in her slippers from her madam's house. She has come to visit Johanna, and they will gabble and drink tea stiff with sugar from their enamel mugs. She is an army of one, neat in her apron that is always faded more than her doek. She opens the gate, as she has so often before, storming the citadel, hooting her greetings. She turns to close it behind her and so she only hears the furious click of nails on paving and the growl of a big dog with an enemy caught in its nose and eyes but not between its teeth.

My mother looks up from pressing plants into their proper places when she hears the sound of a woman screaming, high and hard so that it hurts her suburban ears. What she sees is Susan clinging to the gate with the bitch's head fastened to her calf. She sees the silver stretch marks behind the knee. Blood spatters as the dog tries to shake her from side to side. By the time my mother manages to pull Sheba away there is no more screaming. Susan is saying, 'It's all right, it's all right,' over and over again in English. Sheba has been dragged inside, where she goes placidly back to the cot, licking her black doglips at her job well done. On the path lies a small lump of what could be raw steak.

Susan is taken to hospital, and after that she will limp for weeks. Underneath her brown stockings her calf is a funny

21

shape. Sweeping is hard, especially under carpets. My mother goes back to gardening in the evenings, banking boundary bricks between the grass and the flowerbeds. This side, that side. Inside the house the baby begins to cry.

Houston, We Have a Problem

My mother and a friend of hers have gone to see *Condorman* at the drive-in. My father is at the pub, where women with raccoon eyes press themselves against him on their way to the Ladies where, if there were a bouncer, they would not get in. I'm in the back seat with my brother and his steel-wheeled Matchbox cars, bathed and shortie-pyjamaed. He's making me crazy because he keeps running the green car over my arm. 'Dooon't,' I niggle, knowing he won't stop, knowing where those cars have been. 'Mooom, make him stop.' She leans back and tries to separate us back-handed with her hisses and I squinch as far away from him as I can.

We cruise for parking away from the potholes. Maybe all the moving and sighing in cars over the years has worn the tar thin and bumpy. We test the curly-tailed transmitters next to each parking space until there is as little distortion as possible. We've brought the remains of Grampa's chocolates, which are only still around because I refuse to eat the thin white slabs; we don't go near the fluorescent restaurant unless we need to use the toilets.

As soon as they're settled in I jump out with my bare legs into the cold and crackling night, walking on the moon, with the loose stones crunching and the air so still it feels like you're alone. The only sound is the dull murmur of voices and tinny notes squawking from the speakers as they work their wire guts into space. I don't have a trailing flag for my country or even a brother for once, because the roundabout makes him puke.

The drive-in has its own playground, done out in tarmac under the eyes of sadistic stars and cheap managers. You have to really *want* to play here, and we do. There are always about ten kids scattered and crawling over the equipment, chunky Afrikaans boys who do the running to power the roundabout, and girls hanging upside down with their panties showing. And everywhere is dark, with only the restaurant lights twinking out at us, like the mother ship, reminding us that we have somewhere to go back to.

I get off the roundabout because I want to go faster; there are only three of us left on it, and no one wants to do the pushing. Round we go, panting and over-stepping, and I hop back on, except that my foot catches underneath and I slip on the gravel and fall into the damp underworld. Over me the roundabout scrapes, once, and then again. I see its bottom for the first time and it is black and smells sharp, like weeds. There could be *anything* there, waiting to catch our ankles, and we never thought to look.

I limp and cry my way back to the car, my side burning through my pyjama top. My mother looks at the wound and says, 'Well, I don't think you'll need stitches. Just lie down in the back.' So I do, pushing my feet extra hard against my sleeping brother and snuffling into my pillow against the door. On the screen Condorman swoops down in his fiery cloak to smash through office windows and save the girl.

Passover

Half and half, I am sent to a Jewish nursery school, where cork-heeled gentile ladies feed us matzos and play shabbat on hot Fridays before naptime. I am used to being part of the screaming boys' gang, noses running in time with our Bata feet, our cardigans falling and our ears cold with the wind rushing past. I manage to live quite happily here, a refugee from the girls' camp, not quite having got the hang of dollies and being too quick to poke at people with the scissors, too good at whistling. They huddle in a corner and stare accusingly at me, their fingers itchy with spankings and apron strings under the guidance of Bronwyn with her pursy little mouth and poppy Pekingese eyes. They scare me but I know where the power lies; I know I can be a boy if I want.

The burst pipe in the corner of the garden has made the boys decide to build a dam, but once they start digging Fat Hilton reckons we can dig a tunnel under the fence. We could reach China. I don't see how China could be under the synagogue but I don't say it. They scrabble in the mud with their stubby boyfingers like Robotech claws and I hang around on the edges, kicking away stones, because they don't seem to mind. The sun beats on us and I think of that story about the bet between the North Wind and the Sun about who could make the traveller take his jacket off. The boys pull their mothered laundry shirts off – Sjoe, this is hard work, hey? – and dig faster. We know that what they are doing is going to get them into trouble.

I also want to take my shirt off. I'm the only one left standing; our chests are identical, flat and warm and sharply kid-white in the sunlight, tiny nipples like one cent pieces, not valuable enough for anyone to want to pick up yet. On holiday my mother lets me wear only bikini bottoms and my brother would only look if I grew fur. But these are the days before we have seen *I Was a Teenage Werewolf*.

The girls totter over and ask us what we're doing, heads to one side like budgies. Bronwyn's eyes get even bigger than they usually are and she says, 'I'm gonna *tell* that you have your shirt off, Diane, and you are going to be in *trouble*.' With that they scatter, all flapping arms and ruffled feathers and the next thing I know there is a cold grown-up hand pulling my T-shirt back on and Mrs Smith saying, 'What do you think you're doing?' No one defends me. The boys don't have to put on their shirts. They carry on digging but I have to go inside and not eat the play dough. It's not fair.

Neither Fish Nor Flesh

The weekend scenery flashes, spinning my eyeballs back in their sockets like a pinball machine. My legs are out straight in front of me; they stick to the deep Citroën seats. We are going fishing, with the stripy rods and the Official Fish-Yum Bait, soaking in Castle in the back. There is no way that the fish will be able to resist this. I can't either, and there will be a chance for me to sneak some of it into my mouth when the men are distracted. But you have to watch out for the hooks.

Riverton-on-Vaal is brown and shallow. The kinds of fish that will be pulled up will be weedy and whiskery, no handsome Hans Christian Andersen princes magicked into scales. The only people who will eat them are the little black kids in their big begging jerseys who hang out here. *Their* parents don't make them wear white sandals with studded flowers on them.

I know we will see my father's friend there when we arrive, young and blue-eyed and tense with the importance of male bonding. He has no children of his own and stares at me in casual wonder. I hate that, being a mini-person with no rights to the conversation; it makes me cross.

His legs have curly hair on them, and his shorts really are. He thinks he's big stuff. He tells me that I'd better not stand in the water because there are crocodiles here. I am scathing but scared, and I look to my dad for help. He only smiles. 'Yup,' says his silly friend. 'Sooo many that you could walk on their backs aaall the way across to the island in the middle. But you'd have to be careful that they didn't swing their heads back and bite you. Like this! YAH!' and he grabs my leg. I shriek and stay away from him for the rest of the day. What a nerd.

We scatter ourselves around with canvas stools that never work the way the shop man said they would, and khaki hats and pointing at wagtails. My father takes forever to bait his hook and cast, but there it is, buzz and plop into the murk, and I wander off, knowing that there will be talk I won't understand and beers I can't drink and haw-hawing all round. This bores me.

The day passes slowly, lapped at by the calm of all large bodies of water and the Fanta Grape from the garage on the way, where you have to dive into the sliding fridges and negotiate the bottle like an Eskimo. It is ribbed and dusty and nestles cold as a torpedo against your chest. The first mouthful will be the explosion of grapes and an instant sugar high. Your back teeth will sing songs loud enough to charm the Tooth Fairy along, with her clinking sack and orders for pianos.

But out here there are only the reeds and hidden nests. On the water there is a motor-boat with a skier made Jesus, half-man, half-Superman, all whooping, and my father mutters into his chest, 'Bloody Dutchmen,' as they whip the fishing lines in their froth, dragging us all towards a day closing low and sweet over the river. The sounds coming over are magnified, skipping like flat stones on the water's surface. You know that there are people on the other side having a good time.

My father decides that it's time to braai. We are fishing but have brought chicken anyway, knowing that there is a pecking order that won't be disturbed by the success or failure of the day's activities. The special Cub Scout tepee formation is built and my father emerges, smeared and sweaty in his victory over sticks.

I need to pee but the White Rabbit hasn't okayed this ablution block, and it's very far off besides. I go a little way off, thinking, Weeping willow, weeping willow, and then squat where I am, careful not to let any warm acid spill over my sandals. My father's friend looks over and laughs, as amazed as if I was the sorcerer's apprentice directing a chorus of buckets and floodwater instead of a five-year-old with her broekies around her ankles. 'Look!' he says. 'Look at her pee!' I look down quickly. What is he expecting? Claws? Fur? But I know my fanny and this cleft is all there is.

I want to burn him with my eyes, sizzle his blond sideburns, but he just turns away. I am not a freak! Later I'm going to practise doing this standing up. I stomp back to the car and sit with my book. *The Sleepy Forest*. The soft purple eyes of the trees on the pages close to the hush-hush of their branches, until everyone in the book is sung asleep, and so am I, to dream of slimy crocodiles in my garden, under the windows, growling in their knobbly voices that they want to see me.

I wake up because I'm sharing my blankie with something heavy in the dark, stretched out like a dog beside me on the back seat, and at first that's what I think it is. Except that the smell is different, sharp and warm and somehow dirty, like pyjamas you've slept in when you've had tonsillitis. There isn't enough space. My hand is resting on a spanspek with big warm knobs on. I move my fingers away, sliding off the seat to open the door on the stale air inside, and stand in the hard, blinking moonlight.

It's one of the street kids, curled up under my blanket as peaceful as you please. My father is still sitting by the water, can in hand, and he is unsurprised by my query. 'It's a cold night,' he says. 'You aren't going to be selfish, are you?' I am not happy but I can't think of a good comeback. I just know that when we get home, my mother will have something to say, or maybe she will only sigh like the Snoopy pool being let down after summer. That's what she usually does.

Bambi's Mother

My father hates the idea of hunting, of small furry things being hurt, but he also knows that if he is going to be unemployed then he has to be friends with the kind of people who don't mind a fight being weighted on the side of large men with machines that blast holes in things.

So he buys big knives and keeps them sharpened, makes leather sheaths for them. He calls them his Hunting Knives; this from a man who is so soft-hearted that he throws fish back after they've blundered, accidentally fishy, on to his hook, so much custardly that he once smacked me over my nappy and then cried for an hour. And so on one Saturday afternoon they sweat and laugh their dirty-fingernail way on to my mother's pale blue linoleum porch. She doesn't want to know what they're going to do. The soggy yeast smell of beer and the shape in the black bags is enough and she goes to her room to read, knowing that at some point they will try to make her cook whatever it is they've bagged. I am not as smart, being about twenty-five years younger than she is, and not as well versed in the ways of bloodlust. I want to watch.

They thump the rustling creature on to the white iron table and spread newspaper on the floor below it. This work will be messy and wives can be unreasonable. The bag is slipped off, bumpity bump, under ribs and horns and there it is, a big buck, smelling wild and dangling its puppet hooves over the sides of the table, eyeballs like marbles near to my own. The face is beautiful, elongated and staring. The hairs around the mouth are stained rusty and the tongue lolls. There is a queer gassy smell, and I think, This does not belong here. The men joke and push each other closer; they don't really know what they are doing, but they're going to pretend that they do. There is a vague plan to make biltong, based on the idea that everybody in Kimberley cuts meat into strips, coats it with their own heart-stopping mixture of spices and hangs it to dry in their garages, where it gets in everyone's way and generally causes indigestion because it is eaten too early.

The short squinty one with the blond moustache takes his Hunting Knife and slits the buck down the middle, trying to gut it. The intestines slither hotly to the linoleum and I know my mother will be furious. They are grey like bubble wrap and transparent as sausage skin, which is, of course, their purpose in the next life. But there is something else that we see when they try to crack the rib cage and open the carcass. There is a creamy sac there, slick and rainbow-coloured, ROYGBIV as it is turned over, and what it holds is a tiny replicant, nose to hooves, eyes closed tightly against what is happening. I recognise it from formaldehyde science labs and scary movies. These men have shot a pregnant doe.

My father loses heart. He steps back and tells them to butcher it at someone else's house. He forfeits image points but seems resigned to that. He goes to my mother in the bedroom; on the way his fingers touch the walls.

I never eat biltong again.

Goodnight, John-Boy

We lie on the floor and watch cartoons and puppets dubbed into Afrikaans before the main evening programmes come on. Maybe tonight will be *Die Waltons* or *Little House on the Prairie*, and we'll fall into a world where your lips don't have to move at the same speed as the dialogue, and where everything that is done can be undone. Moms wear aprons and grandparents aren't senile and John-Boy's mole is not a defect but something to be kissed before he goes to sleep.

The *Wielie Walie* monkey comes on. So why doesn't he ever manage to stay on the barrel? Every alternate day my brother and I hold thumbs that *this* time will be different. We hate that monkey.

Our parents are arguing. My father stomps to the bedroom and begins throwing his clothes into a suitcase. Very little actually belongs to him. My mother stays in the lounge, arms folded and eyes grey. She grabs the heavy glass ashtray. 'Take this to your father,' she says, and I get up quickly, because this time it's serious and she looks like she could lash out quite easily.

I stand at the door of the brown bedroom and watch him making his little ant-trails to and from their cupboards. 'Mommy said I must give you this.' He doesn't even look up and his mouth is white around the edges. 'I don't want it.' I go back to the lounge. I want to watch the rest of *Wielie Walie* and they've just gone to the bit with the flowers calling for Benny Boekwurm. 'He says he doesn't want it.' She turns her head to look at me and shouts loud enough for him to hear. 'I don't want the damn thing either! Go back and *give* it to him!' I trot back and put it on the bed. I don't care *what* they do with it; this is spoiling my afternoon. My brother carries on watching, head propped on hands. Now there is a live-action, documentary-type insert on the screen, maybe a paper-making factory, where unidentifiable men in tan overalls tweedle around huge and noisy machinery, fitters and turners forever. I don't like this part. We want Sarel Seemonster and Karel Kraai back. They always fight but manage to sort things out in their funny voices.

My father and mother have moved to the door to carry on arguing in the garden. She is trying to close the door against him, but he has put his foot in the way and is pushing back. 'Look,' she is saying, 'you're drunk and you're scaring the kids. You can come back when you're sober!' He has dropped the suitcase and is nearly crying with frustration, trying to get back into his house. The dogs are gathered at the door, wagging their tails and stopping, their ears pricked and then folded back. They push against my mother's legs to try and get to my father who they love best. She drags them away and somehow manages to throw herself against the door so that it bangs shut.

My father is shouting, 'Are you trying to lock me out?' and he shoves his fist through the glass in the door. They both just stand, listening to the crunch and the tinkling, strangers without third-party insurance swapping addresses after a car crash. He picks up his suitcase and bleeds droplets down the path to the car. Plink. Plink.

He shuts the car door and we can hear the engine, again and again, as he tries and fails to start it. He gets out and takes his suitcase with the hand that isn't mummified in his hanky and goes out the garden gate. It scrapes over the paving after him.

Between the TV programmes there is the irritating little chalk man who spits and spits and can't express himself so that the controlling cartoonist will draw what he needs. Chalkman is always eventually punished for being rude and throwing a temper tantrum; he falls off a chalk line or is erased. We sympathise with him, against the cartoonist. We know what it is like to be ignored. At the end of the insert, this mystifying word appears: FIN. What can it all mean?

The next morning my mother goes to inspect the car before she goes to work. The floor under the driver's seat has a new mat, the Red Sea, caked dry and hard enough for Moses and all his followers to flee over it to the Promised Land. She asks Johanna to clean it before the kids know what's going on. The maid doesn't ask what happened, but my mother tells her anyway. 'Ai yai yai,' they say, and shake their heads. 'Men.' On the TV screen there is the coloured ball of the SABC test pattern, whining high and thin as a mosquito in the early morning air.

Elvis Has Left the Building

Ssh. Be vewwy quiet. We're hunting – not wabbit twacks, but ex-wives. These ladies require more patience, more sneakiness and tact. Sometimes this means hiding in the garden.

He has chosen the blackness under the fruit trees. Their rot-and-witblits stench is like the pub he has just left, but here it is softer, with good red sand and the smell of home when he has to lie down because his head spins. And besides, the Halfway House is closed. Out here there is only his guardian angel to guide him with her voice over his right shoulder; no one else will watch him, as they do at the boarding house where he loiters in the daytime with the other seekers of unhappiness and killers of time. There is even a skylight over the door frame of each room. They have learned their lesson; sometimes they know that they will have to keep watch. Sometimes a man will barricade himself in his single parquet room until it is too late. By the time they have the door down the police will only find an overgrown foetus curled on the floor, with all its goodness leaked out in bright strides. The maids hate it; it's hell to mop up.

This is an ordinary Saturday night, unwalled and outside, when zipping down the side roads is easy because he has been this way so often before. He is not a homing pigeon but a bat, all bones and soft flapping in the thick air. Her radar reaches him, sure and furry, calling him out of the black. And he has very sharp teeth.

Once he doesn't make it, because there is suddenly a police van blocking the road, glowing daffodil and poisonous like the world's meanest corsage, an emissary from *Little Shop of Horrors*. When the officers step out they are buzzing and gentle. They grin when he offers to tap-dance along the broken white line for them. Workers, with no concept of grace and difference. Guarding the queen bee.

The jail is no hive, but cool as a butchery, the cement floor cracked and quiet under his cheekbone. His belt buckle bites into his stomach. There will be other nights. *He giveth His beloved sleep.*

He goes back, opening the gate, no creeping as if he doesn't belong there. No climbing over the fence this time, like a thief. Inside, she wakes up to the squeaky betrayal of the hinges, and she knows, oh she knows, that she has somehow wished him back. The nylon of her oudoos nightie clamps down, weighs her down grim and damp as an extra in *The Poseidon Adventure*. Thinking about water is bad for her bladder. She finds that she cannot move anything except her eyes, which she can feel growing dry and enormous in her head, searching out the Donald Duck nightlight in the kids' room. Quack.

The animals outside whine and wriggle; they have always loved him, even though his own children can sometimes look at him as if he were an alien. Blame Spielberg. Once he put his fist through the glass of the front door because she was trying to close him out.

Her own ears prick up like an Alsatian's. He is moving out there, saying soft words to the animals, giving them kindness and Beenos. The man is a walking doggy treat. Soon, soon-soon, he'd make her love him again (how can she resist?), take him back into the kitchen and lounge and bed with the Mexican bedspread on it. He thinks that the cats probably sleep there now. They never liked him.

Her stomach cramps, innards contracting as efficiently as the maid twisting out bath towels in the choking Kimberley heat. It stops her getting up to check on the children and going to the toilet. It's such a long way to go and she is sure, with a cement certainty where the muscle of her wet red heart used to be, that he will hear.

He has supernatural hearing, you know. He has Elvis down so well he could have sent the King himself to an earlier grave in shame. The comparison is not lost on him. He is coiffed and pelvised too, so that when she shows Johanna the front page of the *Diamond Fields Advertiser* on the day after that hipster heard the judgement call, the maid's horrified reaction is, 'Hawu, Meddem! What has the master done now?'

And now her body isn't playing *Love Me Tender*; by now there's a concerto down there. She plays host to tiny men in tails, violin parasites, death-watch beetles with drums. He has always been able to hum the tune of her body, sing the words to her brain scan. Some days she can feel him stirring her guts with his conductor's baton. Just to twist that DNA ladder. Just to show her that he still could.

He croons gently below her window. He is serenading her, dear Jesus, Romeo in sideburns. He is sure that she will come around if he can just show her that he is sorry and that he really does want to come home very badly. He thinks that if she understands how serious he is, how very much he wants to please her, then she will slide on out of their old bed and come over to the window. Maybe she will let down her hair so that he can climb up and stand in their room and place his hands on her birthmark, on her limbs, as before.

Then he remembers that she has short hair now. Probably she has cut it off to spite him; she has always been perverse. And he also remembers that *Rapunzel* didn't have a happy ending, either. It's so hard to tell who the witch is. He thinks all of this as he slides the window up and spreads his fingers on the sill.

He looks up then, into the orbit of her face. The smell of her electrifies him, frazzling his little nostril hairs and exploding light bulbs in his skull. She leans forward, slowly, slowly, and kisses his open mouth. She draws back. He remains, moon-white and untransformed, on the ground. She remembers that he told her once, before they were married, that as soon as the Afrikaans girls called him Swartoog, he knew that they would surrender their soft parts before morning. At that point she simply steps back and slams the window down on his waiting fingertips.

Two by Two

I am dreaming about the dogs under our bedroom windows again. They are not our dogs, who are kind to white people and let you stick your fingers in their nostrils, even, which I would never let anyone do to me. I don't let my mother cut my fingernails any more, but my brother still does; he's a baby.

The dogs are brown and muscled, like their insides are too near the skin. Their black lips are pulled back further than a Noddy golliwog's, but they aren't smiling, they're growling, with their wet mouths quivering. They jump up nearer to the window every time, but they always just miss. They can't get in, but I can't close the window because if I stick my hand out I know they'll get me.

In the dark my eyes are open now. We're practising sleeping without the Donald Duck nightlight; it's my job to switch it off when Duncan is asleep. I've learned to wake myself up from the bad dog dream even though I'm always thirsty and I have a headache when I do this. I lie under the blanket. But I'm not safe here, either, because my brother and I have taken our mattresses off the beds to see what it's like to camp on the floor (and that really shocks my teacher who drops in on us this afternoon – drops, like a bomb in those run-for-cover exercises they make us do – on her visit of consolation and social welfare. She just stands with her handbag, her mouth still for once. Now she thinks we're poor whites, even though I tried to explain).

Being this low down means that there aren't any bad dogs, but there are more things that can crawl on you, like snakes and spiders, and we've all seen them in our backyards. They're there, and you know it and they know it, and there's nothing you can do because they're so small they can live anywhere, and there are thousands of them with their little snake and spider sons and daughters, like 3D board games without the ladders, because they don't need them. Their legs work, and there are eight or a hundred to your two, or maybe they don't need those either.

My skin is itchy now; it's hot and damp under the blanket and moving around just makes it worse. The pressure in my head makes me feel like I've dived to the bottom of Karen Muir diving pool, where no one else ever swims, so that if your head did ever burst, no one would know until the cleaner came to work the next morning. It's so deep your blood would attract sharks.

My brother sleeps, with his limbs weighed down like a drowned man's. My legs are definitely itchy now. I reach down and scratch, but it doesn't help because the itch just comes back.

I turn over on to my stomach, but now it's all over me and rubbing won't stop it. Little legs, everywhere, the burn and tickle of them like being kissed by an early-morning father; it doesn't make me laugh but it does make me squirm and eventually I can't take it any more.

I jump out of bed and shake myself without moving my head, switch Donald Duck on for his round yellow help, and bam, there is the room with its rusty burglar bars. There they are in their marching columns – ants in ant-time, with their ant-steps, all over my bed, and nobody else's. Why do they want me? Don't they sleep at night? Maybe my sweat is so sweet they can't help themselves. Maybe nightmares taste better, maybe they're caramelised toffee treats for ants. I am the sugar baby doll with my brain a balloon. Maybe I'll pop.

I feel along the passageway to my mother's dark room, where her smell of shaved legs and empty biscuit tins meets me. I reach out to shake her, but she is already awake. She reaches out and touches my chest and pulls out my heart, but then I realise that it's just that my nose has bled again; that feeling of my lobes dripping down to join my belly button.

She pulls my top off over my head and I get into bed with her because my father is sleeping in the boarding house and he is not coming back. She says, 'Go to sleep, puddy tat.' In the garden there is the sound of shuffling, the sound of someone grazing themselves on the apricot tree. It must be the bad dogs, going home.

PART TWO
VENUS FLYTRAP

Baa, Baa, Black Sheep

We think outside the city is probably cooler, but it never is. I am going to play on the farm, where my friend Amanda lives on the weekends and her grandfather lives all year round. Her hair is curly and spongy, clown's hair, and she has a gap between her front teeth. That means that some day she will be rich. I am sick of adults saying that.

I am quite excited. When the Famous Five go out into the country they eat ham. Enid always says, '. . . an enormous ham, pink and gleaming in the centre of the table, which groaned under its weight.' My stomach groans, but not under the weight of anything; the last time I ate was at lunch time when Mrs Gallagher forced me to eat the burnt bits on the cottage pie she made. After school when we go to her house there is always talk of starving children. I am secretly one of them. She watches us constantly, her gold bangles like handcuffs waiting for me to misbehave. When my mother comes to pick me up, Mrs Gallagher titters and smiles in her strained way with her teeth that face backwards, like a shark's.

Oupa's farm is flat, with dust the colour of the new skin under scabs. On its surface Amanda and I move slowly in the heat, without Lego, without Barbies. Where are the grown-ups? I want a grandfather at least so that if anything bad happens there will be a grown-up to sort it out. We are on Mars without oxygen; it makes our feet grimy; it makes us fight. We wander round the rooms, tracking the tired outside indoors, where there are old exhalations rising from the lacy pillowcases and sonbesies sending their shrill afternoon irritation in through the

41

windows, under the doors, so that even if you lay down with your head under the pillow you would still hear it. I understand how men on farms can slaughter their families in the middle of the day, after church. They do the *slagging* themselves. Oh, there is nothing to do here. Even the bookshelves are empty.

We go to find juice. Oros would make my head shrink and everything would be okay. The fridge is huge and smooth-cornered and empty, a space capsule. The freezer is full of carcasses. Amanda is proud of it. She says, 'We *slag* them here.' This disgusts me but I also can't see any blue and white aprons like the one on the Pick 'n' Pay butcher. Do they use one of the rooms?

The juice is also old, weak but scratchy on the back of the throat. On the table there is a bag of oranges and I want one. I reach out for it and Amanda makes me put it back in its rough brown place; she says that Oupa doesn't like it when they eat things without asking. I am not happy here. Even Mrs Gallagher lets you eat.

We bumble outside again into the sonbesies still at it, bush radio for a captive audience. Maybe if I make my nose bleed they'll let me go home. I think hot thoughts. I picture myself gushing from the nostrils and down my T-shirt; that will impress them. Over the screaming insects there is another sound also repeating itself into the afternoon, also in discomfort, also struggling for an audience.

'Come,' says Amanda and starts to run. In the rooms across the paddock there is at least coolness even though there is struggle and stink all around. And the flies are unbearable, insistent and disappointed in my thin tired sweat. They tickle and then lose interest and settle back on the smears of blood. The mystery of Oupa is solved; he hangs over the railings and shouts and points, adding his last-meal-breakfast breath to the heavy air. Maybe he eats children, too.

There are four black boys, each holding down a sheep. It looks like they are tickling their tummies. Ah, sheep are like dogs then. But should the boys be allowed to carry knives that big? What if they turned on us and did what I see now they are doing to the sheep? The boy nearest to me whistles me over and, stupidity in sandals, I go to him with his quick hands and his cat-piss armpits. 'Kyk,' he says and grins down as he whips the knife across its nude grey gullet. The sheep bubbles and gives a stiff-legged twitch like the man we saw once lying in the road after he'd been flung off his bicycle in an accident. It doesn't stop even when you know they ought to be dead.

My stomach curls in on itself. I'm not hungry anymore.

Clutching at Straws

My mother has taken us over to her friend Helen's house. They are sipping drinks that don't have straws and laughing like donkeys every few minutes in the lounge. We are given Coke. The treat fizzes up our sinuses and burps down our gullets like a drink in a Roald Dahl children's book, and we feel in touch with our heroes. In the boys' bedroom there is a whole stash of Walt Disney books to read, with the dragons safely squashed between the hard covers. We sit behind the bookcase, concealed behind the door, but they don't want to read. They live here; they always have access to these books, so we have to play something else.

It occurs to me that I want to try kissing, the way they do in movies. With tongue. The obvious choice is Ricky, who at ten has more teeth than the rest of us in his big red-lipped smile. We kiss. His mouth is warm and exciting, like a teeny Kreepy Krawly. He tastes of Coke and I want to go back for more. The deal is that I have to kiss all the brothers, to make it fair, but the most I can muster for the other two is a peck. Eventually they lose interest and wander off, leaving me to scuba as much as I can before our mothers start asking questions.

We emerge, dizzy and happy, to find their uncle Allie is there. Allie is a grown man with an extra few chromosomes. I know this now but back then he was just a mongol. He doesn't ever say anything coherent, just sits in the sun in his place against the French doors, groaning and rocking and grinding a drinking straw between his teeth. The evening sun makes funky patterns in the tufts on his flat ginger head. Imagine never being able to comb your hair down. What if my children are like that?

He doesn't move from his spot, and this bothers me. How does he get into the house? Do they carry him in or attach secret wheels to a place we can't see? Or drop him in by crane, flat on his brown polyester butt? He's nowhere near dying. Granny gives him all her greenhouse tenderness and Pops drinks more and more whisky. He is their very own hybrid, a science-fiction creature (flesh of my flesh) bred carefully in her body's incubator. All that enamel and freckled skin and rushing blood to service a brain as soft as fruit. When I get nearer I catch traces of closeness, of rotting. Morning breath. Yeast. Compost bins. Gardens.

He sees me watching; he pulls faces like the man enduring incredible speeds in the *Life* photographs, his lips stretching so far back that I'm thinking that maybe they will meet behind his head, like Prince Charles's smile. Nobody will ever want to kiss this mouth. Especially with tongue.

Allie opens his mouth wide enough to flash his molars and groans loud as a strongman lifting his own weight, loud enough to bring my auntie running. Allie has to go to the toilet. So do I. His is a process that can take half an hour, with people keeping watch and much careful wiping of parts. Mine will be much quicker. Preparations to move him are beginning, so I make my break and dash to the bathroom. With my healthy hands I can slam the door on him.

The Colour Purple

The house is quiet except for the sound of my brother spray-painting the kitchen cupboards purple with the leftover cans from my father's last mechanical adventure. When he packed his things he forgot these. Or maybe he didn't care anymore if the mags matched the bodywork.

My mother is sitting in the lounge with her special gold and blue crockery and her friend Pat, which is a good name for her because her flat grey bob looks like someone has done just that as they passed by her. They are having tea and pretending that the apple pie isn't burned. My mother's concentration is slipping; we have eaten enough viennas and fish fingers in the last few months to make zoos of our stomachs. That's how it feels. Things with tails and claws turn around and around in my intestines to make themselves comfortable before they go to sleep, which usually only happens at the library now. They are wide awake at night when I want to sleep. It is impossible to reason with them. They don't speak English.

I am not allowed to be in the room while this friend is there. She is a teacher at my school, and says things like, 'Little pitchers have big ears,' and makes her eyes big so that they press against the flesh on her face, like the wolf at Grandma's bedside. Ah dur, I know what that means.

The tsss sounds still coming from the kitchen draw me closer. My brother may as well be a snake; for a four-year-old he's incredibly cold-blooded in a deliberate sort of way. I can still win in a fight. My mother warns me that when he comes back from the army it will be a whole different story. I feel safe; that's years away.

The kitchen is a mess. There is absolutely no way that he's going to get away with this, and the funny thing is that I have no desire to split on him. I know that my mother is going to crack when she sees this. It's badness beyond naughtiness, badness beyond anything I can make up.

And that's exactly what happens. My mother is a smacker, usually on the bum. Just don't tell her that it doesn't hurt, because then she gets really angry. Even though I am in the passage when she comes into the kitchen I can hear the air whistling between her front teeth like the sounds the warplanes on TV make when they drop bombs. She is holding a *Diamond Fields Advertiser* in her right hand but she manages to yank my brother down from where he stands on the counter to spray the tins and the rest of the gold and blue crockery on the top shelves. But he's slippery, well practised in finding his feet under other people's, and he scrambles down the passage with my mother chasing him. She is crying and shouting, 'Are you kids going to ruin everything I own?' and saying, 'If your father was here, you wouldn't behave like this!' and trying to whack him with the rolled-up newspaper. Eventually she just lashes out with her bare foot and kicks him, hurting her big toe so that she is the Grandma for the next two days, hunched over and cross. Her friend must have left.

She is not in a good mood when the policeman comes to the front door. He wears Noddy shoes. They step through the doorway and I wonder if I should tell him that she kicked my brother. He wouldn't believe me. My mother is a charmer; she has a way of speaking and joking in Afrikaans that I will never have. But they are not joking or laughing. Her face is pale and her mouth is a zip keeping her two sides together.

Hope Chest

A few afternoons later she drops me off at Pat's house. I know something is wrong because my brother is at somebody else's house. The floor tiles are so cold they soak into your heels until you are frozen like that penguin in the Disney books, the one whose ice floe broke off and floated away. The walls are unpainted brick. I have never seen that before, a naked house. Huge arrangements of dried flowers stand on the floor. You have to walk carefully where everything is dead. I am Scott of the Antarctic. She offers me cooldrinks and then wobbles off across the ice house to make pottery, her flesh jittering under her chin like an Eskimo wife's.

I thaw my feet and wander through the house, too. I stop to plink on the old piano. Her son plonks himself down next to me and asks me whether I can play the piano. What kind of question is that? Anyone can play the piano. I crash my hands down on the white keys until he gently closes the lid and I have to move my fingers or let them be squashed. I can't read music, another language that is not familiar to me.

He is old, twenty years old, he says. We go to his room because he says he wants to show me something. He lies on his bed with his hands behind his head. My mother would never let me put my shoes on the bedspread like that. I want to know what is so interesting in his room, and he points to the wall above him. There is the longest gun I have ever seen in my life. He takes it down and lets me feel it. Heavy. Slippery and cold, like a snake. He even lets me pull the trigger. He shows me the bullets; they come in a little cardboard box. They are heavy, too, iron sucky sweets.

My mother comes to fetch us. Her eyes are swollen into slits, the same colour as the barrel of the gun that split open to show me its empty holes. I wonder how she can see to drive. She says, 'More drama, kids. Daddy Jock shot himself.' We are stuck to the seats. I am confused. Maybe God finally struck him down with lightning after all that swearing and drinking. My brother says, 'Mommy, did his tongue hang out like a dog's?' She keeps driving.

All the things of his that my mother wants to keep are in her white and gold jewellery box. Inside there is pink satin like a coffin. I covet that box. Every so often we take it out and spill everything on her bed. We count the treasures, her diamanté bracelet she got on her twenty-first birthday and the cherry pin stored in tissue paper at the bottom.

My brother gets cufflinks, a watch. My father didn't have a jewellery box; he said we were his treasure. He has left me his tiny leather purse. I should wear it around my neck but it's too ugly. Inside there is still a ten rand note. This I like much more.

Over the next months and years my mother slowly deals out the cards of his death (The Fool, The Hanged Man). The police broke the door of the boarding house down to get to him, little pig, little pig, because he could not let them in. He was on the bed in his underpants, drunk and dead. The death certificate says, Koeëlskoot (kop). It was a small, very clean wound. He was not a troublemaker. The maids were relieved.

It's weird to see your own surname on a headstone. There's a space for me that he didn't get to use. They buried him on the boundary between the Jewish and Christian graveyards; suicides aren't loved in this world or the next. My mother cries when she tells me that. But I do see that there are little white stones around the grave. The old Jewish ladies have sneaked out in their tight black dresses and powdery faces to say prayers for him, so I do, too. *Hail Mary* is the only one I know that has death in it. Maybe I'll keep him company there when I die. I don't want him to be alone.

Bush Telegraph

With my father finally gone, his friends come courting. Maybe the cinnamon of my mother's embalmed misery summons them like a perfumed love letter on purple paper; her white-bandaged loneliness sends out signals instead of heart beats. Maybe it's just that Kimberley is so small that everyone knows what each one of their kind is doing at any given moment. Bush telegraph, or a scent on the wind that makes the community eager to pair her up again so that the other husbands will be safe.

In the garden my mother buries her sadness with the roots of the slips of other people's plants. It is so hot that she has taken to wearing her silky pink running shorts (with white piping) almost daily, emerging from her wrappings. She is girl-thin with the heaviness of divorce and night visits and jail and suicide; this has withered her insides, taken her back to what she looked like ten years ago. A chance to start over.

She bows and scrapes, nips and tucks, until the plants wave their limp green arms in defeat. Men take to driving out of their way so that they can spy on her smooth new legs in the bushes, and the routine is always the same. First the drive-by waving and the shouted greetings. My mother stands up in her shiny pink shorts. She is sweet with sweat and pants back to them, cheerful and false to their faces. She says, 'Bastards,' when she bends back down, like the Chinese man in the fairytale who had to tell his secret so badly that he whispered it to the wheat.

Then comes the day when they park their cars. Bow-legged, paunchy, married or not, they bring us their commiserations and gifts of stale pink marshmallows to trick us into going away to play. After they go my mother tells us not to leave her alone with them. How they must have hated us with our small fingers and sharp tongues, like Oliver Twist pickpockets. We want some more.

At the gate one evening, we all stand around in our warped nuclear tableau. Two adults, two children. I swing on the gate between the grown-ups, with my toes hooked into the thick white wire, backwards, forwards. Squeak. Squeak. I'm wearing the blue halter neck my mother has sewed for me, armour on my chest and insults in my head. Who would call their child Godfrey? It is a name that has come true. He tries to look past me to get to my mother to where she stands on the inside, laughing weakly at his sweaty jokes. 'You're fat,' says my brother, sudden and sharp out of his silence. 'This', says Godfrey, 'is not fat. This is muscle.' He flexes his chunky arms. 'I'll model for you in my underpants if you like.' Stale pink marshmallows. The faces we make must be enough to put him off because after that he gets into the car. He doesn't come back, the flabbiness of his biceps blocking us from further intrusion. Fat guys can't leopard crawl, after all. Many years later, when it's just the two of us, she says, 'It always makes me wonder if they lusted after me all the while I was married, or if they just saw their chance for a quick pomp.'

So the man who sells her a used car is interesting, perhaps because he already has a wife and three children, perhaps because he is Afrikaans and cannot be taken seriously, perhaps because he seems concerned. He comes to check up on her more than he needs to. It is raining one afternoon when no other cars have passed by and slowed, with the streets steaming and empty and the grass deliciously itchy when you roll in the wetness. The air smells of ozone, of the insides of science labs, where mad doctors try to direct lightning. He stands at the gate, calm in his curly hair, streaming with rain and testosterone. He grins at her with all his teeth, leans on the gate with his elbows pointing the way forward. She can see that his arms are round and muscled, and his forearms are brown. Maybe she is tired of saying no, being poor, struggling all the time with two small children always at her side like burrs; maybe she thinks she can trust him. She invites him in for coffee and they sit at the speckled kitchen table, where their adult feet touch underneath it.

His brown suit makes puddles on the linoleum, and she says, 'Wouldn't you like something drier?' and in his head the answer is no; from her he wants warmth and wetness, a sea of it against the cracked lips and dust of Kimberley, enough to sail him out of the screaming and drinking of his ugly marriage. But what he says is yes, because he doesn't want to scare her. When she goes to see what she has, she realises that (the cupboard is bare) she has long ago thrown out the remainder of Jock's clothes, and that the only item that could possibly fit him is the pink running shorts. It is a test. He changes in their bedroom, smells her young widowy smell, of buds and beginnings.

And he passes, of course, because when he emerges she sees that his legs, like his strong arms, are muscled and furry. He used to be a gymnast, using his strength to swing himself up and over in the rings above the heads of the audience. Just like he is using his strength to grab hold of my mother's heart. When we come back inside with our grass stains and yowling, we find them laughing at the table, my mother's face pink. My brother says, 'Are you going to be our daddy?' and my mother blooms even redder, red like her geraniums. They laugh. And he didn't even have to bring marshmallows.

Travelling Blues

And what must it be like, really, to be a used car salesman who also travels around the country, selling parts for machines and parts of yourself, trading in bits and loving the Alfa Romeo you drove but knowing it would never be yours? And knowing that Olivia Newton-John was the kind of woman you really wanted but your wife was not like that? Tell me about it, stud.

She was, instead, your high-school sweetheart who had to leave her sweetness and hearts because that's what falling pregnant in high school does. And back then her hair was shiny and black and now it's something she does in the bathroom every week, each time for so long that you give up trying to get in to shave, and just go to work the way you are. Scratchy. Some days the men at the garage call it rugged, but mostly this is how people know your marriage is not working.

The other ways they can tell are the sedatives that she's renewing more and more often, and the telephone calls from other married men, and the seven white tennis dresses hanging in the cupboard. She never plays tennis, but she likes the way her legs look in them. You don't. You like the way other women's legs look, though. Sometimes you tell them this when they've come to you, helplessly looking at second-hand cars, trying to trade in old lives for new models. But mostly you confine your affairs to out-of-town women, the ones who only know you on the road which stretches out also like a woman on a couch.

You like them because they don't smash their whisky glasses and scream at you. You like them because they didn't take your handgun out of your cupboard – your cupboard! A man has no privacy – and point it at you and say in a wavering voice that they were sick of your affairs. They didn't fire a shot into the bedroom door because you managed to slam it at the last second. And they didn't shoot the little toe off their right foot because Valium makes you weak that way. They didn't seep red into the thick white carpet with its other blushing stains from the wine that no amount of Handy Andy will remove. They didn't have to be taken to the emergency room to the tune of a crying baby and wide-eyed daughters still in their school uniforms late at night.

A man needs his peace. A man needs a woman who is good and quiet and gardens in the evenings with her shorts rolled up and her hands bare in the dirt.

Bluebeard's Wedding

It starts with a smiling kiss on a balcony. A flash of throat and the sports stadium roar of the crowds below, or maybe it's a Roman mob, just like us, herded into the hall to watch Lady Diana marry Charles, no Prince Charming, he. We know them well, from their flat faces on the plates that have found their cold china way into display cabinets. All the world loves a British wedding.

She in her flesh and flounces is waving; she sparkles and rustles with what must be true love, like the crown jewels that will be hers too. Precious. Protected by institutions and men with halberds, so that even when she forgets his name – *his name* – we forgive her because she blushes. It should have been a sign. Red cheeks, red as the carpet they have rolled out for her like a long tongue in a lion's mouth.

It is strange to be collected here to watch the Royal Wedding. Afterwards we will have to write a composition on it for News. The hall is a sacred space for assemblies and prizegivings, where a cough will get you sent out for a drink from the taps. Usually the juniors are kept apart from the seniors as if we have to be cattle-dipped before we can be considered safe. Foot-and-mouth disease, like immaturity, spreads easily wherever a few are gathered together. We shift on our uncarpeted floor and gather splinters in our panties like burrs; we cannot sit still. Wherever we go there are things with hooks that cling, and we carry them with us; blackjacks, fairytales, manners. We are pleased to be watching the Royal Wedding because it must be important. All the young teachers are excited, but we do not know why.

What is important for us is the panty inspection we know will happen in the same hall this week, where all the girls have to lift their heavy green skirts until the female teachers can see our panties. Perhaps if we pass this inspection we will be allowed to wear white frothy dresses at some point. And there's a reason they have to check. Our regulation panties are enormous and hated with little-girl hatred; they swathe us from neck to knee in thick green Elastoplast, like being lost in a sticky polyester forest. If we ever had to jump out of an aeroplane, our panties would unstick and parachute us safely to the ground. (Unless, of course, one of the engines was on fire, in which case, we'd be melted like marshmallows before you could say, 'chastity belt'.) But we won't be jumping out of planes; we won't even be jumping up and down.

Danielle's mother is an undercover revolutionary; she is the Amelia Jenks Bloomer of Sub B. She won't let Danielle wear the bandage panties the other mothers make us wear. Danielle has been blessed with cotton panties. I am deeply jealous of this. I go home and complain to my mother, who tells me crossly that she's not Danielle's mother, and if I feel that strongly about it I can wear ordinary panties under the balloony ones. So I do. No more splinters for me, but I am bulky and un-princessy.

My mother is preoccupied; she is also getting married. I have a dress in my head, frothy like beaten egg whites, the opposite of my school uniform, one for her and one for me, nearly the same size because she is so thin lately. Her face is pointy; her shoulder blades are wings. She does not have round princess-cheeks. Just as well, because when the day comes she does not have a princess–dress.

Or a prince, either. He turns up in a brown suit; the shiny pink running shorts will not do for this day's work. She doesn't mind. She is doped to the gills on Calmettes, she says later. She doesn't remember a thing. I am appalled. My mother is marrying a man who doesn't have a tuxedo, or even the urge to rent one. The wedding photos of my real father are different. Then she had a veil and confetti and a man in a black suit who always walked as if he were dancing. But this one has gingerbread-man eyes behind his glasses, and curly Afrikaans hair. And a beard. Not a blue beard, but close enough, Sister Anne, Sister Anne. It should have been a sign.

The Naming of Parts

The West End house in general is tense with whispering and planning; the walls suck in their sides. Something is up. It all makes sense when we are told, after asking questions about the Zoo biscuits – I don't eat the green ones – and Oros being laid out, that my stepfather's children are coming over. They say, 'your new stepsisters and brother'. Duncan is pleased not to be the youngest any more, but I am sick of girls. I want to stay the eldest.

We have heard tales of maternal neglect and madness, with my mother making her eyes big and saying, 'Yes, she's an alcoholic,' and saying, 'Shame,' a lot. Later, much later, she is sorry for being this judgemental, for always taking his side. Later she says things like, 'Ja, what goes around, comes around,' and sighs sadly.

We wait, and of course there they are, hesitating on the path in the garden, two skinny little girls with noses that turn up like cuphooks, and a tiny red baby who, apparently, the monster ex-wife tried to abort with a coat hanger. He looks angry already. 'Mad,' says my mother, and makes whirly gestures next to her ears. And I wonder what their mother has told them about us.

They all have French names and bruises on their sucker-stick arms, as if someone has taken them, one by one, and shaken them hard until they fizzed up like the inside of lollipops. We stand and look and the grown-ups push us towards each other. 'Do we have to live together?' says Rochelle. She is the smaller girl, with black curls and eyes like a pug. 'If you want to,' they say, and leave us alone with our alien visitors.

We don't know what to say. We sit at the kitchen table. 'What is your *van*?' says Rochelle. 'What?' 'Your *van*, your *van*. What is your *van*?' We may as well be Dingaan and Piet Retief; we've just done them at school. I know she wants something from me, but I don't know what it is. And I wonder which of us is going to survive.

Adele leans in with her gym biceps and her boy's hair and interprets, 'Surname. *Van* means surname.' And I realise then that this is going to be difficult. We don't look like brothers and sisters. We don't even speak the same language and we're going to have to share a father. Will there be enough to go round?

When they have gone, my mother is keen for information, and our sulky faces don't impress her. She tries to make us feel sorry for them, she says, 'Did you see those bruises? She gets drunk and then she hits them with a coat hanger.' I don't believe her. There are so many other ways to hurt people; you can break their things, you can not love them enough. A coat hanger is a silly thing to use.

Katberg

We come down for breakfast, and know that our new-married parents will be late, staying upstairs in their hotel bed, rolling around and trading their second-flesh smells and tastes. The dining room is empty because it is the off-season and nearly nine (hang your broekies on the line), though the sun is not keeping score.

Outside there are clouds, crenellated and greyish pink and always wet, like a brain in a failed creation experiment. The smarter diners have eaten and gone, leaving bits of their scrambled egg selves behind. Behind the swing doors there is the muted clinking of washing up, like the bit before a concert where everyone tunes up and there is clashing in the darkness and the gnashing of teeth. Here they would only be able to play the spoons. Steam hisses under the door from the steel vats of boiling oil on the other side of the swing doors, where bad children must be taken, because there aren't any others in the dining room.

The carpet is sticky and thick, a pattern of leaves in autumn colours that makes us feel like we are always falling down as we try to cross it, swallowing our ankles without a sound as we pull against them. Our aunt is waiting alone at the table, reading a curly paperback and crunching her way through brittle toast. Her teeth make dynamite in the silence. The waiters, with their coffee-jug arms and frayed sleeves, watch us as we pick our way across. They are waiting without smiles for us to knock over the cooling buffet plates or pull on the thin linen tablecloths. It's hard to know where you'll be welcome when you're a child. They are waiting, probably, for the last lazy bloody guests to feed their faces and get out, so they can march the dull and sulky cutlery to their places for lunch. They are thinking of the weekend.

The coffee is weak, the fried eggs are runny, and there's nothing to do because outside is just like the eggs and the coffee. It hasn't stopped raining since we got here three days ago. I have had to wear my new tracksuit with the floppy collar these three days in a row, and my mother looks disapproving whenever she sees me, doubly doubtful because Mrs Gallacher cut all my hair off before we came here on this communal honeymoon. I must look like a tiny Russian athlete before defection. Three-legged races. Hurdles.

I have had enough of wandering around the empty hotel; someone always wants us out of the way because they have to vacuum, and the TV room stinks of pinkly wrinkly men with their cigarette smoke and horse racing. I leave the table and skip brushing my teeth because if I'm going to lose my slow, whiny brother I have to be quick. There is a path through the forest between the hotel and the tennis courts, and I duck down there, counting red leaves and looking for money that might have been dropped. A cent is worth two Wilson's toffees – they are the only things keeping me going, my sweet and chewy link to the outside world. Cola. Or maybe the black ones.

The path is slippery and dank with the idea of moss and blind creatures crawling on their stomachs, and some with no legs at all, never being able to escape and having to live under their stones forever. But not me. I hear footsteps and the important rustling of large bodies pushing their way through the growth. I hide and a woman's voice blows forward to me, squealing with laughter and panting. She is saying, 'Not here, Rod, Jesus!' and there is a man in tennis whites chasing her and trying to tickle her. His fingers are really long as they stretch out to catch her round the middle. They have no wedding ring on them, and look as if they will hurt when he grabs her. It's funny, because the tennis courts are under four centimetres of water, and nobody will be playing tennis there for a very long time. It's just as well, because they must have forgotten their tennis rackets. They barge into bushes and break little branches; their clothes are getting stained. Only her gold bangles are shiny. They jangle like Christmas presents and the promise of things to come as they stumble down the path on their biltong legs, doubled over each other, thumping on.

I wait until I'm sure they've gone and I hop out on to the path again. There is a big tractor tyre near the tennis courts and I want to see how much rain has collected there. But in the distance I see that a little boy is already in it. He is doing what I want to do. I come out of the clearing and we look at each other, north to south. He must decide that I'm okay, because he says, 'Hey, who are you?' and we're off. His father's name is Rodney and they are here on holiday like us, but his mother got sick, so she's resting in bed. I have to explain my complicated family to him in return. My father is not my father, but he's with my mother. I am getting used to helping people track my dangerously slippery relatives, under our new stones. They always ask me if I like him, if it's strange, but the truth is that there is a small rhythm to households, and getting up and going to school and ballet and piano doesn't leave much thinking space for brothers being born and having to share your mother.

The Boy seems nice and we spend the whole morning without fighting. We can share the tyre. Our favourite cars are Matchbox. I beat him at movies because I've seen *Raiders of the Lost Ark* and his parents wouldn't let him. I describe how their faces melted when they opened up the ark, and his face changes shape too. 'Bleargh,' he says, 'I don't want to hear any more. I bet I'm stronger than you,' and then we have to arm wrestle even though the grass is wet. I let him win about half the time. It seems like the right thing to do. I have to go back for lunch and we split up. My mother is miffed with the damp tracksuit, but pleased that I have a friend. 'I don't want you to be bored,' she says.

The next day I go back. Maybe today he will tell me his name, and he does, in between jumps on and off the tyre. It's Robert (on), and Robert wants (off) to know what (on) my name is. I say, 'Diane.' He stops (off). He stays off. 'Diane is a *girl's* name,' he says. 'Yes,' I say. 'I know. I'm a girl.' He stares at me in disgust. 'I don't play with *girls*,' he says. I stalk away and then slip and slide in reverse up the path until I'm back at the hotel. I slink to the TV room and sit in one of the armchairs. Silver Pieces and Miss Priss are neck and neck. Silver Pieces wins the race. I knew he would. I dig my fingers under the cushion, just in case, and there it is: twenty cents.

Clan of the Cave Bear

The bodies of the library ladies are shields from horrible brothers; they stand between us and our faraway parents, just in case, and show us *The Faraway Tree* instead. Their woolly chests mother us from a distance. With their books outstretched like bait they trick us from our hiding places. They are fishers of gingerbread men.

They let us sit in the light, a proper place for us, on the cushions, near the windows. I want to stay here forever, devote my middle years to alphabetising other people, putting books *here* and not *here*, cover things in clear thick plastic, give spines to the jellyfish books that flop in after being borrowed too many times, so that I can send the word back out into the world, not made flesh because paper is enough. And you never have to send a book to the gas chamber because nobody wants it. You never have to put them down.

When we move houses to parallel that other family shift, I lose the Beaconsfield Library, where they smile and let me use my mother's cards to take out six books at a time. The carpet is worn through at its entrance, from all the kids being dragged in backwards, maybe, their parents keen to force-feed them literature even if it ends up coming back out through the nose later. The library ladies leave you alone here, don't try to chase you out of the Adult section where you hold the books by their spines to find the well-thumbed pages. Those are the sex scenes.

There is a series of books that starts with *Clan of the Cave Bear* and ends up ensuring lifelong sexual dysfunction because only ten-year-olds can stand to read them. Ayla and Jondalar may as well be entomologists for all the anatomical confusion they cause, with his proboscis dipping into her honeyed well on every tenth or so page. We are trying to find our totems, like Ayla, who has scars from that time she fought the grizzly. I read these books at Danielle's house, where we lie in her bed at the top of the stairs all through the weekend. Her parents try to shoehorn us out, but it's no good. Sometimes we make a mess in the kitchen, or blow bubbles in the dark pool with its sides that scrape your shins, but mostly we are curled like snails under the duvet. She says, 'Listen to this,' and reads a scene from *The Valley of Horses*. I hold myself very still so that she doesn't think I am excited, and she stops and says, 'Jesus, Awerbuck, why are you so stiff?' and we laugh on our bed of nails. I hope I haven't left a silvery trail. She makes me feel like a boy.

Sometimes we go to the Pony Club, a little patch of culture in the Kimberley scrub; everywhere else there are thorn bushes with white spikes perfect for poisoning. She rides her horses and I wander around with a book in my hand until the sonbesies make my head fuzzy, avoiding the mothers with their infidelities and their sunglasses on the tops of their heads. They spend too much time draping themselves over the railings around the stables, trying to catch the attention of the black men in their gumboots as they push their brooms through the smelly straw. The dust makes us sneeze.

Danielle has tried to make me like horses, but I can't understand why you would want to bend an animal to your will like that. When she gives me a carrot to give to Frosty Tom Thumb, I don't bend my thumb back far enough. He gets confused by my vegetable fingers and nips me. It stings and goes numb immediately, so that I think he's taken it right off. I think, We're too far out here. It's going to take half an hour to get me to hospital and I'm going to bleed to death. I hate him, but it's not his fault.

But I'm not the one who needs help. The riders are practising their jumps, and I am not watching even though I'm supposed to pretend that I'm interested as they go through their paces while the fat-bottomed instructor in his jodhpurs shouts at them to do it again. Their heads must be itchy because they sweat under those hard velvet hats even though you can't see that from here; they are middle-class construction workers building a monument to pre-teen frustration.

Danielle is doing her round and Frosty Tom Thumb is slow and jerky in the dust today; he has tasted my blood and it makes him stray into the thorn bushes that haven't been trimmed back because they are supposed to stay on the track in the ring. I think about her muscles and her joints, how they should have been cushioned against all that gracelessness, how she doesn't have enough body fat to protect her. He rears at a jump, and she falls, which is nothing unusual, except that she lands directly on those white spikes, twisting and screaming round so that one pierces her temple. People are up immediately, spilling gin and tonic. They lift her off, as gently as they can, and now she is making soft little sounds.

On Monday she is back at school, although she is stiff and

scratched, like Ayla after her struggle with the grizzly. She shows me her back, where there are bloody indentations. I suppose this counts as a totem.

In Sickness and in Health

I get tonsillitis every winter and have to stay home, feeling my body shrink to only a throat under the stale duvet. I dream the same dream many times: I am in the car with my brother while my mother is in Pick 'n' Pay and she has told us to wait for her. She has also told us not to play with anything. As soon as she moonwalks over the melting tar my brother bumps and slides into the driver's seat. He fiddles with the steering wheel, makes driving noises. And then he shifts the gear and the car starts rolling back. It rolls faster and faster and he doesn't know how to stop it, and neither do I; I do know that we are going to crash. When it reaches blurspeed I always wake up.

When you're sick, getting up to bath is always a mistake. It retards healing and makes everything heavy and sore. You wash off the good germs with the baddies. My stepfather tries to be kind to me, but he doesn't know what to do; his sphere is more leather belt smacking and concentrating during the hymns in church, when he puts on his fake English voice. It is deeper and slower than his Afrikaans accent.

When he comes home from work he makes me tea. Of course it's too hot and scalds my insides so that tears come, but I don't show him because he's trying to be nice. What I want is jelly, is custard, and not the sticky kind my mother makes, but the kind that is smooth and cool and comes in cartons from Pick 'n' Pay.

Instead there are orange Strepsils and they always remind me of that advert with the Christopher Lee vampire and the woman on the bier with her too-full lips and her too-white throat. Asking for it. It makes me afraid to have my neck outside the duvet. Underneath it is sweaty but worth it.

My mother has had enough, and she decides with Doctor du Toit that my brother and I will both have our tonsils out before winter. I think that maybe this decision is based partly on irritation with us, because my brother has caught himself in his zip on his way back in the elevator after giving a urine sample. I am laughing hysterically against the wall, and my mother hisses at me that it's not funny. My brother is in tears.

The soonest the hospital says they can take us is on my birthday. My mother pretends sympathy but then makes jokes about losing organs and so we laugh against our will. She buys us cloth puppets with rubber faces that smell like Ken-and-Barbie's babies would smell. We aren't allowed to eat, and spend our time guiltily colouring in each other's favourite books and snarling at each other. My brother blames me for the fact that we both have to go to hospital and to punish me he cuts up all my panties, which I have carefully packed into a little suitcase in case I need to escape.

In the hospital they make us wear dresses like the puppets' and give us pills and a teeny cup of water. I say, 'Nothing's happening,' as they wheel me down the corridor and leave me there, but the little holes in the ceiling boards come closer and closer until I dissolve.

When I come round my mother is there. My face is puppet-rubber and the sides of my mouth are so sore I can't speak. When I go to the bathroom I see that they have been ripped. It scares me that I can't remember anything that happened in there. My brother is still under anaesthetic; he's not as tough as I am, and I am discharged after a disappointing bowl of melted vanilla ice cream and green jelly so hard it hurts my new throat.

'Ha ha, you're lucky,' says the fat nurse. 'We usually make you eat cornflakes.'

The Sound of Music

My mother in the flush of her second marriage has decided that we all need to learn to play the piano, but somehow the others squirm out of it or give up and only I end up going to long-term music lessons. The black squiggles mean nothing to me in real life. On paper I can make my little tadpole replicants in the bars left open for me, but how they translate to the keys is confusing. I keep thinking, I'm touching elephants' teeth. They must have an enormous elephant tooth fairy, or at least one with a big set of pliers.

I can do a rousing version of *Chopsticks*, and I'm working on the song from *Beverly Hills Cop*, but I hate the new pieces, getting harder like Maths sums and talking down to me on the succeeding pages of the skinny book. They poke out their tongues. So far I have managed to get away with memorising the sound sequences, but this is getting harder as I have to play pieces with more notes in them. I have to learn to play the horrible ones with clangs and pauses before I can get to the good stuff. My heart does *not* want to sing every song it hears. And now she wants me to use both hands at the same time.

I dread Mondays because I have to walk down over the cement of the empty quad with its cold steel poles squaring in the sunlight. This much, and no more. If you fall here the grazes will last for weeks. Everyone else is inside, wielding scissors or tying shoelaces, and I have to pretend to go willingly to where the music teacher lies in wait like a Disney dragon. You never see her teeth but you know they're there. She has the deepest voice I have ever heard on a woman, and her slow English is smothering. She has hermited herself far away from the main block in one of the new rooms, where she keeps the heater on high enough to make your collar prickle. She say it's to keep our hands warm in winter, but the sun never seems to shine here at all. Her ruler lies close at hand on the table, woody and threatening. It is slightly rounded on the top and that side will hurt more when she hits your unpractised Sunday-night fingers.

She wants to know how my mother is; all the teachers in Kimberley know each other, and this is why I am too afraid to bunk music. I know that they would hunt me down sometime over afternoon tea while I was under my mother's bed with the metal springs pressing into my back. I have to do some scales. She makes me do the hard ones and my fingers stretch apart until they look webbed like in *The Man from Atlantis*. I bet *he* would say no to the piano.

We are about to have our usual conversation that will follow my playing a piece and having to start over and over, but the bell trills. God is calling on the world's biggest telephone. It stops and rings again. We won't have to answer but everyone knows from repeated assemblies that three short rings is the signal for a bomb drill. Maybe when the terrorists come I will have to say a thank-you prayer. I shove the sheets back into my bag, all the while with her bloodhound eyes on me, and we get to go outside. I run under the pale sun and over the dead grass to my bobbing class, where the teacher is taking register and then we all have to sit down in an alphabetical column and wait for break. A is for Awerbuck, although I am never first on the list. A is for alleluia.

Off / Spring

In our new-marriage house, our three-family ('ha ha, yours, mine and ours') house, there are many rules. I am the smart one. My mother tries to make my stepfather come to Prizegiving but he won't. He says he's tired and these things bore him. I try to stay out of the house on the weekends. Our family never does anything like go camping or horseriding. They are always tired.

My elder stepsister is the sporty one. My mother buys her shiny peacock-blue gym leotards and hockey socks by the truckload. Her body stretches and scrunches and she is always wired because the coaches make them drink Mina Mino, which is a tonic they say is made of liver and calf brains. She hates her thigh muscles because they are too big. She says the gym coach pokes them in the stomach with a stick to see how hard their muscles are. She makes us do this at home. My mother says she is her father's child. I think my muscles are on the inside. I hope so, that people can be strong in other ways.

My younger sister isn't really good at anything. She misses her own mother too much, even though before she lived with us her school uniform was never washed and there were always fingerprint bruises on her arms. She enjoyed moving from house to house and here she is stuck in the long bedroom with two sisters. My stepfather can't look at her; she makes his eyes sore. He says that she is too much like her mother. My youngest stepbrother still lives with this mother, the only one too young to decide which parent he wants to live with. In real life, all her children look like her, with her green eyes and her pouty lips; they are the word made flesh, and that word was 'unhappiness'.

My real brother is chubby. He eats the animal fat on chops, and my mother can't make him stop. He locks himself in his room with his friend and they play Super Mario Brothers. He's always Mario; he's fat enough, all he needs is the moustache. He looks a bit like an opera singer too, which is part of the reason he is always cast in one of the lead roles in the school musicals. In this way we are able to keep ourselves out of the house, where my irritable mother lies exhausted on her double bed in the afternoons with her glass of Coke beside her and her absent husband not.

There is a phone call from the school to ask her to come and see them. She goes in and there is my brother in the office, smelling suspiciously of smoke. She wonders if he has been caught with cigarettes. She is ashamed. She is a teacher here, too, and now everyone will know that her child is a criminal.

But it's not cigarettes. He and his friend lit a fire under the stage in the school hall. It was a small fire, but that wasn't the point. The headmaster in his cassock suggests that my brother be psychologically evaluated. My mother is shocked. Nobody in her family has ever been in therapy.

She and my stepfather and my brother go for one session, and come home and tell us that the therapist says we should stop picking on him. My stepfather sits in front of the TV, shirt off, face blank. Perhaps he will mow the lawn later, when it gets cooler.

Kuifie in the Upper World

But the most beloved child is the new one. We understand this because their real mother is staying in an institution for a while after she came to our house at night and screamed at my mother who wouldn't let her through the front door. Their mother screamed, 'You stole my husband!' and my mother shouted back, 'That's because you had your eyes closed and your legs open!'

My mother is carrying my youngest brother on her hip, the blond evidence of this new marriage. The fight started when their mother said that he was a fat baby. It's true. He is a fat baby. He only drinks Coca-Cola because he's been in hospital for surgery. His knees are curving the wrong way (always he is different, going backwards, warped even in the bone, a beanstalk baby with his head in the clouds. What will he find there?) and Coke was the only thing he wanted when he came round from the anaesthetic. He stretched out his arms as the nurses swished by him and croaked, 'Co-o-o-o-ke!' He is a giant baby. He takes up more space than we have, a love-child, above-child, the youngest, with his sweet tooth and rotten mouth he will suck us dry. More, he wants. He wants more.

He is driven home, this little prince, and clumps irritably out of the sky-blue station wagon even though they said he would not be able to walk, encased in plaster from hip to toe. A miracle baby, descending to us with his new limbs, stiff with sickness, with starch and importance. Underneath its mask the knee is changing; he is being made into one of us. In the sweaty evenings he flickers blue under the TV screen, miserable with the itch, or perhaps it is just *Dallas*. These things we can't get to, but we know they are there.

All this effort, a king's ransom in medical bills and bargains with God – is this normal, Doctor? And this? – trailing him through schools, nursery and junior, senior and out, when one morning he finally wakes up and understands that he is special, and says, No. I will not get up. I will not be going back to school. And my mother, bewildered beside him, with the cold coffee in her hand, saying, Why? What did I do wrong?

And then finally the last day, which came much later. She comes in and sees that he is lying on the floor and streaming vomit from the mouth. She tries to turn him over, help him past the sixteen years that always seem to stretch *away* from us when we are that age, and not *towards* anything; how it must have taken her back to the day when he was seven months old, still at the breast, at the age when we can all still remember how to sigh and swallow at the same time. Like baby animals we open the red caves to our other worlds without choking. The nether regions. She was showing us what her milk was like. It was in a cup, thin and blue and surely not strong enough to stand between all the germs and infections that were in the world and her baby son. We tasted and spat. It was vile. Alive.

And the next time she feeds him she sees that though the small pink piglet grunts on, there is an incredible pain in her breast, so she yanks him away from her. Part of her nipple goes with him and the part that remains seems to gape at her as she stares down at her chest; it gives her a view of her own red insides. And equally red is his open mouth, with its new teeth.

PART THREE
RED-HOT POKER

Ballet Afternoons

Our parents try to occupy us so that we won't have time to think about sharing our bedrooms with the strangers living in the house. Cubs, karate, piano, ballet. Pick and mix for your crowding sons and daughters, filling their frontal lobes with Japanese counting rhymes because English is too close to home.

My brother tries all these grudging afternoon activities and drops them one by one. My mother shouts about paying for outfits but he won't listen. His eight-year-old lips clamp down and his eyes pop. I feel guilty that he won't play along, so I carry on being the good one, hating Christelle the ballet teacher, who makes us wear scratchy tangas so our panties won't show. After school I wait for the thumping modern class just before ours to end, and secretly chew and chew peppery plastic meat sticks that always give me heartburn.

It's not like the books I read where the heroine is already on points and miraculously gets a part in *The Nutcracker* when somebody falls ill. The girls in the class are skinny and never sweat. They have long feet that point properly, like extra fingers, but I am not jointed in this way. When I dance I try to keep my arms down so that they can't see my new underarm hair. That's hard in a ballet class; you get shouted at for lazy carriage of the arms. We stare out of the double-storey windows of the rented space, at the fumes of the afternoon cars and the frying pan pavements. Inside, we are just girls angling our heads like weeping willows, pretending to droop into the fantasy goldfish pond Christelle says is over the shoulders of all good ballerinas. Our feet work separately from our heads.

But I like the tarantella, where you can slap your feet on the ground and swirl; the notion of getting rid of tarantula poison appeals to me, and my flat feet do their work. Ha ha, says my stepfather when he sees me practising. You can see she comes from the plaas.

I am waiting for my mother one day when two girls come over to me and say, 'Lift up your arms.' I clamp them down like a Lego man and say, 'Why should I?' One of them says to the other, 'She has hair there already. I told you.' Her friend finds this hard to believe; her pretty clips twinkle as she bobs in surprise. I turn away and go to the bathroom, wait in the stalls until I hear my mother's Sierra in the street.

That night I ask if I can borrow her razor, and she tries to stop me by saying that it will grow back prickly, but I have had it. I want to be able to lift my arms up and not be afraid. On Monday one of the boys in my class called me a werewolf, so the legs are being done too. My mother stands outside, watering the grass. I wait for her to come inside to show me but she doesn't.

The razor has a double blade. I didn't expect that. It doesn't look very sharp but it is, and shaving is easy as long as you have a steady hand and your legs don't go numb because you've waited until the bathwater is cold. The ankles are tricky and I press too hard and drag upwards, not seeing that the skin has peeled away and is being dragged with it, over my Achilles tendon and far away. Because that is what razors do. The sting is like Dettol, and the bleeding won't stop. It gathers and plops into the water like Kool Aid made too weak by your friend's mother. I shout out the window and my mother tells me to put some toilet paper on it, and not to get any blood on the towels.

The next ballet afternoon Christelle is defeated; she flips her Dolly Parton hair and tells me that I am just heavy on my feet. I am pleased to give it up, tired of getting Pass and Pass Plus for exams, but never Commended, but my mother is cross. She says she wants me to have all the things she didn't when she was growing up.

Jules Verne and the Merman

I'm better at swimming, maybe because the water holds you up, and here everyone is transformed. Fishy. Our coach is an otherwise jolly man with a glass eye. When he has to do an errand, he pops it out and puts it on the edge of the pool. He says. 'Twenty lengths! I'm watching you!' The older boys cheat, but I'm always too scared. I have seen *Indiana Jones and the Temple of Doom*. Besides, I swim slower than they do, so I never have to do a full set, anyway.

They say that sometimes you see things down there. I always see sharks – it's the silence and the idea that you can never see all three hundred and sixty degrees at once. They keep flicking by on my periphery. But that's what you get for bunking swimming practice and going to swim by yourself in the Karen Muir diving pool. The pool is named after a twelve-year-old girl who broke a world record for *backstroke*. For swimming backwards. Touching the bottom is impossible. Nosebleed territory. And on the way home, back to my sulking, shouting, Maths–homework-ridden family, my legs shake with fatigue and my eyes blur. They always put too much chlorine in public pools. Trying to disinfect us. I think it's going to take a lot more than HTH.

Some days in the diving pool, I think I can see my real father doing crawl and sometimes backstroke. Some days he just paddles and his skinny legs flash white and eerie underwater. He wriggles down to the cracked white tiles on the bottom. I feel his ears as if they are my own, ringing with the depth until our mutual head wants to burst.

He seems to be able to hold his breath endlessly. I wonder if he has gills. I am a biologist, poking at this freaky creature that breathes differently. I really do believe that he has escaped being as human as the rest of us. He floats in his own amniotic fluid with a smile on his face.

My mother snorts and says, 'He was pickled in *booze*, baby child. Your father was an alcoholic.'

She has no feelings for mermen.

Little House on the Prairie

Talking about my father is difficult. All the fathers I know in Kimberley seem to be insufficient, with flat eyes and booming beer guts like *Bitterkomix* paedophiles. My mother doesn't really know what to say, but the subject seems to come up inevitably, like a dead goldfish that refuses to be decently flushed.

I am keen for information, looking for the genetic finger-prints of my father, the burglar in the night. Over tea cups and soggy Ouma rusks we dissect his thin body, perfect for slipping in through windows, look for footprints, measure his shoe size to see whether my feet will follow.

'I felt sorry for him,' she says. When I asked her why she married him, she says that she thought that she would love him enough to make up for his family, that it would change him. These clichés pull the corners of her mouth down in the arcs of divorced women everywhere.

'After he died, I was sure I could feel a presence in the room with me.' She turns to tell me this part full on; she is serious. 'In the last few months of his life he was *evil*. It used to just be when he was drinking, but then, that hanging around in the garden with his gun . . .' Her eyes are big, shiny as stars with distance and disaster. 'Once he blew a hole in the wall. The dogs wouldn't go near him after that. They used to wet themselves with fright when he shouted.'

So I go out because it's true, there *is* a fire in my head; but not to the hazel wood, because there are none in Kimberley. In the flatness we learn to look for other hiding places, for sanctuary. I will find out where he has gone. At my fat friend's house her mother knows the boys come over to drink beer, but she doesn't say anything. Perhaps if it happens between her walls she will not have to worry about the bits between our legs and ears.

We squash like preserves in her tiny room with the side-table in the middle; we squat down with our worried limbs looming and glooming Alice-large in this room that seems meant for midgets. We are playing glassy-glassy. 'Who should we call?' the fat girl wants to know. The only dead person below seventy is my father. 'I'm sure he's in the upper world,' she says. I want to make sure even though I am afraid. I would rather know than have this doubt, this dad-shaped cartoon hole in the wall.

On the table is a small glass. We are all meant to put one forefinger on it while she asks the questions of the spirits. 'You're not allowed to move it,' she says. 'It has to move itself. That's how you know.'

She opens with a kind of prayer for protection, an anti-prayer, because who is she really going to ask? 'Jock,' she says, 'are you there?' Nothing happens. Our collective breath is a helium balloon; it carries us higher than the ceiling. 'Jock. Your daughter wants to know.' And of course the glass moves to this, a skidding little dance across the surface. She asks if I want to ask him anything but I am numb with fright, with realisation. We are in vibrating communion with the spirits; we are in Dead-Dad-time.

'Are you in the upper world?' she says, and this is what I

should have said, I know it as the words leave her lips like the fortunes inside cookies; they trail upward too, they show us where to go. The glass jitters. 'If the answer is yes, then move the glass,' she says, and it does, and we all drop our fingers suddenly and look around and laugh in rips of stale air from the lost lungs of those left behind. Burned. Shy. But she is not, she is leaning forward and grabbing us. 'Wait! Wait! Hold hands! I have to banish him!' Her hand is crushing mine. It's like getting your fingers caught in the car door, forcing the blood away in white patches. 'I rebuke and blind you in the blood of Jesus Christ.' She says it again; maybe the more you say it, the truer it is.

Afterwards I stare at the wall. It is absolutely white, like being dead must feel. Blank. She has done this before, she says, and once she didn't banish the spirit. Esther stayed with her for days, smashing the little china cats on the dressing table until the fat girl's mother got a priest in to consecrate every room in the house. The fat girl says that she was hit by some of the shards. 'Look,' she says, and shows us her wrists. They look like plain old knife scars to me. My sister has taken to cutting herself. Inside hurt on the outside. I know it when I see it.

I walk home on my wobbly legs; I need to tell my mother that he's in the upper world, that he's happy where he is, but this will never happen. She'd probably gate me for months.

Material Girl

In Standard Five Madonna frees us in a way nobody expects and that our mothers dislike. Mine refuses to buy me a black bra or even to let me wear my underwear on the outside. She is appalled at the idea of wearing a rosary as jewellery. It's *common*.

For the same reason I can't have a perm or pierce my ears, which was why we end up one Friday night in Gida's house, devoid of her upright Portuguese parents but stuffed with their bric-a-brac. Little ceramic dogs and the sad eyes of Jesus in the embroidered *Last Supper* turn to follow us balefully. All these accessories to denote the comforts of being middle-class in a foreign country, and behind the burglar gate their own child paces down the passage to prick the atmosphere with safety pins and medicinal spirits. In my Father's house there are many mansions.

The night is lit by the coloured bulbs strung up in the entertainment area and by the pool light, wavering and dull as alien headlamps. Maybe we will all be taken away.

When we were much younger we used to have pool parties here in the daytime, when we would try to break the under-water kissing record; fun when you're a contestant; not so fun if you're the one with the stopwatch. Someone would always stuff themselves with birthday cake and Chipniks and run round the pool in their Speedos, yelling while everyone else had gone inside to watch *Cannonball Run* videos. The sudden quiet right after that would indicate that he'd thrown up in the pool. How *immature*. But all that is gone now. The only way we'll let that chlorine bath wash off our Sixth Sense deodorant is if the boys are stupid enough to throw us in.

The boys are going first because they have seen Martin Gore on the cover of the new Depeche Mode album and they have realised that men have nipples too. Gida is chief piercer because it's her house and because we said so. She is shaky and brave in her lime outsize t-shirt while we loll on our fathers' army sleeping-bags beside the pool, our double layers of lumo socks rolled down so that both colours are visible, too scared to go next but too cool to say so. Thinus holds my hand under the sleeping-bag, his pinky nail scratching me because he's growing it for a reason he won't tell. He says he's going to pierce it, too. Being here is doubly bad, because my mother says Thinus's family is especially *common*.

There is some story she half tells, about illegal diamond-buying and my father being roped in as an alibi for them. He ends up spending some time in jail because it's obvious to everybody in the courtroom that he's lying. He was never good at keeping things on the inside. The cops tease him about being there for something other than drunk driving for a change. He writes beautiful prison letters to my mother, promising love and reform. This makes me feel quite *Romeo and Juliet*-ish, but I'm hoping that nobody will have to drink poison.

The sherry is finished and Gida's parents have wisely taken the keys to the booze cabinet with them, so Dean has to do this cold. He goes first; he's always been a bit weird. He keeps licking his lips and laughing; he is so tall that he has to bend down so that she can make her mark on his lobe in ballpoint. Left is for moffies; right is for drug addicts. Or maybe it's the other way round. Nobody really knows.

Gida is shrieking, 'Bring me some ice! Bring me some ice!' and I have to unwind myself from under Thinus's hands and obstacle race to the kitchen, hopping over the backs of the dogs, hoping they won't go for my ankles. Dean's ear is pierced. She's pushed the safety pin right through and then pulled it out again. He lies on his side, pale and sweaty and needing a drink so much that he swallows the disinfectant. It's alcohol, right? I think of the street kids in the park with their meths, straining it through white bread to purify it.

Ten minutes later and Dean makes a trip to the arum lily beds, spewing and coughing and shaking his head like a dog eating ants. He is careful through all of this not to splash on his kaffir takkies. Everyone must learn to purge.

Mario's

We are driving back from Mario's. There have been the usual admonitions not to drink the double thick now because then we won't eat our supper when it arrives. There have been the same old awkward moments where I want to slide under the table because my meaty stepfather asks the waitress whether monkey gland sauce is what it sounds like, and bends forward to examine his half-jack of Johannisberger. I pretend to want a taste because I know I should start getting into wine, but the truth is that it is thin and bitter, and Appletiser still represents the height of good taste as far as I am concerned. The bottle bulges out obscenely in front of my face if I squinch down so I won't have to watch my family yawling and whining in the restaurant. My mother debates the merits of sour cream over butter. She won't let me bring a book.

We come here every Friday night, even though it's run by moffies. They know how to cook a rump steak, and they let my new brother crawl around under the tables. I go to the Ladies a lot, even though it's cheating because I'm not a lady, ha ha, so that I can look in the mirror at my self in the see-through skirt and think about what Madonna would do. The conclusions I come to are all rude. I have a nice church voice but I know that belting out *Like a Virgin* would make me look stupid. There are not even any good-looking English boys to brush past, only families with broad mothers in tired eyes and pink lipstick or lumpy twosomes holding hands. Even the ugly people have mates.

But now it's time to argue about the tip and take more sweeties than you should, even though they don't have little plastic wrappers and not a whole lot of people wash their hands around here. Mario's has teeny little liquorice suckers on green sticks. They are pirates' treasure in a place where pocket money goes on Charlie Sexton albums instead of Bar Ones. We stock up and nip out the door, feeling clever and dancing away from my parents, out to the parking lot in two-tone shoes. *Live to Tell.*

My stepfather decides to take the alternative route behind the baby bird buildings that will become the new private hospital. We bump along the gravel of the site, back to Belgravia and the Friday-night movie on TV, sleek and well fed and sulky. On the side of the dirt road is a black woman in a stretch outfit, not particularly fleshy or sexy or big, just standing there with her eyes down and her lips very red in the headlights.

My stepfather slows, winds the window down and calls out, 'Hoeveel?' She doesn't answer. She does not want to trade with this man who has a car full of family. He persists. 'Twintig rand?' She looks up as he leans out further, arm resting on the rolled-down window and glasses glinting. 'Te veel!' he shouts, and laughs uproariously, 'Dis te veel!' We skid along the gravel and race off.

Café Society

I tell my mother I am going to the café, and I do. But I also know that Graham and his friends will be hanging out in the sloping underground garage at the back, smoking their cigarettes like men and curving their backs against the cement. The inside smells of cat piss and spilled oil; it smells dark and cold. Sometimes grim businessmen will chuff out, fat faces glaring at the kids loitering in the alley, halfway between real places, but for the most part it's just our secret selves.

I know when Graham is there without his girlfriend because

I can smell Old Spice; that sweetness sends blood to my skull, beating stars behind my eyelids so that I can't see where I'm walking and I trip over the cracks in the pavement. Break your mother's back. He is an ecosystem all to himself; he makes me feel like I'm top of the food chain.

The others eventually disperse but I hang on grimly; I know that he will wait with me for that sliver of life in between the sun going and the bats coming. He gets me into trouble because I am not home by the time the streetlights come on. I am hanging from his lips like another cigarette, always standing on a slope, so that the left breast gets more attention from his practised fingers, always on tiptoe. My muscles flutter with strain like DO NOT CROSS tape around the scene of an accident, and he likes that.

But there are no bullets or chalk outlines; we are not still for long enough and I am not a victim. I am twelve and I share a room with my sisters. I am not a smoker but I am a drinker of Coke. I am a good student. I am a fast runner. I am a wearer of hoop earrings and pale lipstick. In five years' time I will probably hate me, the dislike shooting both ways like Cupid confused. This is how I get my kicks, by sneaking out in my pink lace takkies to kiss a boy who is six years older than me in his body and right where I am in his head.

One afternoon we are surprised when we cannot jump apart fast enough, and there is James, Anthony's brother, who has also crept out for a smoke. A gathering of thieves. He draws in his breath, fast and hissing, and then stands with his hands on his hips and laughs and laughs, shaking his head and then his finger at Graham in a you-sneaky-dog kind of way. I am looking down, secretly proud. I made him risk this.

'I think', says James, 'that some blackmail is in order.' He pauses, trying to put his finger on something he wants really badly, trying to put this precious moment to its best possible use.

He looks at me. 'I think you should make me sandwiches.' He means every day. I don't think he understands what I could do with a knife. He starts to tell me what his favourite fillings are but I dodge out of the alley and down the road, where the tar feels level and hard under the balls of my homing feet. The streetlights come on and if they catch me they will splash me with their real light and real life, dissolve in their acid daytime all our dreaminess and desires.

Bunny Girl

The school swimming pool is so much deeper than it has to be; it was made in the days before metres were the way we measured space. It is never clean. Always there is the slick feel of the underworld on the soles of the feet, the idea that every scratch could be poison. Afterwards your blood would not be pure. And we swim there in the afternoons in the potential disease, lie in the sun with the cement under us until we melt like ice cream, vanilla, then chocolate. Neapolitan. Hoping that the people we like will lick us, eat us up in spoonfuls.

The boys in the hostel climb up into the clock tower, measuring their own spaces in handfuls of flesh and cement. We never see them but we know they are there with their hunched backs and jerking hands. The clock never works. Perhaps it is sticky with their juices. The river of dreams. Wet ones. Sometimes the Matric boys venture down to us; in their Speedos and goggles they are foreign with bumps. On land each one has a defect: skinny legs, a pigeon chest, a birthmark on the face, but in the water they can all do equal laps like Scalextric cars. Their muscles buzz with effort – if you put your ear to the chest you can hear it, that familiar music of the spheres – and they breathe cleanly to either side.

Afterwards they dry themselves off and saunter back in their Adidas slops, wrapped in smug towels and the dampness between their webbed toes. They will shower in the bathrooms that have no cubicle doors; they will make jokes in the steam about dropping the soap, and especially they will try not to think about any encounters with other boys they might really have liked. They will think about being perfect.

I have a white costume but it is not transparent. In the water it turns into dough. Will I rise? The boys in the tower think so. Through the summer I turn darker and darker, like a stain on a carpet, so that my stepfather says that I look like a coloured, and my mother tells everyone that the postman is my father. I wish he was. I could deliver messages from the other side of the Colour Bar.

One afternoon I am sitting watching the Matric boys rotor through their own waves. Their bodies are relentless. One of them pulls himself out of the water and comes to sit next to me. His body has pointy pink nipples and flat brown muscles but his face is pebbly with acne scars. They form shadows on his skin as if he has been burned. He is not twice shy and he is not from South Africa. Always he says that his parents will come to fetch him and they will go back to the UK. Perhaps their skin is like that there, a whole nation of people whose insides show on the surface.

He leans in to me and I wonder if he is going to try to kiss me. I will be kind but I will say no. I will tell him that I am in love with someone else. I will not say, Because you're ugly and I am afraid of you. I will not say, I do not want to be like you. His breath smells of spearmint as he says, 'You know, Diane, you could be quite pretty, but your nose really spoils your face.'

Lord, Dismiss Us

Sunday is churchday and cleanday and fightday all through the eighties. It takes an almost Miss South African effort to organise my enormous family so that everyone has brushed their teeth and will make it to the ten o'clock service in time for the first hymn. It always takes so long to bully my lagging, nagging brother out of bedroom and bathroom that the station wagon is already moving off as he pulls in a last foot.

Inside the car tempers are thin, as bristling as our damp hair. We stare out of the windows misted with our huffing and secret hangovers, wondering if there will be cute boys in the congregation today, dreading the moment when we will have to kneel and inhale the fumes off the chalice of communion wine and the vapour of the Holy Spirit coming down will turn to a mouthful of burning.

We are always late, and march silently in our God's Army ranks to the third pew from the front (public enough to be noticed as the First Family; modest enough not to look too ostentatiously pious), cutting through the standing singers like a Rolux Magnum lawnmower. After the relief of a quick entry, there is the tedium of the lip-service. I change all the Hims to Hers, saying them just loud enough so that my mother will glare sidelong at me, her speciality in sacred spaces. I am sixteen and I lost my faith when I walked into the bottle store and saw the communion wine there.

During the sermon my sisters and I exchange scathing looks when the portly priest pauses and titters at his own jokes, cueing the congregation in to God's laugh track. Some of the service is beautiful; then we say it like we mean it. I refuse to do the raw references to cannibalism.

The queue up to the altar makes me acutely aware of the

number of eyes trained on us, the communicants, whom no number of new shoes can camouflage. I shrink and creep through the stains of the coloured windows; now blue as Mary's mantle; now red as the snake in the grass. The incense swirls, rich and improbable. Burnt offerings from people preserving their seedless-raisin souls.

The sub-deacon zooms in, but not like the angel Gabriel, because the white scalp showing in his parting gives him away. The host, amen, is thin and dry and clings to my panicky palate. The diluted muscadel is still strong enough to evoke choking flashbacks to thirsty Saturday nights in the park.

And back the way we came; relief at absolution and at not throwing up. And now, newly cocky, we stare in pale and spotty envy at the coloured girls, with their lacy knee socks and ringleted hair, wondering at how early they would have to get up to wash and press and shape and curl themselves. If this was a dog show, they would be poodles.

Afterwards, with my sore knees and stiff smile, I wash up the tangible God in the fusty chastity, among the stripping priests and the banter. My mother is an equal-opportunities flirt, bustling and hustling as she deftly counts out unblessed wafers and hangs up chasubles.

It is a tradition for old ladies to leave their jewels to the church, and the priests, bewildered as Aladdin with these shiny stones, have them pressed into the chalices. My fingers feel the clasps and hardnesses as I wash them, shocked into obedience at the thought that I am holding hundreds of thousands of rands, and also at the sorrow and love of the brides of Christ who have left their most precious possessions to someone they knew would appreciate them.

The drive home is punctuated with sniggering and stops for the *Sunday Times* and enough Coke to feed my mother's habit. We are greedy with the idea of making Brown Cows when we get home.

This doesn't materialise, mainly because when we arrive, the safety gate is open. My parents go in first, ears pricked, but our intruder is long gone, the scent cold but the air blue with my stepfather's rantings about kaffirs. There are squash rackets missing, and briefcases, some jewellery. Nothing major except the idea that the our-ness of the house is gone. Someone has been watching us. And we were not watching them.

The policemen, one English, one Afrikaans, both blue burghers who have shaved too closely before coming out, are understanding and polite but essentially unhelpful. There is shrugging and laughing about the state of this country, the suggestion that we are lucky that the burglars didn't smear excrement on the walls. 'They're afraid, you see,' say the policemen. 'They're kakking themselves.' And then we have lunch. The Ice Cap hardens, a brown and shiny shell over the ice cream.

Flying Carpet

In the house our many sounds bounce off the new cream tiled floors; we are little Barbarellas with my stepfather at the controls. We do not see him except for mealtimes or on the weekends, when he hires epic videos and watches them all in a row, right up close to the screen. With his squinchy bloodshot eyes he watches them. He has started taking the little blue pills for his migraines. They come slowly, gathering in the dust of his car as he vrooms to his accounting jobs where he marches ballpoint soldiers into legal rows – salute – and pound him like a raw steak under a mallet, blood and muscle, flatter and flatter.

He has air conditioning put in although we can't afford it; he is too hot, cooped up here with us like chickens. When our scratching and cheeping gets too much he disappears down the secret passage off the master bedroom, into his study where he is teaching himself how also to be a legal ballpoint soldier. My mother pays for his studies with the money from my real father's shares that his dying left her. She wants my stepfather to have a nice leather briefcase. She isn't speaking to one of her sisters who said that he counts other people's money for a living. They have set up a small accounting business for him and even though he hasn't passed his exams yet, people come to him because they trust his chunkiness and his rude jokes. The pork-shiny farmers and the hollow-faced businessmen bring biltong and Klipdrift to his tiny office where the nineteen-year-old receptionist lisps and blushes. They like that.

We have pool fencing and en suite bathrooms and new puppies. We roll on the carpets when we aren't moving the furniture around in our yawning three-girl bedroom. We go away to Jeffrey's Bay in the holidays and eat and eat and eat so that the two small incomes from the grown-ups are translated into the language of adverts. We have cheeks and tummies and thighs like wedges of processed cheese – Mum, remember Melrose! We jiggle when we walk with the good things that are ours. We are the seven fat cows in a king's dream.

I walk home from school early one afternoon and there is a big white truck outside the front garden; the men in overalls are stepping all over the careful soil beds my mother has worshipped in every evening since we moved from West End. She says to her large-nosed relatives over the phone, 'Yes, we live in *Belgravia* now.' They are carrying out our furniture. No one else is home. It must be true; I never believed all those stories about how one day the blacks would come into your house and steal all your stuff. I tell them to put the couches down but they hustle past me with frowns that stretch into the hairlines on their dripping faces. They struggle to and fro; their job is heavy. They are the Four Horsemen of the Apocalypse without their trusty steeds. I push my way inside and sit down on the carpet that smells of puppy; I will not be moved.

In twenty minutes they have cleared out everything that some other family could possibly want. They have left the carpet, so I stay there until my mother comes home and tells me to get out of my school uniform because we aren't poor whites. I think I can spill out this rage at her but I find that while my voice wants to shout, my eyes want to cry. It turns out she knew that they were coming today. My stepfather has been declared insolvent. Yes, that makes sense because he is like that. Stubborn and insoluble, he will not blend in, like lumps of Nesquik that won't be dissolved in the milk.

He stays away until late in the evening. He goes to her in the garden, where she is sitting on the step. From now on he will spend the whole week in Postmasburg doing the books for the Foundry, where metal from fire is pounded into usable tools, and he'll be able to speak Afrikaans always with his red-tipped secretary with her hot hair and nails. Perhaps there will be sparks between them. He will come home on the weekends with his fingers burned from wrestling with the demons who stoke the fires in closed Afrikaans communities. He will smell of smoke and there will be dust on his car again because he has no magic carpet any more to allow him to fly above all this.

Deuce

In the garden I watch my mother move from bed to bed, watering her plants by hand even though there is a sprinkler. She is absorbed and lonely, marking time in her class's workbooks with neat red ticks waiting for Friday (Friday's child is loving and giving), waiting for my stepfather. When he is home he shakes the house to its English foundations with his sport on TV and his aftershave that says, Men were here. When he is home we have to dress properly and not leave our empty glasses in the lounge. When he is home the doors of the cupboards have to be closed on the chaos of our girl-lives.

The only sport he plays now is squash, with a concentration that slicks him down with sweat and teeth-grinding. It's Biblical. With his tiny white shorts and his metallic racket he is a superhero in his own head – see how he leaps tall buildings in a single bound. He oozes out all his weekday weaknesses and lusts. He oozes us out with our bird-voiced demands for new pencil bags and tapes. He oozes out his toddling son with his leg in plaster from the operation. He oozes out the medical accounts. He oozes out his secretary with her curly red hair and her straight red nails. Lately she comes to work in shorts that allow him to see just the edge of her round divorcee buttocks as she bends over the bottom drawers of the filing cabinet. He oozes and oozes. And sometimes he tells my mother about his secretary, and how ridiculous she is, how *common,* and they sit snugly together on the couch in front of the TV.

Some nights I go to watch him play squash because I am bored and because sometimes there are good-looking boys also in shorts. They heave and grunt while I look down on them from the cement stairs that cool the backs of my thighs with their icy blunt ridges. Afterwards the rubber ball is so hot it smells of burning, of things being destroyed. The men on the court yell insults at each other: if I'm lucky I'll hear the 'f' word and be able to hold my stepfather to ransom. He is always so self-righteous. The white soles of their takkies squeak as they lug their heavy stomachs from wall to wall. This is boring. I think, I am never going to let myself get fat like that. I am never going to gurgle when I walk.

There is a sharp popping noise and my stepfather falls forward on his knee, shouting, 'Ah!' I run down the stairs that bruise the soles of my feet with their cold, with their hardness. He is clutching his knee. *Is he crying?* His face is wet. The other wives jiggle down in their own mid-life flesh and crowd around him so that I have to peer over their shoulders to see. The skin around his knee is dimpled, and there is something sharp pressing from inside. It wants to get out, but he doesn't want it to. There is no blood. One of the heavy ladies in her pleated white skirt is going to drive him to the hospital. Another one drives me home.

At the door my mother's face is the colour of old dishcloths. We explain where he is. I have almost lost my breath from all the excitement, and the lady squeezes my shoulder in her strong squash grip until I calm down. My mother doesn't seem perturbed. When we get inside and the lady goes back to her car, she turns to me and says, 'You didn't put a curse on him, did you?' Ah. If only.

Purple Valentine

My stepfather is making lots of new rules as we get closer to something. We think it may be womanhood but we can't really tell. He gets very upset with me when I wear a t-shirt and my bikini bottoms inside the house. He is insisting that we wear shorts over our costumes, but won't tell us why. The rule is lifted once, when I have a horribly itchy and disfiguring case of chicken pox, and wearing a shirt is unbearable. My mother dabs me pinkly with calamine but isn't stern enough about telling me not to scratch, so I still have lots of little raised scars. I think grimly about the story of one mother at school, who insisted that her daughter get her inoculation on her bum instead of on her arm, so she wouldn't have the daisy scar there. My stepfather laughs at me as I run over the cold blonde tiles in my panties. He calls me Spotty.

His other new rule is: no boys in the bedroom. I don't know what he thinks is going to happen there, because he won't say, but mutters darkly that he remembers what he was like 'at that age'. I don't want them in my room, either. They'll go through my stuff, they'll see me ordinary. They irritate me enough during the week, with their anarchy symbols cut into their forearms, and their Sex Pistols tapes. When I kiss them I scratch their initials on the back of my pencil box, and give them a score out of ten. At the moment only Anthony escapes; he is the best kisser *ever*.

But now there is Blake, who is different. For a start, he doesn't go to my school. His mother is a hairdresser so he has access to all these cool products. At the moment he has Andrew Ridgeley streaks, and his fringe is floppy and thick. Hair other boys want.

We look similar. When we go out, people ask us if we're brother and sister, and we say, Yes, and then lean against a car and kiss with tongue. My mother is not pleased. She tells me that that boy is trouble. So we usually end up at his house, where *his* mother lets him have girls in his bedroom, and he puts his hands under my shirt and down my panties as we writhe on his boy's duvet to Def Leppard. I always leave when I think he's getting too turned on; he smells his fingers as he walks me home.

My parents, miracle of miracles, go out one night to see a movie, and Blake comes over, uninvited. He walks in and I notice that the shape of his head is different. Shaved. All his beautiful hair. He looks like a convict, like those photographs of Auschwitz where the Jews peer through the bars with their Charlie Chaplin eyes and their Adam's apples. I hate it. I hate

93

him, then, for destroying what I liked about him most. He doesn't get it, and says, laughing and shy and proud of himself, 'I'm going to the Army soon. I thought I'd practise.' But I'm *not* going to the Army, and I want a boyfriend with hair.

My brother spies on us on the brown couch, so we go to my room, stepping over the threshold of everything I know. On the bed he gets my panties off, and everything is still fun because this isn't anything that hasn't happened before. But then he takes his pants off too, and I start to get nervous because nothing on him is familiar anymore, and for a moment I panic, but his hands are smooth and warm. I think, I want to know what it's like. Nobody will tell me and the books talk in metaphors, and my parents shift in their chairs when there's a French kiss in a video. I want to know what all the fuss is about. Maybe this will be something I like.

Above my head there is the sound of a condom packet tearing, and with that ripping is the knowledge that I can't stop him now even if I wanted to. I can't waste a condom.

He is squashing my lungs as he fumbles with his penis, and then there is an incredible pain. He pushes his hips against me so that now there are three areas of soreness, one for each sharp hipbone, and one really big one for the knife inside. I say, 'Ow. Stop. You're hurting me,' but he shakes his head impatiently and grips my knees. He tries to cross my legs over his back to let him go in deeper, but by now the pain is so bad it's like the time I burned myself on the stove. And he won't stop, just keeps pushing as there is a tearing inside me, like the condom packet, and he now he wants me to grip his buttocks but I struggle against his hardness until I manage to kick his weight off me and vault up and run to the window. My legs are shaking and I hate him so much I almost want him to come after me, because that will give me an excuse to hit him.

I get my shorts back on and say, 'My parents are home.' He

94

lies there on my bed and he says, 'Well, that's not the most exciting time I've ever had.' He gathers his things and stalks slowly to the toilet past my brother, who says nothing.

I tidy the room, switch the light on to get rid of anything my Sherlock Holmes mother will sense. The next day he phones me and wants to see me, but I tell him that I have too much homework.

A month later I get a Valentine's card in the post, from Tempe, the Army base outside Bloemfontein. Inside it says, 'I hope this is the only Valentine's card you're getting, as it is the only one I'm sending.' On the duvet there are still the two scrunched-up places on the material where my hands have gripped and sweated, and a smudge of dried blood halfway down.

The Stationmaster's Arms

And it comes out, one day, when my stepfather is away and my mother can be generous with her attention, why he is so obsessed with the idea of sluttishness, why sex is something that must be kept away from his daughters.

They have always said that his parents were poor. There is the story of how they wrapped him in newspaper to bring him home from the hospital on the day he was born. Perhaps even then other people's opinions were seeping into him. Osmosis via the *E.P. Herald*.

The parents are both dead now, his father last. My stepfather refused to see him when he was dying. Under his thin sheets his father must have realised that he was alone. Was he sorry? Or perhaps it didn't occur to him; they say the man had an IQ of eighty, which got him a job reserved for whites on the railways with a shiny steel ticket puncher but not much else. A maker of confetti. And when he drank he was worse, smelling inside his scratchy grey uniform of heat and rot like a compost bin.

On the side of each hand were the places where the midwife had chopped off the beginnings of his extra fingers nearly forty years ago, and buried them under the frangipani tree along with the placenta. Now the scars just looked like warts. He was so used to them that he didn't notice them, even at night when he cleaned his gun at the kitchen table. So many of us bear these signs of breeding.

And maybe this is why he thought his wife was having an affair, that she was looking for a better man than he was, a richer, smarter man who would whisper words in English to her and touch her with all the fingers on his piano-playing hands. This woman had the same name as my mother although there was a generation and a culture between them, and perhaps they provoked the same blindness in their men. With her smell of dirty hair and her skull poking out through her cheeks in its honesty, his mother didn't have the time or the hope that an affair requires. Perhaps all he really needed to do was look at her in the daylight to see this.

Back then women didn't leave the house unless there was some chore. But they were allowed to visit each other's temporary hire-purchase kitchens and drink Five Roses because coffee was too expensive, while their tongues were coated with tannin and gossip. It was protection; it kept their hearts strong.

Their lungs were a different story. They puffed in and out, more tenacious than Van Hunks and his pipe, sending proof of life up into the atmosphere in their smoke signals to God, saying that Adam hadn't been for nothing. Saying, In our children we start over. In the Port Elizabeth dirt the frangipani bloomed upward too. With its thick white trumpets and memories of weddings it grew wild and this was just as well, because gardening wasn't going to happen when water was needed for boiling kettles.

One of these friends left her footprints in a trail in the dirt as she opened the chicken-wire gate. A jackal, stealing hens. Her red lipstick bled into the wrinkles around her mouth and splashed on her whiskers. My fifteen-year-old stepfather, with his curly hair and his biceps moulded in the free gymnastics classes at school, would wash out the cups she used and saw the eclipses of her mouth, always on the rim, as if she had taken a bite out of the china. And he wondered about that.

One day, while he was doing his press-ups in his bedroom, she came slyly in and stood watching him bulge and groan on the floor. He had made the Eastern Province team for gymnastics that year. He needed to keep fit. Then, of course, she came closer. He got up and sat on his lumpy bed because there was nowhere else. And she sat down beside him and took off her sandals. She asked him if he had ever been with a woman and he laughed, thinking how kind she was to be interested in his teenage life. She grabbed one of his bare nipples and he stopped laughing after that. And then she fucked him, oh yes, she did, with her thin biltong arms and her smell of raw meat.

And sometimes she came back on other afternoons. His mother went out for cigarettes.

But one evening his father came home and he was wild with Klipdrift and rumour. He took out his gun and he pointed it at his grey wife, who sat at the kitchen table with her tea and wearily repeated that she wasn't seeing anyone else. At the sink my stepfather turned around. One day he would stop his father.

But this time was different. Maybe it was the smell of sex in the house that burned up into his father's stunted sinuses and made his head ache in bursts like electricity; maybe he was tired of this conversation. So he shot her twice and she slid down the chair on to the floor. He made sure she was dead and then he walked back to The Stationmaster's Arms where his brandy was still on the bar. And he did not ever say sorry.

The Butcher Boys

The song is wrong. Out here on the perimeter there are always stars. They allow six drunk boys to see their way clear to hauling their meaty bodies over the side of a bakkie. They have cricket bats with them and they drive off into the darkness. There are no streetlights or other authority figures because this is not a laboratory. The animals don't need to live under fluorescent lighting on game farms. It does give them an unfair advantage, though. We should all have pupils that expand to fill space on the sides of our heads. The boys make up for being night-blind with their other senses. Their heads swivel at the scurryings of small things under the tyres of the vehicle. Their breath is anaesthetised and their voices are scratchy with perceived targets. It is too dark to wear mirrored sunglasses.

The trick is to be as quick as possible; pin the dassie in the sunburn of the headlights and jump off as close as you can. Sometimes, if it is really frightened, it will crouch and quiver but it won't run. This is the part where they swing the bat down, like when you play swingball in the garden to the tune of the lawnmower, only here it's the engine of the bakkie that vibrates in the veld. There should be a crunching as the spine gives, and after that, it's vital to get into some sort of rhythm so that everyone can say they got a chance to batter at the heap of fur and paws scrabbling at their feet. It's important to wear the right sort of shoes.

The boys are sweaty and spattered when they throw the lumpy body into the back for the dogs. Epol isn't all a dog needs.

This is what Philip is thinking when he twists round to look at the dark patch where they have just been and falls out of the bakkie, flat on to his back. There is a singing sound in some vertebra below and he is numbed by the laughter and clumsiness of his friends as they haul him up and, in the process, snap his spine completely. He is the world's biggest fish, he thinks. Born slippy. They don't have any feeling either.

It is only when he can't sit up that they realise that he is hurt and not drunk – an easy mistake to make – and race the half hour into town, death and damage suddenly closer than they thought. The permed nurses at the hospital are reluctant to let them in; they are familiar with the scars on chins and broken bones these boys send to them in the daytime. But they see that Philip is crying, and they call a smooth-faced doctor, who makes them take him straight for x-rays. Here he is made transparent, and all the operations over the next months and years will do nothing to make him substantial as other boys with their organs in less useful places.

There is a theory that adversity is somehow conducive to spiritual growth. You suspect that there's more Calvinism than compassion there. But nobody in Kimberley hunts dassies anymore. And Philip has the arms of Atlas, except that he doesn't have the weight of the world pressed upon his shoulders. It wouldn't fit in a wheelchair. But he does say that he has bettered the world record for javelin. Except that he was by himself at the time.

His two-legged friends come to see him, but it is also amazing how many people there are like him. You don't see them in the daytime, in a rampless world, but they are there, bristling and self-sufficient. Jason says that they went out drinking a few weeks ago, and clearly there were many things to celebrate (the most obvious of which is still having a functional liver) and this ended up with his not being able to drive, or not being able to find his car keys, which is not the same thing. Jason stayed over, face-down in the lounge, and came to in the morning to find three boys fallen out of their overturned wheelchairs, snoring gently and dribbling on the carpet. His first thought was, Jesus! Did I do that to these okes?

There are an awful lot of people in Kimberley who think that tragedies are tests from the Almighty. The rest of us just hide the cricket bats.

Pythagoras's Theorem

And there are always the Sunday evenings; we are doing our homework at the dining room table after having avoided it the whole weekend. What this means is that I am drawing roller-ball mermaids and leaving spaces after writing out the questions while everybody else watches the M★N★E★T movie. I just have no idea of what I am supposed to do. The letters and numbers stare up at me; they must be boys, they are good at keeping their secrets. I flip through the pages of the textbook, looking for the unfunny Maths cartoons, and there she is, Pythagoras's girl, the squaw on the hippopotamus. She looks as irritable as I feel, waiting and wearing my life into grooves until I can go to university.

My stepfather swings past on his way to the fridge, and I stop his accountant steps and whine, 'I don't understand how this wooorks.' He looks at me and says, 'What's one plus one? Two. That's all that Maths is. One plus one.' I give him the death stare and say, 'Not when it's geometry.' He carries on going, hearing the roar of Lion, calling back, 'What are you, stupid? One plus one.' It trails after him like the arms on the flag of the self-righteous, the ranks of computer geeks and white collar-wearers. It makes me angry to think that all those dorks who spend their afternoons playing Super Mario Brothers might actually inherit the earth.

The next day is worse, because I have enough time to copy the homework first thing in the morning, fingers cold with cheating, but then we also have a test. My stomach is empty. Fear and no breakfast. I bet other people's mothers make them muffins and fruit salad, but mine is always rushing around in her underwear, hair half dry, telling us to leave the Coco Pops. I write down columns of numbers like family trees, link angles that can't possibly be connected legitimately, bring on the bastards and prepare myself for the sticky red failure that will come my way in a few days. I'm not brave enough to throw these tests away. I console myself that I'm smarter than Richard but dumber than Meagen. So what. I have nice legs and a file of poetry. And I've read *Dracula*. Surely this will mean something in the afterlife.

At break time we trek to the hostel, shoes crunching, pushing each other into the street, to herd after the first Judas goat into the tuck shop, where the mothers won't serve you unless you say please, and a boy pushes his hand up my skirt. It is worth it to get close to a packet of Jelly Tots. We lie in wait for the boarders with their syrupy scones the size of their own heads and beg for bits. Things we would never eat at home take on new status here. This is my Body. The boarders deal in guilt and promises; they navigate our salivary glands. When I leave school I will never eat these things again.

On to Guidance, where the girls and boys are split up. This is how we know this is going to be a Sex Ed lesson. God knows what they tell the boys, those brothers in their fluttering robes, trim guardian angels weighed down with crucifixes that make you hesitate before lying to them about your homework. The girls watch a video called *Our Friend the Clock*, which has to be explained to us by Kerry as the rhythm method. This is Lifeskills in a Catholic school at the end of the twentieth century; a female index finger and thumb rubbing together to test the elasticity of morning vaginal secretions. There is some thermometer action as well, but by this stage the teacher has left the room and everyone has dissolved in disgust. Next week there will be a visiting nun, and there will be anonymous questions on scraps of paper drawn out of a hat. Ha. Messages from the centre of the earth, or at least the pituitary gland; messages from the devil.

Last period is Cadets. Girls get away without holding bugles and dressing in little Boer War replica outfits, but have to pay the price by doing needlework or ceramics or make-overs. I can never decide which is worse, standing pins-and-needles while an overshaved army captain spits and roars, or having to twitter and titter when someone's mother comes in to lecture us on cleansing and moisturising 'in little circles, girls, because we don't want to help gravity now, do we?' I am biding my time, and the kind of things I need to do won't require mascara. I look over at my friend Michelle, and she rolls her eyes and passes me a peach-coloured tissue. On it is written, Rum, Sodomy and the Lash, and I think, Yes. Save us, Shane McGowan.

Back to Nothingness, Like a Week in the Desert

In the desk in front of me there is Randall, with his headgear that is supposed to straighten his teeth, and his teeth, which don't look that skew. The Velcro harness has flattened his hair into a cross shape. Perhaps it will never come out and everyone his whole life through will think that he has come to Jesus. I hate having him in front of me. With his oil-slick eyes he watches me sidelong, with his long legs he takes up too much space. He is Bambi and Nosferatu in one, a vampire twat. He is always saying strange things, like, 'Diane, do you think I could be described as tall, dark and handsome?' and me, thinking I'm funny, saying, 'Two out of three isn't bad.' He smiles, slow to understand malice.

But the worst is that he has dandruff because he can't wash his hair properly. Maybe he never takes that harness off; maybe it is what keeps him together. The dead skin flakes gently back on to my desk, because everything he does is gentle and inoffensive, and everything ends up being unwelcome, like his unseasonal snow in this southern hemisphere, snow under the Southern Cross. He twists backward and manages to bob at me in his chair. He hands over a tape and says, 'I don't know how you feel about this, but these are my three favourite songs.' I am afraid that people will think he and I are friends, so I take it quickly.

When I play it at home there are the Moody Blues songs and a Crowded House track, *Better Be Home Soon*. When I take it back to him the next day I ask for a copy. Somehow the quietness of that track, that yearning to be scraped clean and start over, surprises me. I thought that he didn't know what we said about him, that his skin was thicker because there were more things wrong with him on the outside than with us. And after that I can't be mean to him any more; I see that his giraffe limbs are dignified, not gawky, and that he is a gentleman. A gentle man.

But when I am sent out of English for 'enrichment work', I go to lie down on the splintery planks of the stands and it's Anthony I think of, hard and lovely in his Pipe Band uniform, the blond hair on his arms shining like pot scourers. Rumpelstiltskin, spinning the ordinary into the extraordinary, and then back again. Wanting something different from what is being given.

Guilty Party

I have to stay inside and study. The day has been so dry that there isn't enough saliva in your mouth; it has been too hot even to cry. People in Kimberley don't bother to water their gardens before sunset, because it all evaporates, sucked up into flat clouds that never deliver. They say that it's the fat-bottomed clouds, 'like women', that are the ones to watch for. When I was small we ran through the sprinkler. Now I spend my time resenting dogs, hating everyone who doesn't have to study, wishing years off my life withering here behind the Anglican lace curtains at nine o'clock. My desk looks out on to the night garden beyond the curly burglar bars designed to keep others out and daughters in. Ha. The white jasmine sweetness is warm and thick as new jam cooling on counters. I want to keep it in jars so that I can dip into it when I am old. Preserves. Matric 1991. But right now the last thing I want is breakfast.

All this is not conducive to memorising the workings of the kidney. When I try to think back to what was happening in Biology when we did these organs, all I can think of is the boys chopping little slices off the sheep's hearts we had to bring, and daring each other to eat them. Ian carefully wrapped up his group's heart in newspaper at the end of the lesson. He was taking it somewhere but we didn't know why until after break.

Apparently he had found Kerry and told her that he had a present for her. 'Here is my heart,' he said, and gave her the damp bundle. 'Aah, sweet,' she said, unwrapping it and then splatting it on the floor when she saw what it was. He was doubled over with hysteria at his own funniness, which was just as well because when she punched him he didn't have that far to fall.

My sister comes in with a smile and a screwdriver. 'Get out

of the way, please,' she says and crawls over my kidney notes on the desk. 'What are you doing?' I ask, fairly stupidly, considering that she is twirling the screws on the insides of the windows. Her wrists turn, rotating tan and white as she works, all those hours of flicking hockey balls finally being put to use. 'I have to go to the park,' she says. There she will be able to lie back on the grass so that it prickles through her shirt like pins and needles; she will wait near the moondial for her girlfriend to meet her.

She lifts up the bars and wiggles out, her breath minty and her eyes bright, and I am jealous and afraid, back in my chair with my high IQ and my empty chest.

So it is no surprise one night later that my own escape also happens, when the air from the jasmine outside pours in again with its sticky messages like wasps. I find that it's true, the burglar bars unscrew quite easily, and the side gate isn't as slippery as you might suppose. We hop over in our stretch jeans with no giveaway girliness, into the street like the nursery rhyme and it's all true, the moon *is* as bright as day.

It lights up our bleached English faces and the trench coats in the middle of summer. Maybe Anthony will be there, with his crocodile eyes and slow amble. We huff cigarettes in the park and the white bakkie that zooms by is no one we know. So when it reverses in its own dust and the spidery boys on the back jump off, we are a little bit scared. But no one moves. There are five of us. 'Engelse!' they whoop to us, and the down on the backs of our necks rises. The Wit Wolwe. We understand that there will be taunting and pushing and taking of cigarettes, and that we will have to listen to the boys for the rest of the evening, saying how they could have taken them on if they'd had the chance.

They take a dislike to Seth, insolent as the Sex Pistols. He is gripped by the padlock he wears around his neck and choked.

The other boys scuffle to stop this, and we girls shout about lawyers and human rights, but it's no use. They punch Seth with white knuckles and kick out at the other boys. Some kind of chivalry or disdain for cross-pollination stops them touching the girls. We look on, and it's never the way you think it's going to be, where there is a clear body part to aim for, in slow motion. There is only this undignified flapping, and the sense of being pinned down and deliberately hurt by people with arms like rope on a boat, tethering us to ugliness. They decide that we have been humiliated enough for the evening, and one jams his cigarette out on the inside of Seth's forearm. He doesn't react in the way they expect – ha ha on them, there are scars there already.

Seth brings his fishbowl face to school on Monday and people are concerned but not surprised. There is a lot of talk about lawsuits but nothing ever happens even though we can identify the guilty parties. Our parents tell us to stay away from dangerous places after dark, under the illusion that this happened about six hours earlier than it actually did. My mother makes a new rule; I have to be home before the streetlights come on. I tell her that I'm not psychic. This is how Kimberley works – there is no real retribution for anything truly upsetting in the greater scheme of things, but for getting home two minutes after curfew, there is house arrest. I didn't know about Robben Island at the time.

Do Ya Think I'm Sexy?

It's a Friday evening and we're fresh from a Prefects' meeting in the hostel with its smells of old semen and incense trailing after us, trying to stop us with our Going Out shoes on, made of rubber, and clipboards in our hands. Kerry has decided that karaoke at the Kimberley Sun is an option for us under-agers. You never know who might be staying in the hotel. Steve Hofmeyr was there once. And the Cover Boys another time. It is a place for grown-up misbehaviour that goes with making a special trip into town for the night, the kind of place where you hope there aren't mirrors in the room to reflect what you're doing right back at you.

The bar is dim and smells of rich travellers on dirty weekends. We colonise some bar stools, polished with the bottoms of hopeful drinkers and fondlers, and we watch the cricketers out of the corners of our make-up. They are sent here from the UK, part training, part punishment. They call themselves pros, and their noses are always peeling. They have pounds. We have to be sharp so that we are not picked up by any of our parents' friends; it's happened before and it's hard to say no.

People drift in and soon our friends appear, having bunked out of the hostel with their Aramis aftershave and their pula from Botswana. They are telling blonde jokes, even though these are beginning to be replaced with a variation: Stupid Men jokes. Not as funny. The boys drink faster than we do, but we buy in rounds, so there is no time to really think about what you're doing. Jon and Morgan make us play Quarters, drinking to sharp clinks. Table, glass. Table, glass. Do they practise this at home? Faster, pussycat.

We have collected enough people to move to a couch and a table, and it is here that the business of betting starts. Kerry says whoever grabs first tonight doesn't have to pay for drinks because the loser gets the bill. And at the bar, by chance, stands my friend's friend Craig with his floppy fringe and his wide shoulders, and before I can think it through I am up there, and his arms are around me and his lips taste of Bubblegum Lip Ice because he hasn't even had a chance to order his beer yet. He steps back and smiles and then ducks into me again. And then Kerry is right there beside us, 'Jesus, you win! That's the quickest I've ever seen!'

Craig drops his arms and although he's still smiling, his mouth is turning down at the corners. He says, 'Was this a *bet*?' I'm sober enough to nod but not enough to care. He turns and goes outside, those lovely shoulders rounded over so that when I turn I can see the knobs of his spine against his cricket shirt. I'm starting to feel a little bad, my conscience in my stomach.

The karaoke man has his equipment set up now, and Gillian is singing a song about birdies, going chirpy chirpy cheep cheep. My friends are laughing hysterically and pulling at me; I don't understand until I realise that they have all sung and that it's my turn. I've been looking for my Prefects' clipboard which has disappeared. In another-morning-world I will be in trouble for this. I don't want to sing. I know I'll look as dumb as they did, shuffling their big feet in their Doc Martens and mumbling off-key. Even drunk, I know this. But it's no use.

Eventually I'm half dragged across the floor in a way that is more humiliating than getting there on my own, so I walk. Gillian stands there, for moral support and a decent tune. Jon is sniggering through his nose and shouts, 'Diane, we've chosen a song just for you!' On the TV screen with the little ball bouncing out the lyrics appears the Rod Stewart song, *Do Ya Think I'm Sexy?* and I am stupefied with betrayal and surprise. I can feel my teeth grinding into the bone of their sockets, like those death's heads on that first Guns 'n' Roses album. I think, I don't care if you think I'm sexy! And then I think, Craig must be laughing somewhere. This is my punishment. I stumble down off the platform, managing to make it to the Ladies before I cry. What I want is to sit down. Actually, what I want is to lie down and stay that way, without goose bumps, for a very long time. I thought they thought I was cool.

At the bar when I come out and get myself a new drink is a man with MacGyver hair. He is humming a song about lighting fires. He has scars on his hands and the guilty eyes of someone who doesn't intend to unpack all his suitcases. Women can smell this; it excites us. It's the smell of heartbreak and new beginnings.

And so we are going to his room, our footsteps muted by the carpeting everywhere, even up the walls; I'm not sure what I intend to do once I'm there. My brain is muffled with sambuca and the nodding of the hotel's potted plants. It's like being lost in a drunken forest. *Babes in the Wood*. In the elevator there are tinted mirrors.

In the room there is a bed, of course, with a duvet that doesn't smell like him. 'Whose room is this?' I want to know, and he says, 'A friend's.' We roll around half-heartedly and I am confused. Men usually press themselves up against me right at the start, their jeans knee hard between my legs like a see-saw, but not this one. I end up straddling him while he laughs with his arm flung up over his face. I am sixteen and angry and I still have my takkies on and I say, 'What?' and he says, 'You remind me of my sister.'

Vision Thing

Sleeping is difficult; there is too much time in the day. We visit each other because we are alone at home, supposed to be studying. (The maid doesn't count. She only pushes her shiny brown legs and vacuum cleaner around and makes you lift up your own legs when you're trying to watch K–TV. It drowns out the sound of the Smurfs and it is very irritating.) We walk endlessly to one another's houses, and the tar is always hot but never hot enough to melt and stretch and swallow us up so we don't have to write exams. Nothing so extreme ever happens so that our routines will be interrupted; we are hamsters whose cages are lined with the scraps of notebooks and experiments; hamsters in wheels. Wheels within wheels.

We eat bucketloads of popcorn because we want to feel fuller; we want to put something in our mouths. The salt puckers our lips so that we look like the old Catholic ladies we have to visit while they lie in their beds at Nazareth House with their limbs like carrot sticks and wonder what these school-children are doing there. No more salad days. We know how we're going to end up, with too many brooches on our bed-jackets and the urge to sing in our warbly birdvoices.

We watch videos in the daytime, in the carpet quiet and furniture polish of other people's houses while they are at work; we could do anything and they would never know. Instead we watch *A Nightmare on Elm Street* and *The Evil Dead*. They should give us nightmares but they don't, because what could be worse than our real lives, where we have to write finals?

The video is scratchy and the voices fade in and out – is this what real snow is like? – and I say, invested with stepfather-and-screwdriver authority, 'It's the heads. The heads are dirty.' I must sound very sure of myself, because my friend has flipped the video machine on to its back, like the scene of a car crash, like a black plastic dog wanting to be scratched.

And we do scratch, and nothing works, and so we end up with the parts spewed out on the mottled upstairs carpet. They won't rearrange themselves the way they should and they only lie there with their smell of electricity and dusty insides of machines. Nothing fits. I jam everything back in and amazingly they find somewhere to go. The only clue – how good I am at hiding things – is the rattle that sounds when we shake the machine, a toy for the world's biggest baby. We won't be watching anything today. I'll have to go home now.

I flop on my bed and there is Stephen King, who always saves me because everyone knows that fear is better than panic; he talks about the switchboard of my soul and it soothes me to sleep.

In my dream I am at the field at the centre of the school. There is a grotto in the middle where the Virgin stares sadly out at us; every day she learns more swear words at break. My Geography teacher is on the other side of the grass and he is smiling his ratty smile under his moustache, and beckoning to me. I know that if I can just get across the field everything will be all right. I look down and the grass has changed; it is suffused with a yellow light that blurs everything underneath it, the kind of light you see in *Ghost* when they're trying to show you heaven. Like pollen it will rub off on you, knee-deep in the light. Like baptism, like bathwater, it will make you clean and make you glow in the dark, it will never, ever go away and it is nothing at all like my real life.

I don't cross to him because I wake up too soon. I am crying horizontal tears into my vertical pillow like a husband back from the border. The pressure behind my eyes has gone, leaked out through the tear ducts in a way that no video ever evoked.

Abbatoir

The McManus Hall is quiet, with the man in his black dress smiling and frozen and grown up, looking down at us from his canvas, looking down at our bony bums on desk seats, bony skulls crammed with shapes. They scrape new places inside us. Rough. Smooth. That's why brains in experiments are always shaped like pecan nuts. Geomorphology pie.

There are one hundred and eighty of us in rows, like mielies, although I don't know what kind of harvest we'll be. Children of the Corn. We send up our breath and our frustrations; they hover in carbon dioxide clouds above us, where the ceiling is far away. The empty inkwells go deep into the desks, wormholes to woody places. And none of us wants to be here, having to come inside from the sun, from sleeping late because they let us stay home now because it's so near the end and so they trust us to study by ourselves. All that time I spent scratching over 'DA is a slut' on the science lab desks, hating the smell of the nervous teacher's sweat when he sat next to me in his stripy shirt and his thin leather tie to show me an equation, hating the ranked wooden desks in the lecture theatre where they thought they were showing us our futures on the screen, hating the blackout screens on the windows, hating all the hopelessness and dread of that final term. But now I would go back, because at least then days were knowable. You could drown your familiar sorrows with two beers on a Friday night at the Mohawk Spur. And they could not learn to swim.

I know I am going to fail; my neck is stiff with it, vertebrae ticking clockwise by degrees (and it stopped, short, never to go again, when the old man died). Last night there were more tears at the desk by the window, and the idea that this must be what growing up is – knowing that crying doesn't make Maths exams go away. Crying anyway so that I can be tired and go back to bed, curled up and shaking with the lights out.

The numbers toyi-toyi across the page with their backs to me, spiky shoulder blades keeping me out like a paper game of Red Rover, each in its place, certain of its steps. They link arms so that I can't move them from where they already are, a demonstration, a sit-in to protest my English brain, my sleeping in class. So I don't move them (they will not be moved). I'll write out the question. Do the division bits.

The only bright thing in the room is Lambro's leg. It leans out from his desk in front of me; it slouches, it is a leg with bad intentions, sulky and blasphemous in the aisle, waiting to trip invigilators. We are alphabetical soldiers, and sometimes there is an advantage to having a surname that's near the top of the list; you get to sit near all the Greek boys, with their furry legs and muscles like Caramello Bears. Attention. His calf flexes as he shifts in his tie and his cheekbones. At ease.

I lean forward; my head is feeling tight, like I'm still wearing my boater, but I know that I can't be because we're all inside, Hi ho, hi ho. And then there is the terrible sense of *letting go*, like dreaming that you've peed during the night, and then waking up to find the bed wet like litmus paper. But I'm too old to wet my pants, so it must be something else, and the sound of droplets hitting the page makes me look down, and there it is, bright red splatters all over my empty equations. And I think, That's what comes from thinking too hard.

Of course they hustle me away to the office, and of course they call my mother from her class at the junior school, and I've had enough nosebleeds to know that I don't have to stop it if I don't want to. I can only see up to people's knees. The brothers' robes make them look like nurses, replicant Florence Nightingales. They make me bend over a metal bowl, a dog's dish, and the drops hit the bottom with a ringing like raindrops, like the triangles they used to make the tone deaf kids in the orchestra play. Ting. Ting.

I have to go to the doctor because this will happen all summer if I don't, my insides appearing on the outside like flags, saying, Disease! Freakishness! No self-control! He jams a triangle on the end of some probe up each nostril and cauterises the little blood vessels; it feels like he's pulling all the hairs out, and if I'd known that burning would happen I wouldn't have let him do it. My nose is an Indian wife, a princess saved from the pyre by a man travelling the world in eighty days. Ha. I didn't have to write the paper. Ha. In eighty days I will have finished Matric.

Wicked Game

The air is damp with the kitchen fires and the black workers are sweating like dwarves, not digging but frying, hidden away in the back behind their sizzling screen; their silver spatulas twinkle for help in the thick atmosphere. Semaphores. Tweener waitresses bring us beers even though we are also underage smugglers. At the Mohawk Spur we are too young for Klipdrift but not for Black Label. Under the stained-glass lighting we are safe, stuck to the leather booths but not to our daytime selves, drinkers in a saloon waiting for the stranger to walk in. His boots will clack on the floor, and the smell of burning will attend him. The world may be on fire, but rescue comes with ten fingers and toe-caps.

There is a boy with a white guitar, perched on a bar stool in front of the artificial plants. Against them he is impossibly rosy, filled with blood and movement, filled to his fingertips. He is a collection of separate movements taking their turn – tongue in mouth, fingers on strings, foot on the pedal below. We are so close to him that watching him sing is like seeing a strip show; his eyes glitter with the intimacy of it and his lips move in slow motion. It's true: he *has* never dreamed he'd meet somebody like her.

Next to me Danielle shifts. She has come out here because Greg has asked her to, sat at this table because this is where he will sit when he has a break from singing out his boysoul to the fat farmers and their squawling kids scrabbling at each other's Chico the Clown ice creams under the tables.

Usually on a weeknight Danielle would be studying, absorbing the words off the page in her wing of the house, where her mother pins up quotes from Goethe about boldness and magic. Settlement geography, algebraic equations, excretion and reproduction trickle into the mental reservoirs we are all supposed to have in Matric. Hers is fuller than anyone else's and her hair is silver blonde with the force of it, with the rush of waters waiting to be let out in a time of dryness. Greg knows this, recognises that she will be his counterpart. Together they will be impossibly blue-eyed and even-teethed. Beside this I am a collection of averages. Some people radiate perfection; being near them is enough.

The song is over. Greg eases himself off the bar stool and slowly puts his guitar down. Everything is meted out; a spoon of honey, a pinch of nerves. He saunters over and slides in next to us. They talk. I can't look him straight in the face, and I am not meant to. I send my mind away; looking at him makes all my other senses numb. I watch him eat when his food arrives. His steak is so bloody it trickles pink from the redder muscle. He carves it up and eats quickly. He transforms everything he does by touching the ordinary and leaving it different after he's gone. His steak knife is a light-sabre; his serviette could be used by bullfighting men.

When he leaves, Danielle leans out and says, soft in her girlness, 'Play that Chris Isaak song again,' and he does, his voice breaking when his eyes close, as if looking away from her leaves him less measured.

Out in the street she grabs my hands and says, 'He asked me to go out with him sometime!' We squeal, the sound bursting out of our throats like egrets with somewhere to go, bursts out under the orange streetlights, even though all the smart birds would be home in their nests by now. 'I said I couldn't. I have to work,' she says. 'Exams are coming up. I said maybe afterwards.

And anyway, he has a girlfriend.' We let go of each other. I look at her at a long time because she is new to me in her self-denial. 'I bet she's sleeping with him,' I say. When her mother comes to fetch us Danielle looks out of her window on the passenger side with her smooth hair gleaming and underneath, her untidy heart. In the back I am still, the tar smooth and quiet under our tyres. Thank you. Goodnight.

A week later there is another car trip, this one away from Kimberley on the night of the Boys' High School Dance. It is after midnight and Greg wants to go gambling. He says that he can feel it. It's his jackpot night.

The road stretches out, empty and wide, with the sound of the engine felt but unheard because the *Twin Peaks* soundtrack is playing in the tape deck, and so it seems as if the Fish River Sun, as the man said, is not a place but a feeling. They just rocket blind into the dark. Greg is a fast driver and he doesn't wear a seatbelt. He always says that it's not going to save him if it's his time.

The Sun may as well be in a different dimension. It takes forever to get there, boundaries more than physical. Crossing over. Fewer streetlights flash past, no cars attend them to drive in escort. In the back the others are sleeping; he is left alone to see the huge truck in front of them, loaded with bales of hay. He slows, jerkily, and the others wake up with curses tripping on their lips. The fear of falling magnified because it has really happened, that jolt that makes you wake up at night safe in your own bed with your lungs between your teeth and your fingers curled into claws.

A bale falls without warning, bounces and scatters stalks across the tar, the world's biggest game of Pick-Up-Sticks. Greg doesn't try to pick them up; what he does is slam on the brakes, his famous foot bearing down, and they screech across the road until the car lurches forward and into the back of the truck. Its rubbers finally stick to the road as the truck drives on, motoring animal feed to farms everywhere. The car's passengers are thrown forward as the windscreen shatters. Greg, going through it, sees the white stars as they happen, the birth and death of a supernova in two seconds, and he is shot into space.

On the side of the road his girlfriend sits next to him; she cradles his head in her lap and cries. There is nothing else she can do. The other people are bent into positions where their limbs are like wishbones, but they can all speak. Only Greg lies with his head smashed, looking up into the night sky where he is still seeing stars. And then he closes his eyes.

My mother hears first. It falls to me to tell Danielle and I walk over to her house with my fingers prickling and my face red. I don't know how to say this to her. At her front door I stand and say, 'Is Danielle here?' and I know that she is, sequestered in her paper nest like a hamster. She comes to me, stretching, and I can only say, 'Greg is dead. He was in a car accident.' She says, 'Are you joking, Awerbuck? Because if you are, that's not very funny.' Then she inhales and inhales and starts laughing. I look at her as her ribs expand and contract; she is having trouble breathing. I spend my life looking at her. I don't understand her, but I want to be near her. And then she says, 'I'm going riding,' and wheels her racer past me. I walk home.

The church is the fullest I have ever seen it. The coffin is closed so that we don't have to see the mess that is his body. We must only think of him in terms of white teeth and wholeness. Entire schools have turned up; in our uniformed ranks we are a box of blunt crayons, our faces damp with the knowledge that it could be us lying in there under a heavy lid, carried by our brass handles to a place that will press down on us as our mothers and fathers throw handfuls of earth on the top instead of helping us to stand up. His mother laughs upwards as she weeps through the eulogy, filled with Remember-whens. Danielle stands with her stiff secrets beside me. And it *is* a wicked thing, to be tricked into dreams of love and bull-fighting.

After that, Greg's parents divorce. There are stories of his father sleeping with that white guitar beside him, such a reminder that it dissolves the other survivors. He moves away and marries someone else. New job, new woman, new shoes to fill.

Danielle gets six As in Matric. And then she moves away. I also move away, but Chris Isaak stays with me.

PART FOUR

DELICIOUS MONSTER

Frog Eating Bug

Travelling to varsity – even though technically it is Momspace; she has given me her recipe for love and pineapple beer – is something that happens with my stepfather. He is clearly put out by having to drive me, teenagerness packed in thin suitcases, through the Eastern Cape, a place where most black people are so poor they eat the skin of the orange as well. I do not want to go into this new, raw, juicy life. At other times it seems like the welcome end of the world. It bothers me nightly, this wannabe-bomber in her cool, sweet, single bed. I am wrapped, comatose and ticking, in my parents' sheets, running familiar hands over unused limbs. Preserved. I want to be Tiger Lily, Belladonna, capture slaves and eat their fiddly bits instead of Matric Dancing and yearning for boys who have broken their arms. I have to get to university soon.

The women on the side of the road are also wrapped, but I am not as wrinkled. They hold up their rude punk fruit and turn to watch as the kombi whooshes by. My stepfather drives grimly, as he does everything, with a Calvinist concentration that could bore holes in the dashboard. I slouch against the backrest, teeth rattling, determined not to enjoy myself among the blue gums and the smell of those bushes with their sense memories of I and J adverts ('So fresh it smacks of the sea!') and travelling down to Port Alfred in our carsick childhoods. But this time it is not for holiday bacon fried crisp on Sunday morning, or going barefoot to a foreign church, or that desire to reach out fingers to the shoulders of the brown surfers snaking towards the beach when everyone else is inside.

This is being sent away from home with thin towels and lumpy pillows. When I make my bed and lie in it later, I find that the pillow inners are all blotchy, my mother's high-water marks when she left her own parents; the smell of sorrow. I add my own. No family Bible, but a pillow book.

What she does give me, instead of thick towels and white linen, is advice. That song from *Dirty Dancing* is playing and she says to me in the kitchen, laughing and cross at the same time, 'Honeychild, if you have to call your lover boy three times and he *still* doesn't answer, you tell him to sod right off.' At the time I would have settled for terry cloth.

Perhaps it is because I am leaving that she is willing to talk about heartache and the loss of God instead of why I can't do Maths. She is ironing, and I am watching the muscles flutter in her arms as she presses collars, seams, crotches. Tsss. She is humming and telling me stories, her wedding band flashing back and forth like the light on the roof of a police car. Law enforcement through jewellery.

'Roland was my first love,' she says. 'He came to beg me not to get married, at one o'clock in the morning. I said, "Why should I listen?" and he said, "Because I love you." It was too late.' I ask her if she cried. She sighs and says, 'Ah, sweetie, it was a long time ago.' It's hard to picture my mother in her white knee-boots, the high-kicking centre of a torrid love triangle. I am driving away from this all.

It is a journey that ought to take eight hours, but ends up being six. We circle the depression that is Grahamstown. There must be some kind of cosmic reverberation from being continuously rained on, in a small town, in a valley. Lines of geography convert to emotional damp, rising in the peeling walls of old digs far from campus.

This place is supposed to be a centre for Satanists and New Agers. Perhaps this is why the police get to patrol women who are looking for ley lines and stop to skinny-dip at Grey Dam. Grahamstown-Rini has the highest rate in South Africa for the rape of children. There is the rumour that at the police station there are invitations to digs parties up on the noticeboards. They have been invited. Anybody could be an informer.

The memory of Makanaskop survives. The black people say that the land is soaked with the blood of their ancestors, and the street kids have blue eyes. The white townies all have six fingers on each hand, and the academics ride bicycles in their beige stockings, intent on their pseudo-secret meetings with lovers. Oxford-in-the-Bush, with its streets that always tilt in the opposite direction to where you need to be. And this is where I will be for the next five years, in this place where frozen yoghurt is unavailable and casual violence is endemic. No wonder we behave badly; the-devil-makes-us-do-it.

My stepfather, who is not the devil, just a tired accountant with a bigger dose of fascism than he can sustain, sees that I have the room in Walker House I am supposed to, and drives straight back home. The iron of his will impresses me, and I want him to be proud. The Great Off-White Hope.

Pussy-footing

Orientation Week scares me. The clothes I have are too clean. I am ordinary. There are speeches about academic traditions. Women in floral dresses smell strongly of some generic perfume that follows them like ectoplasm, more real than they are in their garden party outfits. The wood fittings are polished endlessly by workers in blue overalls. We are forced to go for coffee evenings to male residences and mingle with men. It's not that I'm shy; I'd just rather chew my own foot off than spend my nights thinking about having too many pairs of tracksuit pants in my wardrobe and talking about Kimberley ('Kimberley? I was there once, on a school trip. We went to the Big Hole.') We are not yet at the point where Zimbabwean whites terrorise social gatherings with fire hoses. There is the sense that we are being hammered into a certain shape here, and it's probably not going to be a hammer or sickle. Lay me on an anvil.

We sit in a circle on the linoleum in Goldfields House, boy-girl-boy-girl, our bums numb and our legs asleep, playing Small Talk, Small Talk. There are other little fairy circles of intrigue and weak coffee, and I am a blank screen waiting for projection until we start to argue about writers. The boy with the elf face from the circle behind me leans with his sharp and casual elbows into our circle and says, 'I know I'm interrupting here, but Dean Koontz is just as good as Stephen King.' I am horrified and spluttering, partly at the rawness of his haircut but mostly because this amounts to blasphemy. He only grins, evil-tongued and sure of himself; rubs me over with his gravel voice. He has the straightest, shiniest teeth I've ever seen, like a plantation slave.

Hours later, when we girls tumble away over the grass to go back to Walker, safely back to The Land of the Hairdryers, I am buzzing and exfoliated. (Oh Walker House, whoever named you knew what he was doing. All we seem to do is traipse up and down the hill, to lectures and back to res with its boiled meat in the daytime and its raw meat at night.) He is wearing a shirt that says Ireland by Night, but there is no picture on it, just a bright yellow fingernail moon. He wants to take it off to give it to me, there on the steps, so I offer to return the favour. He flickers and refuses. Is he scared of what's underneath? Do I show him the third nipple?

Radio Ga-Ga

In the first week, somebody places a home-made bomb in the Rhodes Music Radio studio. Boom. No one is hurt, but it is unsettling. It is supposed to be. A number of groups claim responsibility; rumours circulate about FemiNazis, and I over-hear a skinny girl in pearl earrings saying, 'Lesbians. They're everywhere.' Her careful, factor-five-tanned features wrinkle. 'We all look the same here, and you just can't *tell*.' The irony doubles me over. I don't want to look like someone who had their ears pinned back when they were twelve – it makes everything negotiable, shifting. She does me a favour. I stop wearing tracksuit pants and feeling homesick.

That night a boy gets so drunk at the Union that he falls over the balcony, on to the bottle of beer in his hand, which smashes on impact. The thing that bothers me the most is that his friends come over to pick him up and carry him away, and they are laughing. After that the Union won't let us have glasses because people throw them on to the Great Field, so it's plastic cups all the way. Maybe it makes us drink faster, the grown-up thrill of leaning against the bar with a drink in your hand gone. By ten o'clock the girls' toilets are flooded. We go to the men's instead and they shout out, shielding their dried fruit packages with both hands. As if.

All in all there is the sense that we have escaped our parents at last, and there is too much freedom here; you can smell it like electricity, like blown plugs in sockets that won't accept the appliances. Dislocation. The idea that you can start over and be anything you want. Drunk, mostly.

We spend a lot of time in the men's reses, where, although the atmosphere is thick with rugby socks and talcum powder, you are allowed to wear slippers in the daytime and everybody disobeys the curfews. What's that smell of burning? I want to say, 'Nerves,' but it's toast. Always hungry, boys pile bread from the dining hall like the world's biggest deck where every card is the joker. Resources are scarce, and a drunk man will eat anything. So will a drunk woman, judging from the blowjob jokes doing the rounds on a Sunday morning.

I find out that Elf Boy's real name is Mick but everyone calls him Irish. Because he is. He entices us to his room with Quality Street and Led Zeppelin tapes. We cram on to the bed in the artificial closeness engendered by panic and the scramble for friends in the New World, and the music pounds through us, vibrating us into wavelengths we know; the old chocolate sweetness dragging us back. I think, 'What is he going to do when the sweets run out?' but by the time they do, his room is home base for fresher girls and other carrier pigeons, a ring around my own ankle.

One night I stay late to watch *The Fabulous Baker Boys*, not because I care about women lolling on top of pianos, but because I will get to sit next to Mick and watch his profile in the safe darkness. He has the smallest nose I have ever seen on a man; he fascinates me. He is as fearless as the boy in the fairytale. He can turn cartwheels even when he's drunk. He exudes a weird energy, like an acrobat, that makes you think that his skin will vibrate if you touched him, and his eyes glitter.

His hand lies casually on the armrest between us and I have to sit on my own to stop myself from grabbing him by the collar or pressing my fingers against his jugular so that I can feel his happiness rushing through him. But mine are soon numb and I have to find somewhere else to rest them, and this is when he lifts my hand from my knee and holds it, and grins and grins. The force of that gladness pins me to my chair; my face aches with the way my mouth is split from its stretching.

So he walks me home, over the fifty metres of grass that

separate the buildings, and we dangle outside – he because it is after curfew and it hasn't occurred to me that you can ignore this if you want to, me because I know I will not be able to fiddle my key into the lock in front of him. We stand with the cement tiles between us and our arms folded. A moth flickers down, dizzy with its own wings, and I am startled with spiderthoughts and squash it with my shoe. Mick is horrified at this brutality, the lightning of it, the instinct to lash out. I have to apologise over and over before our softness under the barley sweet security lights can be recovered and he will kiss me, tongue and squeaky teeth. Ha. Mine.

You Make All the Others Look Like the Sahara

We are back in Mick's room and there are no more friends who will hang around there and drink coffee until we are wired like television sets with the sound turned way up and the picture all blurry. I sleep here most nights, watching the galaxy of freckles on his shoulders, listening to his snore. He always smells like strawberries, or beer and strawberries, and his saliva is silver; it washes off my skin in the shower. He alters my pH so that I itch and burn but I can't stay away from him.

Now we stand next to his single bed, like the Bob Marley song, and he watches me not being able to say that the only sex I've had so far was the worst pain I've ever felt. I don't know why people do this with other people. How it must scare men to have the faces of women underneath them with their wide Bambi eyes, saying, Don't let this hurt. Maybe that's why they always want to get away so quickly in the morning, like robbers.

I am sure my fear will prick him like splinters and stop him halfway. It will protect me. He always says, I just want to see the colour of your skin. I am *naked* for you. He says, slow and close up, I am going to fuck you so hard that you bleed all over my sheets. And then, I'm going to show you how it should be. And I can't explain. It's better just to go to the safety of his chest and the wetness inside his fierce, sad mouth.

When he slides his jeans down he turns and smiles, cool and pale as vanilla ice cream, and as welcome. Tonight I plan to swallow him in mouthfuls. I won't be needing a spoon. I am huddled on the bed in my tan stripes. Above me he is warm and solid with the roundness of his biceps as he holds himself over me, and I think, He could crush me, just like that. But he never does. The slickness of his tongue makes a trail for himself; he will be coming back here later. I stare down at my hands cradling his head, fingers in soft hair and that tiny nose buried in my soft parts. I know that I taste of orange peel. His stubble scratches the insides of my thighs and I start to shake. All the hair on my body stands straight up. Is this how the electric chair feels? He grabs my hipbones and transforms my nipples to marbles and now there is no going back.

His tongue tastes of continents and we travel, sweat and tears glue us into our time capsule. We shake with the pull and thrust; there are no seatbelts. The smell of blood, of the insides of plants. Pollination. That searing shudder pulls my shoulder blades back and I can't close my mouth. I am panting and jerking; I can't get enough air into my lungs. *I didn't know it could be like this with another person.*

He lies beside me, our valves opening and closing. We stick to the sheets. I look down and see dribbles on my thighs. They look like yoghurt but taste like salt. Breakfast will never be the same.

On the phone I lie to my mother and say that I am thinking of sleeping with Mick. 'Oh Diane,' she says, with that falling intonation and I know she is not happy but that she will not stop me. 'Don't tell Dad,' I tell her. If she does, I will not be able to be his girl any more. Surely she will keep my secret.

But she does not. When I am home for what turns out to be our last family holiday in Jeffrey's Bay, we walk on the beach and he turns to me with a smile that shows his faded adult teeth and his fillings, and says, 'Mom told me about Mick.' He tries to make a joke of it as my heart bounces off the walls of my cavities like a squash ball. A lump of black rubber, burning up with the heat of being beaten, and still beating.

'It's nice, isn't it?' he leers at me. 'Breakfast in bed. Heh heh.' I am furious with my mother; this is the only thing I have ever asked her to do for me. When I ask her why she told him, she shrugs and says, 'I tell him everything. He is my husband.'

Better Be Home Soon

My mother calls me every week and the intercom growls and hollows out a place in the girlsteamy air for my name; it booms and swirls up the stairwells, over the linoleum and kettles where we are boiling our bunnies and other fantasies. My old life will settle on me like a damp cloak, like a winter of tonsillitis. I don't *want* to come downstairs, I don't *care* that there's a call for me. Nothing that is happening at home can find me here; she has lost her grip on my arm and I won't come back.

She tells me stories of people I know who have died in horrific ways since leaving my school; she sounds puzzled. So young, she says. It's strange. The worst one she tells me has to do with twin eighteen-year-old boys I used to know, who were driving drunk out to their farm one night and crashed their car. One died in his seat, the breath puffed out of him like a whoopee cushion, and the other wandered away from the roadside and into the dark, where he collided with the newly erected razor-wire on his father's farm, and decapitated himself. Not right off, she says, but the jugular, gone.

So far there are nine that I can count who should still be alive. Only boys, so far, apart from the girl who shot herself in the stomach even though she wasn't pregnant. Her left-behind mother smiles tightly through the days and drinks gin and tonic. She listens to Bobby McFerrin who says, *Don't worry, be happy.* She tries very hard to do what Bobby says. She hums his song to herself all the time. It's Kimberley, I think. This only happens to people who seem as if they might be able to get away from the Big Hole. It's trying to make us stay.

In the stuffy booth my mother is still breathless with horror; over the line she carries it down to me like haemophilia, like colour-blindness, so I will have to carry on bleeding onto my new sheets, so I won't be able to tell green from red. It's a good thing that I don't know how to drive. But Randall, my old schoolmate, does drive. He drives a lot these days because he has had to commute between Kimberley and Bloemfontein, she says. He was accepted at Free State University, this coloured boy in the white Houses of the Holy. With a bursary. Ha, I say. Who would have thought? All that orthodontic work, all the hardship his parents must have endured to send him to a private school, finally paying off.

But that is not what she is calling to tell me. He was driving home one weekend when he wanted to change the music playing in the tape deck (oh, was it Crowded House, Randall, my dear? Were you trying to be home soon?) and as he looked down to check on his hands, he lost control of the car. It swerved and rolled and of course he was killed outright. Straight teeth and straight As could not bring him back. His passenger survived; he was always the gentleman. He didn't suffer, says my mother. But I think he did his time.

Edgars Belly Dance

Oh, I am tired of being me, of being brown hair and brown eyes and brown legs all over. I want to be special and I want to be real, like that Smiths song, 'I want to see people and I want to see li-hife.' Like Mick does. And so in my first year I think that getting a piercing is a way to do this, except that this hasn't happened in Grahamstown, even though it has happened in *Student Life Magazine*, which is funny. That magazine is supposed to be covering *us*.

The only place I know that you can get this done is at Edgars, where the skinny coloured girls ignore you and talk on the phone to their old-man lovers. I don't want to go here, but I don't have a choice. I want to be augmented, made android and impermeable, cross over to where things are shiny like battleships and fast like missiles. I want a belly ring. This beats in my head as I walk down High Street, dodging beggars and choosers in an episode of *Robocop*, thinking about the story of the girl with a belly ring who was struck by lightning at that compass point as she walked down her road. At least, that's what the doctors said. Afterwards she was physically changed, her features rearranged like someone who's had their jaw broken and rewired.

They titter and hustle me into a changing room when they hear what I want. I feel like a drug dealer. I feel like Hunter S. Thompson. And so I am belly up on the carpet, with the three of them huddled round like nuns at a virgin birth, trying not to stand on me or my strange steel limb. With their pouty mouths and boots they stand over me; I am afraid I will be crucified with their heels. They squabble like *Jungle Book* vultures over the metal instrument. Whose turn should it be? They pass it from hand to hand, rolling their Rs. But even vultures know how teeth and talons work; you need a curved needle and not a gun with a blunt stud in it.

I have to pinch the skin away from the muscle so that the stud can pierce right through it, and they pull the trigger. The pain is blind and deaf; it hasn't had a chance to have a voice yet. And I'm thinking, 'It's through. That wasn't that bad,' and that's when they look at each other and one backs out of the cubicle with her shiny red fingernails over her mouth. The other two stay. 'It didn't go through,' they say. 'You'll have to do it again.'

They make me yank out the thick metal stud, the jewellery equivalent of braces, and of course it won't be extracted because it has no point at the end. A stud relies on ultra-quick pressure over a small surface area. I know that now. I managed to pull it out like a loose tooth, thinking, 'I *won't* cry. I *won't* cry.' What still surprises me is that I made them do it again, twice over, because I thought that it was me. And then we gave up and I walked back up the hill with my hand over my stomach.

Home for the Holidays

At about half past nine on the starry nights, you'd drive out into the flatness where the sorry coloured girls and the knife fights are. There'd be music on the radio, maybe PJ Harvey or Barney Simon's appalling metal show on 5FM. And you would be in the back, shoulders touching with hitchers and other people you liked, way back against the sticky leather seat. Past the neon, past the mine dumps, breathing that parentless air, with the night's hysteria gathering like a storm cloud over your shoulders and a little hash in your university veins. Hearing the music your mother can't, dog whistling only to other dogs, in the shirt she hates because it looks like you're *soeking 'n man*. Slipping the leash, holding tight to the seats in front, talking fast or maybe not at all, at all.

Sometimes the best catching up is done in the quiet flashing under the sodium lights, when your throat constricts with the sharpness of everything you see. Grinning. Rubber-faced.

Out at last, skipping in slow motion past the parking piccanins, who are bright as squirrels, hard as nuts. You promise to come back with their money and breathe hard on the pavement outside. Grab a-hold of that brass knob, step in and salute the Star of the West.

You and the rest of the time travellers stand dazed and a little shy on the inside, hands in pockets, feet on other people's shoes. The air is different here. You couldn't stop your nostrils sucking it up even if you wanted to. You should have oxygen tanks on your backs, instead of wings. Dead diggers stare down from their frames and follow you to the bar. Everyone should have a ten-gallon hat.

Head outside to the beer garden, stripy awnings above you, flagstones at your feet. Sometimes they have a schoolboy band playing, and then you have to shout your inanities to make yourself real. They have picnic benches here, under the lovers' and haters' stars and the circus awning. There are no official acrobats or waiters, but you can slide around, as slick or as jelly as you please, or pretend to be a lion-tamer. The wood is worn thin and rickety under the layers of varnish. You scratch marks to show you've been.

Milk Stouts jostle your insides. Sucking them down means a trip to the toilets. Cheers. You get up and untangle your legs from the boy in the black jeans, and follow the track in the human undergrowth slashed by shiny leather handbags, like the native bearers in that advert for lawnmowers.

Girlsweat and unlikely bouquets – the herd smell – forces its fingers up your nose. The clean hair tickles your face as you lean

133

into the queue of women, arms folded, nipples erect. They rap on cubicle doors, all foul mouths and designer jeans, the yawl of nature in their sambuca-soaked forebrains. It makes you want to throw open the door and shout for the men to come on over and see what really goes down. It makes you wonder whether you belong.

Back to your table, squeegeed by the beer boeps of Afrikaners drinking slaan-my-vrou, avoiding the hands held out. They make you as fearful as the Little Mermaid on her way to the sea witch. At least you don't have a cloaca. And you do still have your tongue.

Eventually the lights flicker, the slick-haired band packs up sulkily and drags their chrome away. Most people get the hint. Couples have paired off in obedience to the heavy undercurrent of sex, as bright as the fabled mother lode beneath the slate we live on, and twice as electric. The hairs on your arms salute. This is the grooviest part of the evening, when Jason locks up and smiles, and you stay on after lights-out. Midnight feasts and beyond; ten of us left. We. Go. Way. Back. Our mothers were in pre-natal classes together, while our 1970s fathers went fishing.

A boy you loved in high school holds out his hand; it's a song you used to listen to. He folds you into his grown-up body and the tattoo of his heart is hypnotic. Picture his vital organs, beating the blood to the pads of his fingers. And then you're dancing, and it's not the scalding you expected, but comatose ticking. Behind your eyes it is purple. You sway and there are visions of rock falls in your head.

Four o'clock. The sounds slow down and there is a girl asleep with her cheek resting on the counter. You inhale for the last time and spread your sorry goodbyes. Jolting, out on to the too-hard pavement. Home again, home again, jiggidy-jig, to your sleeping mother and brothers in the fatherless house. Back to creeping around and remembering not to say 'fuck' at the table. Trying to cross the road, understanding too late that Grahamstown traffic is there, and you're here. You kiss your old sweetheart goodnight in the twittering morning. The dew and you. Maybe you'll sit on the steps and have a bowl of cornflakes. Maybe you'll see him again in a year. Maybe you'll have a drink sometime.

Diamond Lil

Jason never locks up alone after a shift; perhaps this is why he wants to keep us there, why nobody leaves before sunrise. He says that the Star is haunted, and no one ever doubts him. His family was only the third to own it in a hundred and twenty-four years. That's Marquez time, enough for sorrow to steep in the walls; that's time enough for kingdoms-rise-and-kingdoms-fall (but you go on). Kingdom come.

He hears footsteps (oh, don't we all, when the lights are out?). He thrusts his fists against the posts and still insists he sees the ghosts, but there's no speech impediment here, quite the opposite. Lots of voices. And ghosts have body language too. Especially yours.

Old Man Geller walks in the rooms above. He is measuring out time the way he and the ones before him measured out change. The king is in the counting house, counting out his money. All bent little Jewish men, but not crooked. Everyone's money counted the same and everyone called them uncle. He is not frightening now and he never rushes. This is his home, he is not afraid. Slowly now, visiting each room where the diggers used to sleep, hoping for what treasure?

They found Diamond Lil, or she found them, and found their

135

wallets too. Why Diamond? Shiny, I suppose. Hard. And precious. So many men never made it back to their mothers and motherlands because of her toenails, also like diamonds as she danced barefoot on the bar and sometimes into the dust of the street outside. The milk and silk of her kindness and cruelty in that heat so dry your insides vanished and the idea of having vital juices was impossible. On her bed, upstairs. Tumble. Weed.

Why Diamond? The treasure of her insides, damp red jewels. On her, foreign pearls of semen, sweat like silver. These travellers all hoping to be worthy, like Columbus at the court of Spain. Why Diamond? She was a whore, after all, and one day woke up and found a front tooth missing, so she had one made of porcelain. And of course the dentist (he loved her too) also had jewels, because that is the currency of desperate men. So he inserted a chip into that tooth as surely as if it were a piece of his heart, nearly a hundred years before Janis Joplin sang about dissecting that most untrustworthy organ. After that, Diamond Lil's smile dazzled everyone she met, little girls in town as well as the men who looked down her cleavage in the bar downstairs.

And of course she gave it up as soon as she could, made other girls give up their fluids in the smothering evenings instead when she became the madam. Tired of filling the hole the men all seemed to have; perhaps this is why they were prospectors, digging to find themselves, digging for water and hope and Diamond Lil, who made her own fortune without ever lifting a spade.

And now? Her portrait, taken for free, of course, of course, because photographers are seekers too, is on the wall in triplicate, and no one knows who she is anymore. Except for the person who stole one, still some man out there with her face in his head. And except for Jason, who locks her up safe each night in the building where they gave her no peace.

There's No Business Like Show Business

In my mother's classroom at the junior school the children are lined up in their rows, ready to have their make-up put on. They are ghosts and ghouls and characters from fairytales and my youngest brother is the most fearsome of them all. He is wearing a black cloak with a red satin inside to it that billows as he stalks up and down, singing his lines to anyone who is interested, and wiggling his false black eyebrows. He is the Dastardly Duke of Spooksville and he likes it so much that his irises are dilated black instead of blue.

My mother pays no attention to him as long as he behaves; from the top of her perm to the heels of her teacherly shoes she is focused on each child as they step up to her in their factory rows. She turns them out with her other-world cookie-cutter — tens of vampires, twenties of ghosties, but only one Duke. She gives black children skeleton faces and knobkierie bones; outside in the trip to the back of the stage they glimmer and caper in the evening. They leap out at stray grown-ups hurrying to their seats and say, Wooo, flapping their thin stocking arms. They are scary, it's true, because we can't see who they are.

After the finale there is complaining and cold cream. Nobody wants to go back to their ordinary lives where there are name tags and baths and school-on-Monday. My mother wipes my brother's face with difficulty; he keeps turning away from her until she loses her temper. Underneath the make-up his skin is still white. She thinks it is the excitement so she lets it go. The next day he is worse. He has slept in the Dastardly Duke's cloak.

At the doctor's we are told that he has developed problems with his spleen. We don't expect organs we aren't aware of to implode, but there you have it. Perhaps he really does have bad blood, and everything we think about Bluebeard his father is true. Or maybe his body is going into overdrive because he is trying to rid himself of all these impurities. Whichever it is, it doesn't work. But it does increase my mother's absolute reliance on the kindness of the Almighty.

In the hospital x-rays my brother's spleen is visibly enlarged. They are worried. It is unusual in children. The doctor especially, with his thick wrinkled forehead and his white safari suit, does not know what to do in the face of my mother's faith in him, this Moses with his stethoscope who has led her in the desert for her forty-three years. He has struck a rock and the water won't come. So she takes my brother the Dastardly Duke of Spookesville to church, where more men with faces under their layers of time lay hands on him and the church is always thick with whisperings and cold as cement. Here is the oil on its cotton wool bed. Here is the chalice and the Body of Christ. And my brother? He lets them do it. Perhaps he likes the feel of those warm hands pressed firm in God's service against his side.

The next x-ray shows his spleen as completely normal again. Imagine having that much faith. Or else being a seven-year-old with the ability to heal yourself. Either way he is special. Either way we should have known. Oh yes, dastardly he is, and oh yes, he haunts us and reigns over us in Spooksville.

I'm Your Fan

My mother takes me out on to the stoep when I am home from varsity and says, 'We're getting a divorce.' I laugh. I say, 'Mom, that's not funny.' She starts to cry, her face red and wet like it was at the vet's when we took Brutus in to be put to sleep. Then her arms were heavy with Alsatian; now they are empty. She says, 'He's going to live with his secretary.' The tiredness of that betrayal, the sheer silliness of his giving my mother up makes us both laugh in high whistles through our sore lungs and blocked noses. And then it all comes out, about how he said he was living a lie, and that he told her he was going to have sex with this woman to see if he liked it, and of course he did. And now he is gone.

I wish I could say that I'm sorry, but the truth is that a household without a bully is a happier one. My mother is given tranquillisers and spends two months lying on their double bed, staring at their new ceiling fan as it goes round, but not moving herself except when she turns her head to let her tears slide into the pillow. They make watermarks that we can never wash out. The bitterness of that grief, indelible. Sometimes I look round the door to see her, but mostly I don't, because I know what I will see.

When I am there for the September holidays – outside it is Spring – I creep into bed with her at night, and she stops crying. She sighs and reads her Bible and her *Daily Bread* and I read something that will not promise me false hope. She rolls over as the mattress follows her body and says, 'Goodnight, puddy tat,' and strokes my hair. I understand that she is happy to see me but that I cannot hope to be a comfort. Her mouth is smiling but her eyes are puddles. I wonder whether we will be washed away in the night, their marriage bed lifted up on such a salt wave of regret and longing that we are swept to his new brick house in Postmasburg, where he lives with the secretary he has promised to marry. Will they be surprised to see us?

His son, my miracle brother, sees him every few weeks in Postmasburg and comes back with stories of how the men go out in groups to shoot birds and duiker. The new Auntie treats him well and they have lots of braais. But sometimes my stepfather doesn't come to fetch him because he gets so caught up in work, and my brother sits on the front wall and drums and drums his seven-year-old heels from five o'clock until it is dark. He will not come inside, not to go to the toilet, not even for Coke. My mother goes out to lift him down but he is too heavy for her now.

She looks sadly over her married garden in the evenings, at her swimming pool and Alsatians and Labradors with their wet smiling mouths, at her youngest son whose hair is turning out to be just like his father's. We are moving to a townhouse that cannot possibly have anything to do with him, even though sometimes he comes back at night. She cooks him dinner and he weeps and then they go to bed, as if he is back forever. He has been in hospital because a blood vessel burst in his eye. Like an Old Testament prophet he has seen things which ought to have been denied him, and now he is going blind. She goes to visit him and we stand awkwardly by the bed. I can't let him kiss me now that I know where his lips have been. She comforts him even though under her clothes she has a continual and raging bladder infection; her body rejects him and doubles her over, burning and burning. Bushfire. I only hope the secretary is equally scalded.

It does not clear up; she tells me over the telephone that she goes to the doctor again and again. She is half in love with him; he has seen all her insides at their rawest point of entry. How can she not be in love with that cool and quiet whiteness and the certificates on the wall that qualify him as an expert on malaria and other airborne stings of feeling, that say, I will protect you? She has to go for a scan and a biopsy; he is not happy with what is happening inside her, and neither is she.

It turns out, of course, to be scar tissue.

Baby Seals

They don't look like brutes from the outside, with their Woolworths chests and Lego haircuts, but there are visiting hours in the women's residences and not in the men's, as if we need to be sheltered like nuns from the outside world. Or maybe it's the other way round. Then again, nuns are always the first line of defence in a civil war, first to be hurt, first up for defilement and aggression. Saint Catherine, save our breasts and our ligaments.

Either way it means that there is compulsory and unpaid door duty for us. At the end of the twentieth century with our contraceptive pills and microwave ovens, there is still no way to stop forced perversions except through the frozen intercom, bold as a voiceover in an episode of *Buck Rogers*. V is for visitor.

They stand at the booth, the wolves, on their hind legs. They are more likely to have red noses than roses but we let them in anyway. Because grievous bodily harm doesn't count if it happens before eleven p.m. on a week night. And date rape is only just beginning to be a term for us, spoken mainly by our skinhead sisters. For everyone else, no still means yes.

The Walker Boys come in on a dark night in Orientation Week, regardless of the curfews and visitors' books. They are here to take back their res, and there will be stomping and hoarse rapping on locked and frightened doors, but no waiting for a girl to come down and get them.

The university designated Walker House a women's res this year. There is a dual purpose here. It is to the advantage of admin to pursue their sixty-forty female to male student ratio. Statistically, girls are more likely to hand in assignments and pass exams; less likely to throw up in the dining halls and flatten the bushes outside the wardens' houses. They are hoping to make the troublesome racial integration process a little easier as well. Girls are mixers. There are all those hair products in common. But those products need desks and bookcases and res rooms.

Also, Walker has had too many disciplinary hearings in the last few years. The solution is to disperse the trouble-makers, with their saliva-soaked overalls and drinking-club chins, over a wider residential area. Because boys will be boors, but this is going a bit far. The rumour is that two of them pissed in a baby's pram during the last RAG procession. There wasn't a baby in it at the time, but the gesture was enough to widen the Town and Gown crack to a chasm. And this isn't good for PR. The Four Horsemen have their place, it is true, but not now. We're not ready.

John Leahy still has his key, and has managed to zig-zag it into its place in the door, where it is meant to be. And so he stands at the foot of the stairs, debating with himself over exactly where to go. The others move quietly, sniggering swagmen. There is talk of panty raids and worse, but he knows that most of the rooms will be locked, sheltering tiny incense and marijuana stashes or pasty Christian pyjamas. He decides to get to the top of the building alone; it's three a.m., the perfect time for a little barbaric yawping across the rooftops of the world. This could be a *Dead Poets* moment.

He thumps up the linoleum stairs while the boys downstairs move along the corridor, banging fists on doors and shouting, 'Fire!', hoping for more skin than you can see on the dance floor at the Vic, all the insides of thighs a man can eat in the parking lot outside. Easier than clubbing a baby seal, as they like to say during those first few fresher days, when wearing Old Spice will remind a girl of her daddy.

No tenderfoot, this boy. He stops only on the third floor, to take a leak in the old bathrooms because those beers will pass right through a guy who's been forced to open his throat at a four p.m. fines meeting. They still haven't taken out the urinals, and there is the reassuring stink of dried piss and Ego deodorant.

And up to the top balcony at last, iron railings and cold floors. The air is sherried with possibilities. He hears the bloodbeat of being young and outside, with nothing to lose except your mind. He inhales constellations; there go the Seven Sisters, straight to the sinuses. Whoosh. He smells of sweat and is weightless as an angel on a pinhead. And to test this theory he climbs carefully over the railing, straddling it a testicle at a time, like a counting rhyme.

He jumps, and it is over quicker than he thought it would be. His bones jar and his ankles crack, and he thinks, I missed the grass. Inside the warden's house, the lights come on.

Bridge Over the River Kei

Smashing both ankles is only practice for John Leahy, who finds that he likes high places.

The rest of us inhabit the low places, because Boat Races are happening today. We pile into complaining cars that won't expand no matter how much we try to squash six people into them. Our cooler bags and icepacks take up space. And so they should, because we plan to be in the Port Alfred sun the whole day, and that's a lot of beer. Mostly we don't see the races at all but that's not really the point. There is very little that is less attractive than sweating students in semi-transparent purple and white all-in-ones with their boats on their heads. This doesn't stop the sexual activity, though. One man is sucked off so hard in the bathroom that he has a blood blister on his penis.

We travel, mugged by heat and the tartrazine residue (it kills fish, but will it kill us?) off the Nik-Naks, enduring the obligatory sighting of the trees in the shape of the rabbit. Pot-holed roads shake our capped teeth in our heads and the Big Pineapple appears with all its spiky warriors beneath. They won't spring from dragons' teeth but they will taste of acid.

The giant bridge hums into view like the title sequence from *CHiPs* and there it is: our venue for the day, along with hundreds of other idle handers and devil's workers. Ace of Base and beer cans drug us too. We wade through them in slow motion to find a spot closer to the water.

Later we go and stand on the road under the bridge and look at the water below. It is a very long way down. Not as far as the Big Hole, of course, but far enough to hurt if you land on your stomach, flopping among the silvery jellyfish pumping casually away from you. There are no railings, but most people aren't stupid or drunk or windgat enough to try to bridge-jump here. Most of us have jumped in East London, but that was about a third of this distance. The sensation of brown water being forced up my nostrils was invasive, the fishy fingers of strangers, enough to make me understand that this is not something I want to repeat.

For John Leahy, this does not hold. He crawls up, quick as Spiderman but not as sticky. He pauses on the uppermost parabola until there is scattered applause and disgust from the landlubbers below, and dives. It is slow and strange, graceful and dangerous. He emerges a few wet feet from where he went in. He pulls himself out, pale and trembly-muscled and climbs up, hand over foot over hand over foot. Once is never enough.

The next dive is just as graceful, and now other boys are doing it, too, plashing large and neat before the rowers come. Except that we don't see the seal head that is John. A minute passes. Ha ha, what a joker; he's swum downstream. But the way is clear, and there is no Johnshape that comes up for a third swoop. Feet shuffle. Questions are asked of others equally answerless. A man whips his shirt off and dives in; my lover follows. The ripping of the Velcro separating on his strops is the tearing of patience, of calm. I am horrified; I think of that Stevie Smith poem.

The boys in the water inhale and submerge; they must work by touch because the water is so murky. Imagine being the one to find this heavy hidden treasure. We are all pressed to the edge of the river, elbows close, forming the kind of armed guard riot police would envy.

Above there is a helicopter. It ruffles the water whitely, obscuring where it should be clarifying. An ambulance screeches to a halt. Drunk men still climb up the bridge and continue to jump. Now the crowd is shouting insults, warnings. Policemen crawl up to stop them, a cartoon chase. A lone boat trawls for what now can only be a body. How many minutes? Ten, fifteen, twenty. People are quiet now, sitting down quick as dominoes, their day spoiled.

The boatman is leaning over, slowly pulling on a thick and floppy mannequin. He is trying to shield it with his own warm body. The boys in the water swim over, heads up like dogs in a swimming pool, to help push it into the boat. I think, How did that get there? It is boneless and blue, even from the shore, and that is how we know that mouth to mouth is a waste of time. It generally is, for people who have broken their necks.

Crossing Palms

It is a winter weeknight and we are all getting blessedly drunk in a sticky pine booth in the Oppie Den like a sauna. It is too cold to stay at home where essay writing numbs the fingers. We come here to drink Black Label because the bottle says it contains six per cent alcohol, so it must be true; we listen to the strains of the Fireside Jam bands from the main room, where two engineering types are unplugging on the stage. The Loomer band has been and gone with the shaven-headed girl and her choir voice, singing high over the rough boys with her finger in her ear and her eyes closed, *Meet me in a tub of Clover / Come on, Rob, come on over*, concentration so pure and straight it is an arrow in our chests and frontal lobes, zinging back to first year in res beds and the Rhodes swimming pool where we drink baby Cokes. She makes me nostalgic for a time I am still living.

Inside, we compare the merits of Puma versus Adidas sneakers on the newbies at the pool table. Everyone is poised and listening. 'It's speedy education and horrendous entertainment,' says Adam. He gets up to click stop-motion pictures of us. Later they will come out with fairy lights swirling around and ghost girls looming. Digit the genderless dog lies quietly in its bandanna; it has finished hoovering the carpet. Eugene and Liz are delving into their bag of treats to distribute magic presents of ashtrays and rolls of toilet tissue and salt shakers stolen from public places they've pirated along the way. Ho ho, me hearties.

Eugene has started reading a book on divination. We are like small children in mission schools, waiting to be smacked with a ruler on our open palms, the stinging of reward and punishment. He turns my hand over and shakes his head; he says, 'I just want you to know that I'm new at this. I could be wrong,' and proceeds to tell me that I have not met my true love yet. I am shocked to the stomach. My true love is right over there, leaning over the pool table with a cigarette in his mouth, squinting the squint of people in Levi's who are prepared to fail first year in return for being a god with a pool cue. Duh, Eugene.

So I also don't take him seriously when he tells me that there's one other thing, and that the lines on my palm break off completely. This means I'm going to die when I'm thirty. He leans in closer and the white streak in his hair is luminous, like the bad gremlin in that movie. 'A violent death,' he says. He makes me think about being caught in the demonstrations in St George's Mall, the day Chris Hani was buried.

We are on holiday in Cape Town, the only white people dumb enough to venture into town after the murder because we want to barter beads and blankets at Greenmarket Square. Maybe we get what we deserve for not paying attention to the news, or not caring enough about the Struggle.

As soon as we are dropped off we smell the weirdness in the streets; sweat and sirens and the broken glass of windscreens in the daytime; the feeling that something big has just happened, and that this is the aftermath. And in the mall itself, all these young black men, jogging with knobkieries and anything else they have picked up along the way. They are streaming like army ants towards the cathedral and the TV cameras. On the outskirts of this column are ANC marshals in plastic yellow vests; the whole event feeling like some kind of marathon except that they are carrying sjamboks that gleam and snap like mambas in the morning sun.

Inside the offices the workers in their little suits have barricaded the doors and backed away from the windows, thanking their stars for vending machines and thinking that the Apocalypse is finally upon us. No horsemen, but war and pestilence for all. Mick and I are caught in a doorway, our faces feeling so white they must blind the people behind the mass of feet and sticks and the caps of the Young Lions. We aren't smart enough to be afraid yet. For the most part they are ignoring us.

What is it that makes some of them stop and try to smash in the windows of jewellery shops even though they are empty? No hope of entering the citadel, but still they kick at the walls. The officials shout and swear and swing their sjamboks, and most of the men keep running. We stand with our backs to the door, waiting for it to be over. And this is when a man decides that I need my face slapped, and so it happens, his palm like a pink glove. And the next man also does this, hits me and runs on, not even looking back to see whether I cry white tears before an official jumps in front of the two of us and stands with his arms stretched out, a crook on a cross. He saves us. He could have given us over.

An old man decides that he is immune, or maybe he just wants to crawl to safety, because he emerges from a building, blinking behind his glasses in the sun, pink and white and grey in his pinstripes, unable to believe that this is happening in his own paved working space, where German tourists drink coffee and fight off the succubus cameras on their chests. Where there are always police officers on horseback and there is handcuffed punishment for people who do things that break the law but not for stealing office supplies. Where everything is always black or white and obvious from the flatness of the nose behind the tea trolley.

He walks slowly, old and bent, and the twos and threes of the young men behind him hit him on the skull as they run past, like horses at steeplechase jumps, with only a brief hesitation and gathering up. His glasses fly off on to the bricks. He would have bent down to retrieve them but he is down there already, blood streaming in the white fluff of his hair as they kick and kick at him until he stops trying to cover his face with his flypaper old man's hands.

Back at the station the train we are supposed to take has been set alight, metal payback for the men everywhere working like dwarves underground to bring up coal and iron and diamonds and gold. We are also sweating, but not for the same reason. People run through the stale air of the subterranean mall, looking for family or something that won't change. There are desperate calls from public payphones and immigrant fathers weaving through traffic blocks to fetch us. Violence. Death. But not ours.

Thirty is not that far away. *Surely* goodness and mercy will follow me all my days.

Swan Lake

On the other side of the telephone umbilicus my mother is breathless again. 'I nearly died this weekend!' she says. Always she has nearly died; by her skin, by her teeth, she lives again, miraculously. She is the New Jew who always escapes, bluffing and huffing herself more Jewish than my father, who had genes on his side. If I ever wanted to swear an oath I would say, By my mother's birthmark. I know it will always be there.

She has decided that my also miraculous brother would be better off at boarding school. He has decided against it but she ignores his sulks and silences; she sews nametags on to the seven of everything he will need there, pricking her fingers. 'Seven shirts! It's nearly bankrupted me! But it's worth it. You should see the school.' It sounds like that story of the princess in exile who has to make shirts for her brothers from nettles because their ugly stepmother has turned them into swans.

He has only been there for a term but she has to go and fetch him because he locked himself in one of the bathrooms and refused to come out. He stays in there for twelve hours before they take him seriously. It is a last attempt; every weekend he phones her and cries to come home. She forces him to stay. The fees are exorbitant and he isn't usually the kind of child who weeps. He'll get over it. Another term, maybe. But this is different. The housemaster has called her and told her to fetch him. My brother won't say why he locked himself in. Later he will tell her in little bits about the Matrics holding one of the junior boys down and raping him, but that is still a way off. When she sees him she will understand that something about him is different; there has been a change. But for now she is on her way.

It is a very cold winter. This sounds trite but a layer of snow has actually fallen in the Northern Cape. People come out to stare at it. If you're looking for signs of the Apocalypse, this would be one of them, thin and greasy on the roads. My mother has always refused to drive long distances by herself. Perhaps this is partly why I haven't learned to drive yet. Maybe it filtered into my bloodstream along with the antibodies from her breast milk.

She and her friend are driving over this layer of snow, and of course they skid. 'Right on to the gravel! I thought we would definitely roll.' But then, she says, she remembers what my father had said when he was teaching her to drive on the gravel at the drive-in before they were married, back when she was braver than she is now. Turn into the skid, he said. Don't try to brake. So she does. And it works because there are no cars coming. They gradually come to a stop and look at each other, panting. Then she bursts into tears and laughs hysterically. She says to her friend, and to me, 'Jock saved my life!'

So maybe they are quits now, a life for a life. Maybe now she can live in peace. Maybe I can learn to drive. I remember how the story ends, about the swans. Just as the princess is about to be burned at the stake for being a witch, her brothers fly over. The nettle shirts have made her fingers bleed, but she throws them over each of their heads and they turn back into handsome men, except for the youngest. Because she has not had enough time before her execution, the last shirt is unfinished and so he has a white-feather wing instead of an arm. It is unchanged, but he gets his human form back.

Voodoo Chile

I am walking back into Walker with my weekend in a bag, and there is twittering in the passages. Big birds bring me news, how while I was away Mick got so drunk that he stripped down to his boxer shorts and dived one night into the swimming pool at Boater's bar. Beautiful, they say to me, these snide girls, who have stopped the buzzing of their hornet hairdryers long enough to snigger to me, Beautiful. He looked like he was flying.

I am jealous, I am enraged. He always does this, makes people believe that they can all do these things, when the truth is that he is different, he has white man's magic, he is cartwheel in the grass and swallow dive from the board. He changes his shape to suit the occasion and the potion of his motion is beer. He will always survive, while the rest of us mill about and look up at the clouds, going, Aaaah. And I want to be magic too.

I am having a new car-and-panic dream where I step out into the road and a massive car vrooms past and cuts me off at the knees. No pain, just the impact, like being caught unawares by the punching bag at my old ballet school building. And then I cannot walk because I have no legs, only thighs, and I cannot get out of the road.

We are on the grass at Brian's new house, drinking pink drinks with straws. The boys' chests are exam-pale in the sun; I can't imagine them being the same chests that must house a heart, liver, lungs to make them sweet, bitter, breathless – they are too smooth, Ken doll chests before Barbie's had a chance to scratch them with her pointy plastic fingers.

The sun has turned our heads and the grass has made us itchy, so when the motorbike appears we welcome it as if it is the only one we have ever seen; it is twice as welcome as the first motor car must have been in De Hel in the 1950s. There are places in the Karoo that can only be accessed by roads so bumpy and dusty that you might make it there, but only blind and toothless by your journey's end. An eye for an eye. The brothers had to carry it in part by part and assemble it once they were there. A Frankencar.

Mick and Brian are invincible; they are always first on the list and fresh for an audience. Mick at the front. He doesn't know how to drive a motorbike but his confidence will carry them three inches above the ground. It will be the first levitating bike. The closest contender so far has been Evil Knievel. I'm hoping no one will be going over waterfalls in a barrel.

We lie around, me stiffly talking with the other girls. They confuse me; they smell wrong and want me to talk about sex. I take the pink drinks into my pinker insides and avoid eye contact. I make Stupid Men jokes until the phone rings inside, even though there is no one sitting by it, wishing for this to happen. They call me to it and I go with my heart descending floor by floor, an elevator of dread like the ending of *Angel Heart*.

The voice is no one I know. He tells me that I don't know him, but would I get there quickly? There has been an accident. He gives me an address. In the time it takes for one of the boys to drive me there, we die and revive, memories of those emergency demonstrations from school ringing through our passages. We see Brian first, dry-eyed and whole, waiting with his legs crossed like a nursery school order and staring at the mangled motorbike. On the grass of this new man's garden Mick sits and shakes. When he turns to me he is blind with grief and drunkenness; all the skin on his left side has been scraped off. 'I drove into barbed wire,' he blabs, 'Brian surfed me over the fence.' Brian starts crying; it is relief. There are women here now.

Inside the cold ambulance Mick leans on me and can't stop

sobbing. It's the first time I've been in an ambulance. He bleeds on my chest. Like Saint Sebastian. Pierced. How I would give him my own salt blood if I could, replace everything he has lost, his liquids, his self-love. I might still have to. My own organs are working double-time under the siren, beating like fists against the rib cage. It will crack with sorrow.

At Settlers' Hospital the boys shiver and swear on the gurneys in the corridor, just like the catfish used to wriggle for my father. For an hour we pace and make loud white demands for a doctor. It is never like this on TV. The one on duty today is playing golf; they will have to call him. Does this boy have medical aid? Why is he so drunk in the daytime? In the wards down the corridor I pace; in the beds there are quiet black people, shrivelled. They make no demands, and they will not be going home.

The doctor walks up the corridor, stooped and snappy on his soles, the Grim Reaper in golf shoes. He is old and irritable, he tells the boys to stop swearing. He says, 'I don't know what *your* girls are like, but my nurses aren't used to that sort of language.' It's almost funny. The three nurses gathered around the half-naked boys in their red stripes like rugby jerseys are cement-faced and flat-arched. A million pontoon bridges' worth of beige stockings couldn't make these women cross over into Ladyland.

The doctor tells Brian that he's fine and gives him an injection. He gets up and realises that it's true: he is fine. The doctor pours peroxide over Mick's cuts; it foams up and he screams; even the nurses flinch then. When it subsides, he is sewn up with a length of metal that is more a mafia steel pipe than a needle. The thick black suture is drawn shaky and slow through the brown skin and gold hair of my lover's bartending and breast-fondling and bread-breaking arms. X marks the spot. And X and X and X. Poison kisses from spiders, love letters from Jack the Ripper.

After that he only lies miserably under the flowered sheets and wants to make love when I creep in beside him, a refugee from my daylife with calculator eyes to sum up the forty-six cuts. An inside-out tiger. So much for Christopher Robin. He doesn't cry often. He doesn't cry at all. Sometimes I wonder if his tear ducts work, if maybe they did something else to him, there in the hospital, while our own eyes were somewhere else.

Spirit Level

The last days at university are about looking for Cape Town schools in the phone directory and licking the sticky stripes on large manila envelopes. It is better than looking out for Mick to come walking to my door or wiping sticky stripes of tequila off the large manila bar counter. I have sent fifty CVs out from the hinterland; they are carrier pigeons with messages to the new land. They say, Our mistress is smart. They say, She is willing to sell this to you.

In the interim I wait and do extra shifts at the bar. My biceps have grown; I am Rambo with my knife, slashing through beer carrier undergrowth, flicking off the bottle top leeches and making it safe for the convoys of Muslim boys, so they can drink enough at varsity to make sure that they won't ever feel like they're missing out again. They have to go back to their parents in their Mercedes Benzes and the girls with their shiny long hair under Chanel scarves, silk tentacles out to take the boys back to their underwater world. Yo ho ho, and a bottle of rum.

Exams happen; in the day we shuffle and sigh our futures through our sinuses. We do not know what it will smell like. We ourselves smell of the Fizzers we've dissolved to make us faster, or else stale beer from the night before. The daylight litres of Coca-Cola and the vitamin C make us walking invalids. We are vats filled with hierarchies of need; our insides bubble with risk and disaster. They strap us to the desks in the Great Hall, where a man with a patch over his eye makes jokes with us. We stare at him in his double ferocity and his eye in reverse, a wormhole into another dimension. We leave early after doing backstroke under the waves of foolscap, heading for the shore and hoping not to bump our heads.

On the telephone the headmistress's voice is plummy and soft; she is used to being obeyed and she knows the way to dry land. Ahoy, matey. I know exactly what she will look like in real life – not a pirate captain because she will have fewer earrings, but something softer and scarier. Like the world's oldest air hostess powdered into her suit, she will warn you to put out your cigarette, to buckle up, and that you must follow the instructions in the interests of safety. It's going to be a bumpy ride.

She says that they want me and I take them on, because I've only had two responses at all. My CV must still be there somewhere, in the filing cabinets of all these schools. Dead letter offices, where we have sent our desires, our messages in bottles. They must pile up, smelling of suntan lotion and growing pains, making the secretaries cover their faces and think of their own children when they're sent to pick just one and uncork it. Most of them are too late; by the time they're opened the message is old. With our wide-bottomed trousers and our tropical diseases we have sailed on.

Silver Bullets

We are camels on wheels on the N2, in our slow hot caravan to Cape Town. There is no stopping now because everywhere there are cars, glinting and stopped, or glinting and crawling, but always sending metal flashes in through the windscreen. They make my eyes water, and they make my brain sing. I am past being excited at the idea of moving here, although I am glad to be alone with Mick. Tonight we'll lie down between cool sheets and stretch out our toes curled with travel; his parents let us sleep in a double bed.

We have spent ten hours together in the car, stopping at a series of stale towns every two hours or so, where it is always late afternoon and the petrol attendants are sleepy and don't speak Xhosa. Bubbly brown water comes out of the taps and sulky teen waitresses serve you salmonella along with the runny tomato sauce. The tape deck stretches everything we put in; no radio signal can make it past Sir Lowry's Pass. The tendons on his hands stretch as he curls them around the gear shift, the handbrake. I cannot drive; everything about the process is always new and impressive. Control. Like the Janet Jackson song.

We are travellers on a new planet. We have rations of peppermints and melting jelly babies and Rubik's Cube maps that can never be refolded, even though you saw them when they were new, and you know it can be done. We are at the mercy of the savages outside our thin metal box; our legs are scrunched underneath our chins. They peer in as they walk above us over the skyway bridges, fenced in and fenced out; their feet don't touch the earth. Lately people have been throwing bricks through the windscreens of white motorists' cars, but the fear is worth it. We are driving away from everything that is wrong. A chance to start over in Newlands, where the trees make you cool and dark because you're so small against them, and the wind rocks you to sleep. His mother will come to the door in her white cotton socks and lilt at me, 'Ah Diane, it's so nice to see you.' There will be enormous cookies she's baked that day. She will smell of Oil of Olay and laugh at my jokes, and his father will be jumping around the living room at a Man United goal. They are my new family.

The day cools slowly from blistering to oven; we squint in our heat blindness and Mick says, 'So. Where are you staying?' I am a little shocked at this strange humour; it must be a joke. Everything I care about is in the back of this car. We talked about this. I'm skipping my Northern Cape teaching bursary and moving to Cape Town to be with him. I've sat on enough suitcases to cripple a porter at an airport. 'I thought I was staying with you. Haven't you asked your parents yet?' He shifts a little in his sticky seat and grimaces, tries to convey sympathy. His face tightens up in his cornered expression and I know that he can't look at me. He drives extra carefully. 'Well, that's the problem. They said you can't stay there.' My vocal cords have nothing to say to this, but my tear ducts won't be quiet. He carries on. 'It's my father actually. He said that you aren't welcome in the house.' He laughs at this, at how ridiculous it sounds. 'He says you broke my heart.' I turn and look out of the window. Blink. Blink. The grid of the streetlights flickers on around the houses floating in their upside-down stars. It's cooled down at last. It's not the strangers at the gate we should beware of, nor the stone-throwers on the bridge. It's the ones you know, with their fur on end and their teeth sharp in their mouths. Keep the silver bullets close at hand.

PART FIVE

PENNYROYAL

Quiet in the Cloisters

The days make me tired and the nights out are too loud. Being in Cape Town makes me breathe differently, deeper into the lungs, like a swimmer, even though that way more carbon monoxide finds its way in. Stroke, stroke, breathe, choke. Every move is calculated so that I can negotiate pavements where there is a speed and a glitter that must rub off on me. It must.

I still don't know how to drive. I've never had to. I've always lived in small places where you join the pedestrian dots by looking for landmarks. It is safe this way; it is controllable. Walk. Don't walk. I still have the dream about the car in reverse, except now I am alone in it.

In Cape Town there is more of everything, especially taxis ready to take off your toes. It is safer to be inside, where the coffee jockeys are magic and Cavendish is a kingdom of greed. The swish of people with their shopping bags makes everything Christmas. You can have whatever you want, but you have to be prepared to protect it. Tooth, claw. Dentist, manicure. Anything ugly can be rubbed off. Our faces are blank slates; we write rude messages on them in lipstick. These say, I am hunting. They say, I am available and I want a four-by-four.

On the trains they are trying to make us say 'Metro' and 'Metro Plus', but everyone knows it is still just Third Class and First Class. I don't want to be a snob. I also think that if I am going to be mugged, at least in Third Class the mamas will protect me. So much for Girl Power. With their fat yellow fingers and their fat yellow shopping bags they are a buffer between my skin and my conscience. There are hymns and sweating women preachers who have come to Jesus late in life, stomping and shaking their heads (hallelujah!) like a Leonard Cohen chorus and it makes sense. God has filled the gap. Who better to spread the Word than the people who have spent their lives spreading bread with apricot jam? Man cannot live . . .

On the train today there are only a few of us. There is a man who has only one arm. His sleeve is not pinned discreetly; he does not seem to care that he flaps up and down the carriage in the wake of the preacher. He is a crow, shrivelled and beady. He picks up the crumbs of attention that fall behind her on her way. He gathers the scraps to his raggedy self. He comes over to me (oh, is it my face? Is it my skin, reflecting like the mirror of the lost climber on the mountainside?) and drags his loose shirt sleeve over my hair. I am too afraid to move. He doesn't smell of wine; his eyes are not rolling. There is no spit. Our mouths are both dry.

He folds his sleeve back tenderly and shows me his stump, not the polony I was expecting but a slender and shapely limb that tapers to a pale point. He rubs it on my cheek twice before the mamas flap at him in their turn, saying, 'Hawu! Get away!' and he goes, smiling at me over his intact shoulders.

At home I sink on to my new bed in my new house before I can find the energy to run a bath. Sometimes it is lonely, but not for long, because that night another man comes to keep me company. I am naked from the waist down and I reach over to close the window and there he is. His forehead is pressed against the window so that it smears when he pulls away, Klingon with fright. Didn't he think I could see him or did he just not care? Doesn't he understand that all this effort is not for him? I jump back with my hands first praying mantis and then covering what they should have been all along. I hit the light switch and pant in the darkness. My eyes are as wide as his were (blue and white, like Delft). I have no phone.

I can hear him rustle under the tree. He isn't going away. I creep nearer to the window and yank it back and there he is, an equal yanker with his dick in his hands, rubbing furiously at himself, more an itch than a fondle as his hair flops and he gasps.

I slam doors and run to my neighbour who has a phone. She tries to feed me pea soup while the woman who picks up at the Claremont police station shrieks with laughter and cries out, '*Mas*turbator!' and there is deeper hyuck-hyucking in the background. They never bother to come, but the man must have, because by the time I get back home he is gone.

Lunatic Fringe

Last night we drove down Canterbury Street and looked from the sides of our eyes into the building where the Fringe used to be. There is a huge car advert painted on its wall but if you look up you can see that the roof is gone, blasted off like this building is the booster on the back of a rocket, and the rest of it has whooshed into space. It must have taken all the cool people with it, along with the blow-up alien they used to have suspended from the ceiling. Maybe it will come to earth somewhere or crash into the Pacific, where all our space garbage seems to end up. I hope this doesn't happen, because it's going to be really difficult to do doggy paddle in a trench coat.

The Fringe was the first place that I knew where they played music with words that you could dance to. The wooden floors made your Docs do flip flops, and even teenage white boys looked like they had rhythm. As the nineties wore grooves in the floor, they changed everything there; rumours about health hazards making the venue into a pool bar, where only jukebox rednecks and Jonathan went, desperate for cheap beer and women in cookie-cutting jeans who couldn't dance even if they wanted to. After that we couldn't go back, like leaving home all over, and then there was the fire that gutted the building with three homeless people burned in their sleep, dreaming of hell, maybe, but not health hazards.

Before that, when the place still had a pulse even when the DJs didn't, they used to project fractals on the walls and the picture of that Vietnamese girl with all her clothes burned off, and that's how it felt to be there. Naked and burning to Smashing Pumpkins, even if we hadn't eaten all our vegetables at supper. This place was the solution to being a first-year teacher, motherless and new in the City, or a boy doing his articles in a blue shirt he didn't like. It was a solution because there were all these other broken people there, with their shiny piercings and fingers of dagga, and you didn't even make a dent in their weirdness. You headbanged and shimmied and jumped around, and the boys had long hair and there weren't that many girls.

On the mattress I sat next to Kurt Cobain Boy, and his hair impressed me. When he leaned in and started asking me questions I knew that old bloodbubble rush was coming on. His pupils had swallowed the rest of his irises; I couldn't tell if they were black or blue or why he even wanted to speak to me, the straight. What I could tell was that I wanted to follow him when he went down the industrial stairs into The Pit, which smelled like a garage and probably was; people got themselves lubricated there. His tongue tasted of cigarettes and I liked the way he didn't pin me to the wall like I was a frog in a lab, ready for dissection. Twitch. Twitch.

I found out afterwards that he was seventeen, and this was a five-year age gap. I found this out because when I started school on sober Monday, one of my grade elevens grinned wide and said, 'Ryan says hi.' I went over and said, 'How do you know that?' She went on, sweet and low as Canderel, 'Because he's my ex.'

Mother Tongue

The students and I are small girlanimals sniffing each other; will we like the same foods? Will we manage to live in the same space without our fur flying? Mainly you can tell that we are different because of our feet. They are the same size but theirs are hooves in their tight black leather at the ends of their decently-shaved and blue-skirted legs, while my toes are allowed to wriggle like the fish in the waves at Hermanus. Like my mother's must have been when she was in her twenties, peeping out with grins on their toe-faces from under her zooty new pantsuits.

I am here to endure the staff room with its smell of spoiled milk and spoiled lives, here to spread the New Age gospel, to tell them about white explorers and the body parts of black women, to dig with my Seamus Heaney fingers and pens into their soft strata to see what is there. It makes me afraid; it makes me tired. There are no assumptions here, I think that is what it is. The things they told you in your HDE year aren't always true and sometimes it is as if your tongue will not move; it sticks to the roof of your mouth (*jou verhemelte* in Afrikaans – isn't that beautiful? The universe inside your mouth) like peanut butter and it will not come back to its root. I sweat and sweat and I jump around. I want them to be excited. I want them to care about evolution and suffragists more than they care about sheep's eyes and soufflés. I am a woman-preacher on the Poetry Train, where there is always room for one more.

The things we have been told that will serve us in our new lives rise up like the lost island of Atlantis. If only we had flippers. Instead we have language and love. My old schooling comes back too and now I begin to understand the memories of the Lord's Prayer in Setswana. We mumbled in our ranks like the army of God, Rara wa rona, Yo o kwa legodimong, because the Christian Brothers understand that knowing an African language means learning to bubble and squirt. Forget your tight-lipped English with its defunct spelling and obscure idioms. It is as though you are blind, but have been given the chance to see again. Amazing Grace, how sweet the sound, only this time the colours will be different. Like Helen Keller meeting Lazarus.

Except that I have chosen Cape Town, and everyone speaks Xhosa. My tongue will not work here.

And I am not the only one. Everywhere there are people trying to communicate. At the café Mrs B is lisping. I lean over the counter to hear her but still it is too thick to wade through without gumboots, without glass slippers, footwear of some kind that will lift us off this pavement of confusion. How rude of her to eat while she is speaking to me, I think. Is that betel nut? Her mouth looks stained. Do Indian people still chew that stuff?

She is tired of repeating herself; she thrusts out her tongue at me and a third of it is gone, like a tree stump, like William Tell's older and lesser-known son. 'Cancer of the mouth,' she says. 'I have to go back to the hospital every six weeks.' It makes me shiver; it makes me shake. She has lost part of herself. She has to teach herself to speak again in the language of the maimed, the survivor; it is the language of resurrection.

Vingertaal

In the car there is more Pink Floyd. We will never escape it. We will always be on the dark side of the moon, mainly because the child-proof locks are on in Norman's car and he chooses the music. But outside it is sunstrike and white lines on the tar, and seeing how many Pringles you can fit into your mouth at once.

The clouds sulk and dither like girls at a social when the DJ plays a slow song; they are low over the mountains. We are on a wine route. What else is summer but a chance to get wasted outside?

The Taal Monument pokes up at us, kisses the sky like a Jimi Hendrix song in cement. It teaches us new words and reawakens old languages, things we've thrown away because we hoped never to use them again. *Die Sakmense. Fiela se Kind.* Books like telephones used by white people to talk to other white people. I have never seen the monument up close (oh, Kimberley is flat, oh, Grahamstown is a hole of another kind) and we want to stop somewhere to line our stomachs before they dissolve completely and take our tempers too.

The man at the entrance wants to charge us two rand to go in. The idea is ludicrous. The whole point of the monument is that it can be seen from the outside. It is an anti-lighthouse; it draws Afrikaners and other sailors on to the rocks. And underneath them spiders live. Rock. Spiders.

We lay out our blankets on the grass. There are no flat places and everything is a struggle. No ox-wagons and marauding blacks today but wind, sobriety, the proximity of other people's summer skin. These are difficult too. The Battle of Blood River in our T-cells, the Day of the Vow on our lips. Behind me there is Gordon with his knees bent. If I lean back on my elbows I can see up the legs of his shorts, all the way up to his red undies. There is very fine, soft hair on the backs of his legs, like the hair at the nape of your neck, like baby hair. I want to stretch out my fingers and stroke it but there is no way that I can. He has a girlfriend in plucked eyebrows and power suits who will protect him. To me he is only ever lazy or evil-tempered; he smokes constantly. This one throws up more veils than Mata Hari and sells his secrets dear. But that ended in front of a firing squad, and maybe he will, too. It is hair that leads to dark places.

Reflections on Ice-breaking

Norman's mother has asked him to housesit in the Spring holidays. So far the ornaments are all still on their shelves, but outside there are neural messages circling faster than common sense. What Norman is doing instead of keeping an eye on us is locking himself in the bathroom with the Junkie Waitress and her ecstasy suppositories. Maybe he's giving her a bath.

The beer has traded fists and gone its good way to our stomachs and heads. We turn to the teat on the five litres of Gordon's raw red dooswyn; we see him swinging the box from his Nick Cave fingers. We drink fast and cold, with our shrivelled tongues and notions of morning shoved into the same place toothbrushes are stored. Home is the hunter.

On the blanket in the night garden we are wriggling and giggling. Behind their little fences flowers spy on us. There is creeping massage and the pressing of hard fingers into muscle, changing the shapes underneath, preparing us for ovens, making us edible. There is also slow touching and fingers warm under the blanket, so that the blood rises to the surface of the skin and turns to glühwein; we are all glowing. Sugar. Spice. People close their eyes for too long and so it feels right to kiss the one next to you, boy to boy, girl to boy, passing on the Braille of our palates, the taste bud message. *Roll over, roll over.*

Beside me on the blanket lies Gordon, who is tired of looking at the Pinelands stars because they are too far away, and is looking at the back of my neck instead. I can feel his sky eyes there, soft enough to raise the little hairs all the way down to between my shoulder blades. I have always liked blue-eyed boys. He sighs as if he has lost an argument and stretches out those arms around and under me, and gathers me to himself. There is never any question of saying no against his chest. He is an emissary from Planet Boy and his message is that he comes in peace.

I cannot get close enough to him; he is so tall that I can stretch myself out along his length and there is still limb length to go round. We inch off the blanket with our open mouths and fingertips and there is all this grass to cover, and so we do, rolling around in the wet and prickle of it, gathering bruises and grass stains – yinyangyinyang – until he lands heavy on my ankle and there is the sound of bones grinding. Perhaps that should have been a sign. This. Will. Hurt. In. The. Morning. Not because he meant it to, but because we don't know when to stop.

Ich Bin Ein Pinelander

Gordon lives with his mother and his grandmother, a chain of being that hands down to him love and clean laundry. He drags home driftwood that looks like crocodiles and his Gogo puts them in her flowerbeds, where they keep watch with their splintery jaws over her indigenous plants. Snap. Birds come to her, and cats that won't let anyone else touch them; she doesn't talk much but she is a siren for hurt things, she is an animal ambulance. And the crocodiles let them live.

In the evening their garden is glassy with the sound of wind chimes and other people's dogs made insane with the idea of being allowed outside. Her birds fly over like a Bob Marley song, and you know it's true, every little thing is going to be all right. We sit in Gordon's rooms with our cold drinks and hot hands. Under our fingers the ice melts. Ogden Nash is right. And so is Taj Mahal. Candy is dandy, but liquor is quicker.

I am staring at the business suit of the girl across the room. She works as a receptionist and likes to wear tight beige pants.

She paints a line round her lips like they tell you in *Cosmo*. Through her crocodile teeth she is drinking screwdrivers and she doesn't know how apt that is yet; she is Gordon's girlfriend, but he says she isn't. He says, 'I never made her any promises.'

She must spend an hour each morning playing Make-Up Snap (but not Old Maid) with her mirror twin, because every feature of hers is curled, like petals – nose, eyebrows, hair. And Cupid loves her lips. Beside her I am cold feet and poky elbows. Gordon sits down next to me on the floor. He touches me and I wonder if he is sorry for taking me on, because at that moment she is looking at us and everything is so obvious it hurts. She stands up on her platform feet and stalks out blind into the garden, where everything is in its proper place and she is not.

Gordon goes out after and I only know she is weeping because I can hear them through the window; a spy in the House of Love. He tries to hug her and she pushes him away and screams at him that she does *not* want to be friends; inside there is loud clinking of glasses and clearing of throats. But her throat is not clear. She re-enters and I push my spine against the wall – cold, but not as hard as a woman whose blue eyes are pink and whose heart we've cracked open. I expect her to curse me like a bad fairy at a christening, but her suit contains her; it holds back her wrath in her Wonderbra chest. She has come back for her handbag made of the skin of some thing and then she leaves, looking taller than she is, clicking down the driveway and into her car.

Gogo comes in with her threescore years and ten and her offers of supper. At least we know at the beginning who Judas will be.

This is My World

Sing die ou, ou lied van Afrika, / Sing dit sag, sing dit lank vir my. / Maak oop jou deur, maak oop jou hart, / Laat my binnekom, laat my bly.

We went into the desert to be electric, to give off sparks to send the rock rabbits scurrying and shock the tortoises. Prepare in the desert a highway.

We went to wait for the zing of illumination to light up our windscreen, to pray for the lightning bolt that would rearrange our features. Druids on wheels, with the holy ground tarred and whispering. It is starry, even in the daylight, even in the mine-dumps. We see the names that we have known for so long, and they feed back to us. Rietvlei. Graaff-Reinet. Moordenaars-karoo. And oh, you know something bad happened there, with the sound of thudding footsteps and the kitchen knife missing. We don't stop to listen. Our dagga bankie bounces in the togbag on the back seat. We are going to the Owl House. Maybe we will be bored.

Farm ghosts attend us, with their dresses for the Peach Blossom Festival and their opsitkerse, small lights flickering in time to traditions that are meaningless to us in our silver Mazda and our sex before marriage. A hundred years ago we daughters would have been laced tightly as boots into our bodices, hiding our calloused feet under the table so that the man across from us thinks that he's seeing a girl with the magic hands of a princess who uses them in the daytime to eat bread and honey and in the night time to brush her hair a hundred times over. What we really have to do is plaster the floors with dung. The pips from the peaches go in.

In the seat next to Gordon I am in my summer dress under the nuclear-winter light, metal and orange, with my legs smooth and quiet on the dashboard while he drives. They are exfoliated, depilated, tanned. Chocolate melts under my hands.

The discovery of our callouses, of our rough parts will come later, when we've given in to the taste bud music of men who promise across the table that they will love us forever while our parents eavesdrop from the kitchen and the shotgun leans against the wall. More coffee will make them stay.

The road is a pale path of sleeplessness in the Karoo. Lightning cracks like the knives of little English children in Robert Louis Stevenson rhymes, smashing open their breakfast eggs and dictating our table manners. Every sound is bigger than we are; every breath is the taste of thunder. It makes the hairs on our arms stand up; it makes him say, 'I'm just looking for the first place to stop and then I'm going to jump you.' I believe him. I believe in him. John the Baptist.

The rain comes, cold and pricking. It pins us to the bonnet of the car. He is a wet animal over me while the aimless cows look sideways over their barbed wire. My eyes are taking in too much light again; everything is open. I am the warm negative of a photograph, wide-angled. We pant with half our clothes off; the insides of our caverns match the moisture outside. The Cango Caves, where everything is slippery and you can only find your way by touch. Vingertaal. I cannot stop laughing, like being held down and tickled so that it hurts. I don't know what to do with this joy. I could suck in the clouds. My stomach muscles are still sore when I bury the tissue soaked with semen under a rock. My ancestors won't like this offering. If only T. S. Eliot were here.

Nieu-Bethesda is easy to find. Most things huddling against the hills are. It emits a kind of radar as we approach in the headache light, taking us in, blinking. Against the sky the cement hands are groping like unmarried daughters behind their high-wire fence; the poems are charms wired and hot-wired in steel. They are all backwards to me, and that's as it should be.

Inside the lion's den there is money changing hands and squat Afrikaans fathers arguing about the couvert charge, going 'Isn't there a fidiyo?' It's like screaming in a temple. The grim mermaids and the flat-eyed travellers are stiff in their postures, crumbling slowly into their disapproval. We regard each other in stand-off, our thousand-yard stares make us equal statues of meat and cement in the sun. Gordon, alive and always twisty, climbs inside the bottled domes and among the glass and cement skirts of the women. He feels at home there, looking back at the outside.

In her house there is the stuffed body of the goat-foot girl lying on the floor, with her smell of mould and other people's husbands clinging, and all the mirrors and candles and jars of ground glass rainbows in the pantry are still only the result of a woman who made mince of her hands with her idea of being beautiful on the inside. She used to hang around the windows of the houses of the coloured people, listening to their music she could not make herself, with her bare feet and her extra toe making marks in the dust. They hated her. Kids threw stones at her statues. And she knew why. Eating caustic soda flakes is only the logical conclusion when being raw on the inside is nothing new.

'Take a left,' says Egbert, with his watery eyes and his dry throat, 'take another left and drive for thirty-five kilometres.' So we do, around the tortoises mating in the road and three lambs and a toddler, all baa-ing for their mothers in a line of demand and open mouths. At the guest farm where these creatures all get their suppers, we are assigned a cottage called the Prison. Ha ha.

The thing is that, after the bath and the braai and the staring into space, we cannot sleep. There is a picture of Helen Martins in my head, bent over her grinder, dissolving jars and her hands. Gordon gets up. 'I'm going to smoke a joint,' he says. 'I need to sleep.'

It doesn't help. Back to bed and still the demon restlessness, playing snakes and ladders in our skulls, or maybe a tune I don't know the words to, because I'm white in the Karoo. This is my world. White on the outside. Raw on the inside.

Standing on the Rooftops

I have arrived with my suitcases of hopeful underwear. Not my father's house, but my lover's. And we will live. Up the crumbly green stairs I have lugged my trousseau of dirty jokes and university degrees, feeling like Nancy Drew, Girl Detective, thinking, I could be happy, higher up. Thinking of that picture they always have in the old *Life* retrospectives, of the girl who jumped from the Empire State Building, dead before she made contact. She took a car with her, landing on its roof and making a dent so deep that the insides were crushed along with her own. She lies peacefully, unscarred, with her hair splayed out like the Little Mermaid and her hands in her lap, decently Catholic to the end even though she didn't mean to be.

The balcony is long and cool, a cement cocktail, a vantage point for lost souls and other wanderers who won't come any further in because lounges bring back memories of Sunday afternoons in parentful places. While you're under my roof . . . What I like about it is that you have to walk its length every time you want to get to the front door; it is the only point of entry, an enforced meditation. Outside. Inside.

Sometimes at night a man strides up to the telephone box outside the café. It cups him like an alien egg, ready to be let loose from a plastic stomach to spy on the rest of us and send messages back to the mother ship. Telkom was here, under his overcoat, on the bottoms of his shiny black shoes.

He grabs the receiver roughly and shouts into it without dialling a number. 'You scuuum!' 'You whore's poes!' His throat is hoarse with his outrage and his spit bubbles up as if there is a volcano in his stomach – a Mount Etna that an equal mountain of Rennies could never damp down. Where his spit lands it sizzles with indignation, burns tiny holes in the plastic. We listen from our balcony; you don't have to strain to hear. He stops to punch in an impossibly long sequence of random numbers and shouts some more, straining forward to get as close as he can to the receiver.

My friend Mark says, 'I bet he has a family somewhere. I bet he waves a cheery goodbye and comes down here to shout all his abuse down the phone. And then it's out. He's purged. And he goes back home again, to his family. It's a really good idea.'

Eventually the man gives up and stomps back the way he came. His shiny shoes reflect the sane gates and trees along the sides of the road.

After five o'clock on any day you can see the soles of Gordon's sneakers propped there if you look up. No diamonds underneath but then again, he doesn't need rocks to make him happy when he has his secret identity and his Indian name – Two-Feet-On-The-Balcony. All through the summer visitors sit on its wall above the street, looking out like lemmings with eyes gone cloudy. In the armchair Gordon holds me on his lap. In our mouths there is the afterburn of chillies and the froth of beer. He says, 'I feel like the prairie and you're the little house on it.' The love words stick in my throat, making me growl; they are also inflamed. They will also not be damped down.

Being here makes up for the thick damp walls inside, and the shebeen queen below. It makes up for having a lumpy futon and floorboards that squeal in the night. It is a place to have drinks in, a shadowed place where you can't feel the kwaito earth-quakes from below because the floors have changed from wood to cement. It is the opposite of a jail cell but there is always the jingling of keys. In the mornings I blink out into an alternative universe, where everything is colder and sharper and girls tell lies about homework. At school there is no beer.

On a ten o'clock Wednesday I am called to the office to listen to a man trying to squeeze his thick voice down the telephone wire. The security company wants me to come home because the alarm in my flat has gone off. I teach another king-on-a-heath scene to the Matrics; there is talk of lightning strikes and divine intervention and then I walk out into the banal sun. Nancy Drew never had to walk.

There is the siren sound warbling to me three blocks away; like a dying diva it begs me to be true. It says, Too late. Even the traffic lights are angry. Over me there is a cloud of sighs and curses like flies; every stone rolls under my feet and every crack in the tarmac widens to meet me. I will be swallowed before I get home. I will be swallowed and the police will put up a poster for a missing person. My mother will be worried and my cats will return to the wilderness. They already eat locusts.

The front door is frozen open and the fat-bottomed policemen don't care who I am. They drive off and now I am Nancy in *The Curse of the Missing Map* with the trail gone cold. Worse than the idea that strangers have been in your space is the idea of how easy it is for them to do so. There are bits of credit card stuck in the lock; with their strange feet on the balcony and their light fingers in the jamb, they didn't care enough to be afraid. And nothing has been taken.

Was it the alarm that panicked them? Or just the surprise that the inside had nothing to offer? How disappointing, to have grown up on the notion of being Ali Baba, and then to find you're only one of the forty thieves. And we all know how that ended.

I traipse back to school, wanting to walk backwards, a saviour in reverse with sweat tickling between my shoulder blades and black magic in my head. But what really happens is that everything is the same, except that you get a security gate. After trauma there is always the morning, always the day after. And then there will be the evening, back on the balcony where the air is thinner and sweeter; it will make us lose consciousness. I say, I'm standing on the rooftops, when he calls out, Baby, are you ready to go?

Mug

Jen over the phone uses her dancing teacher's voice. She is used to being obeyed; she tells me that something has happened to Gordon and we are going round to his father's house, flouting the rules of divorce and Constantia No-Man's-Land to hunt down her son. He didn't come home last night. She knows this because she got an early morning phone call in the kitchen; I know this because it is my house he is supposed to come home to. Little pig, little pig.

I have been waiting there with damp underarms and four a.m. hollowness of heart, picturing car accidents on the ceiling or Gordon being kissed on his soft unfaithful lips since he slammed out eight hours before.

'I knew it,' he said. 'I knew you would react this way.' My eyes are black with unfairness; I can feel the pupils shrinking. 'How can you not take me to your office party?' In my head there are reels that play back scenes from other parties we go to; he is always a magnet for the faulty iron filings of desperate women; they press him up against walls with their shirts casually unbuttoned, and he does not push them away. I drink too much and sulk in the garden, kicking at flowers and scraping my hands on the bark of trees.

This is how I know something is wrong tonight; my arms are heavy with dread and my eyes won't stop jumping with their jails and hospitals and long-haired vampire women, with their plastic teeth and see-through nighties. If you looked at my eyes now you would see the red lights of ambulances where my pupils used to be. If I opened my mouth a siren would sing its way out, one clear note to wake the neighbours in their double beds bulging with the right number of legs in pyjamas.

Our car ride is nervous tension and steering hands, through Saturday morning and beyond, breaking on through to Rondebosch-Newlands-Constantia. Behind the walled garden Gordon will be, eating grapefruit, maybe, or swimming lazy lengths in a cold pool.

We fly over paving and through security gates, stopping fast and shaky. We do the awkward hello dances, needing to see down the passage. He lies curled in guest room luxury, naked as the day he was born, but less bloody. It has crusted and cracked on him, face and arms striped like an extra on a break from *Lord of the Flies*. His mother holds his shoulder and wakes him, slow and numb. She gave birth to him; she gets first touch. She makes him put on his boxer shorts, makes a magic circle around him; now he can tell his New South African story and laugh with his broken face in his hands.

He tried to hitch home, he says, and the bakkie with the five coloured guys stopped for him. He wanted to accept this favour, go with them to show them that not all whites are racist. And he did. They laughed with all their teeth when he told them he needed to get to Rosebank, and for the next two hours they drove him around, pushing their hard hands against him and spitting their phlegm down his shirt. 'Langneus! We could stab you! We could kill you right here!' And then they got bored and he didn't have a wallet on him, so they opened the back and pushed him into the scrub on the side of the road.

On the flat horizon there was a garage, always a Caltex wherever you go, and towards this he walked with the stones pressing up through his shoes and the spaceship lights twinkling hope and telephone booths. The two men had time to watch him. How slowly this whitey was walking! It gave them time to plan their attack, so that he fell right over like a skittle when they jumped on him. Again, no wallet; they tore the lining out of his pockets, looking for gifts from the money tree, but there was nothing except credit cards. These were not enough, and the short one with the scars jabbed the screwdriver at Gordon, at his face, trying to put out his eyes so he couldn't see them, and also because they were blue. Jabbed at his arms, too, when he tried to cover his face. And then the taller one pulled him away, like he was separating two dogs in a fight, and they ran.

The garage attendant was unimpressed. 'Ja, there's lots of muggings here. It's a dangerous area.' 'Where is this?' said Gordon, pink and ragged, and lost as E.T. But he remembered his father's number, and he did what all aliens do. He phoned home.

His father, who is only ever a hero at the other end of the phone line, raced out to find the White Rabbit garage on the empty roads of early morning. Children beep high and shrill on their parents' I-told-you-so radar. He bundled his boy into the 4 × 4. His emergency rations were shaky cigarettes and Johnny Walker. The man on the bottle beamed under his top hat, and kept striding. Nobody ever tries to mug *him*.

Hem of Your Garment

There's a lady who lies in wait for me on the way to school; she is most powerful in the morning with her poison apple cheeks, top and bottom both, and the smile she takes out in the evening so it can live next to the bed, guarding her good manners and grinning at everyone because she's not awake to do it. She makes me think of being a little girl in a gingerbread house, doing housework while my brother lies in his gilded cage, being fattened for the feast, like Hansel and Gretel, like Hotel California.

Her plumpness precedes her; it bulges out like her eyes do when she stops to gossip with the gap-toothy maids on the pavement outside the mansion where she works. She is also a char, but higher than the rest, fat-faced and fairer-skinned, with hair like a Spanish dancer. But she doesn't move quickly, and this is my trick. I can stretch my eyes (oh, yes, we've heard about you at the Corner House, we've heard how you stretch your legs) and rush past her and breathe that I'm late so that she doesn't get me.

I hate the way she makes me feel like a pre-schooler, so that a tune I used to know rollicks through my head, 'I married me another / She's the devil's grandmother / and I wish I was single again / Ta tum.' I hate the way she shepherds me as I shrink and shrink into the past across the road with her. I hate her patience and pleasantries and her flat-heeled shoes.

And also I hate the way she makes me dread being fifty; I will fight this future that smells of poverty and dignity and Sunlight soap, with a wedding band that was never wide to begin with and erodes steadily with each season as if it is impatient to get back to the river it came from.

She has stopped at the café. I can slip past and make my compass legs go wider than they ever have. I am wearing seven-league boots even though this will take me past the school with its morning meetings in the airport chairs and its smell of divorce and unwanted gifts of perfume. Desperation makes me Mercury.

It is safe to cross to the traffic light on her side now because she is so far behind; there is no way she can catch up with me. She is thick with hysterectomy and puffy ankles; she is slow with a lifetime of sweeping. The light, the blessed light, greener than Gatsby's hopes and shinier than his cufflinks, says yesyesyes it will let me cross: I am Elsa the lioness, I am wings and wheels, I am the Little Engine Who Could.

I step into the traffic and have to step back again, with the whoosh of early-morning cigarettes and battered exhausts finding its way inside me. The light is red. And when I exhale all that I am empty; now I am my outsides, I am only tooth and claw.

She breathes in gleeful little pants behind me, with her shiny cheeks full of their venom and her horns hidden under her doek where no one else can see them, 'Jaaa! You always walk so fast and now the light has changed!' And I know that she's right and that this is it; mediocrity and middle age will get me in the end.

Pompeii

On the mountain there are fires. In the day there is always ash in the house; it sweeps through and makes everything grubby. It is a messenger. It tells us all how we will end up. The nights are impossible. Helicopters cannot fly over in the darkness and drop their containers of reservoir water. There is nothing we can do but watch the burning, like the world's biggest braai.

He is awkward; we have been fighting for days, in tune with the summer heat that has evaporated all our own reservoirs of affection and tolerance. He says, 'I don't know what I want,' which means that he wants to fuck other women. What can I do but divide the earth and the water, give him back to the sea?

He is a surfer; his mother says that he was conceived on the beach. I will be a landlubber.

Once we went out to the docks, climbed over the dolosse to get to the sea, and he paddled out on his board, long and thin, too, made to be in an element other than air. Overhead the seagulls wheeled. Did they think he was juicy? They followed him forever, waiting to see what he would do. Beside him in the water a seal swam hopefully, a smaller version of his oil-slick wetsuit, ducking and splashing as he whooped back to me where I sat girlheavy on the stones, thinking, This is a sign. God sent Noah a rainbow. Why not me?

So now I am choosing land again. Dry. Gritty under the eyelids. I have a new car dream. In this one the car rolls backward with me in the back. Without thinking, I reach between the front seats and pull up the handbrake. And that is that. No more dreams about being lost at the controls. Ta daa.

I live in hope, as I ought to, as missionaries do, ignoring the cannibal girls I know will soon come along, buttoning myself up in the tropics, knowing that I am being nibbled away from the inside. I am my own cannibal; this is worse. I cannot make myself go home in the morning.

My mother says that it is a constant source of consolation that our lives never turn out the way we expect. Gordon says that he doesn't want to be lonely. And what do I say? I don't. I am blank, I am the Desiderata, walking, teaching, trying to get my crying over with in the bath before school in the mornings so that the plates of my temper won't shift in class and cause eruptions that will burn, so that my anger won't turn all that I have made here in this separate world to ash. I drink a lot. I damp it down.

Last season at this time there were also helicopters in Newlands Forest, but they were a step ahead; they were spraying the forest before it could catch alight. Gordon and I had gone up there, sat in the long grass which always looks soft from a distance but is spiky and uncomfortable up close. Gordongrass. The buck were strange and unafraid. They crept out on their quiet hooves and waited for the helicopters to whirr overhead with the heartbeat blades beating in time to their own. The buck lifted up their heads and opened their mouths to the drops that sprayed down on them.

I have not been up there again.

Wildfire

I am itchy for something else. I want to be different; I may be pink on the inside but that isn't the only colour girls can be. I want my Braille in the dark not to feel like any other woman's, and perhaps this is a ridiculous want but it is my own. Other people have ways of marking themselves out; my mother has her birthmark but my differences are less obvious. I want to be able to communicate in another language and I don't think speaking in tongues will happen to me: my youngest brother is the miracle sibling and I am the Good Daughter. 'I never have to worry about you,' says my mother, 'I always know that you're just getting on with it.'

I go to the Purple Turtle because there is a tattoo parlour upstairs and I want to be marked. I want to be dirty and this is a good place for that. The men inside are drinking in the daytime dimness; their leathers creak as they hunch over the pool table. Why is it that they only come in freak format? They are shrivelled like peach pits or plumped-out like lilos; their dry bikerlips twitch to music with words in it. Perhaps it is because they are not normal that they have ended up here.

The steps wind up like a dreamtime Jacob's Ladder and when

I reach the top with my visions of being closer to the infinite I will also smell like singed hair and beer. Welcome. At the receptionist's desk they send me away. Wildfire has moved but I will track it down; I am determined to hurt myself.

At the swanky new venue coloured women in business suits choose Chinese symbols to threaten and charm away their lunch break. How can you be sure that they really say what they profess to? What if you have the symbol for Donkey emblazoned on your back? I wait fifteen minutes with the backs of my legs sticky. I want the Batman logo. It sums up the cartoon freakishness of the twentieth century, it symbolises the will to power and it looks kiff. Balanced. I like that.

I am called over to behind the saloon swing-doors, where the slinky seven-foot man gives me a Coke and makes me sit cowboy-style on the chair. I am excited to think that he will lay his hands on me. And then, Jesus, it hurts. Don't ever let them say that you get used to it. It feels like a red-hot knife being stuck into your flesh and repeatedly dragged down hard. Because it is. I think he took pity on me under those hot studio lights; he didn't colour it in. Maybe the sweat and blood were obscuring the canvas; maybe he knew he wouldn't be able to stay in the lines.

For ten days after that it isn't allowed to get wet. You have to apply Savlon twice a day. It heals nicely, oh see how I heal quickly, along with my notions of invisibility and other super-powers. I lie on my blood donation forms about my contact with needles in the last six months. I show my mother much later, who says, 'Oh Diane. Why did you do that?' in her patient voice.

I am at the hairdresser and he is talking to me about tattoos because his left arm is covered with a crucifix. Perhaps he got it when he was very young, I thought. He looks at my tattoo and says, 'Did you know that the bat is symbolic of transition?'

All Gold

Oh, and Gordon comes back, like he always does, saying that he was wrong, saying that if he were the marrying kind that I would be the one. I appreciate the effort of these words, but I do not believe them. His friend has already said that he dumped his new girlfriend because she ate tomato sauce with everything. In the interim he has been involved with this woman, the anti-me – slight, creeping, she wears a trench coat and smokes as much dope as he does. Even her hair is miserable. Why is that worse, that she was simply the first who came along? Perhaps it is because it is such a denial of everything that has gone before, such a conscious blotting out of all the hope and love. It says, You never existed. It says, Anything is better than you. It is the punishing voice from childhood. It is the empty space beside you in the movie theatre.

When I phone my mother she tells me, crossly, 'Diane, no one's asking you to *marry* this man,' and I think, That's exactly it. Freedom works for political prisoners but not anybody else. She tells me the story of the oak and the willow, of pride and storms and learning to bend, and while I understand the message, I want to say to her, Look where it got you. Always those double conversations with our mothers. They probably have them too. She says, 'Where did you get your stubbornness?'

Out on my window sill is the plant that Creeping Girl gave me when she went away. It grows green and leafy while all my carefully chosen babies wither and twist in on themselves. The cats chew the cactus. I do not have that gift that my mother has, of crouching on the haunches and paying attention to what the earth whispers. From your lips to God's ear, she whispers back to them. I do not have the patience for mulch, and decomposition appalls me.

I also try to block out the feminist theory, the idea that enough women have suffered this and learned from it for me not to repeat the pattern, but the trouble with love is that it blows you wide open; it leaves you with holes like a moving cut-out target in a shooting gallery, and the wind blows through. When the hand comes to pick you up again, you let it.

Calamine

I am hot under my skin; I only want to be with Gordon, who is leaving the country in a few weeks. The last night before I go on holiday to KwaZulu-Natal is long, buzzing with the sound of the refrigerator mumbling to itself in its steel brace. He switches it off because I can't bear its fits of rumbling even though everything inside will go bad. He giveth His beloved sleep. His room is alien with suitcases; they are moon craters we stumble into as we try to reach each other. There is not enough oxygen, no Sea of Tranquillity. We are numb with our good-byes and Jack Daniels. He shouts himself awake. I am not asleep yet; I have had a vision of a baby. I whisper that it's okay, and he says, 'But what if it isn't?'

The next morning he makes me coffee with Cape Velvet instead of milk. He kicks off his boxers and dances naked round the room. How strange this is, to love somebody outside myself. He says that he dreamed about babies.

He blows ants off me as I lie there; he lays a teddy bear on my hip, another on a pile of clothes. He says, 'They're there for my company. I hope they speak French,' and smiles.

Adeste Fideles

By the time we reach Hanover the steam hissing out from the bonnet cannot be ignored. We skid to a stop and find that Clare, ha ha, really has blown a gasket. We are trying to get away to Durban for Christmas, where there is the Famous Five house of her parents and presents waiting for us, where there is long grass that will squirt sweet into your mouth when you want something other than Old Brown Sherry and fruit cake. After the dust (*my end and my beginning*) and garage toilets without toilet paper there will be gardens and clean sheets. And plenty of toilet paper. Two-ply.

KwaZulu-Natal is a 3D fairy story, but it's hard to talk about something that is beyond, as the man said, any singing of it. Just as well; the only singing happening here is Massive Attack, thin and piercing because only one speaker works in the bakkie. You understand, finally, how small you are, how your collection of chromosomes is not special because it's yours, but because it has allowed you to be here. The gratitude of space.

Except at the Engen station. It is long and low, a laboratory for breeding mutant insects; it is the centre of a sticky flat universe. There are petrol pumps and a shop and a butchery. Fill up, fill up. Black people in Sunday dress buzz in to buy cakes for Christmas, thick with cream, while the smell of meat hangs over all. We are waiting here for the mechanic, we are bitten by mosquitoes; bloodsuckers both. We wait until the still sunset when the birds wheel up over the Engen sign; they are there in their thousands. They must know something we don't. Or maybe they've finally declared war on the mosquitoes, like an Aesop's fable. Clare says she feels like she's been beaten. My left ovary aches and aches. I ask her if she thinks it can be rotting, and she laughs at me. My insides are sore; my breasts especially are feeling strange and *round*; I hate it when men look at me.

We have to stay overnight in the only B-and-B we can afford, where there are chickens in cages and giant pointers that are angry with us until we let them put their paws on our shoulders and slobber brown dogginess into our faces. The air is lumpy with heat, buckled into itself and up our sinuses because there isn't enough space for temperatures this thick and dry. In the kitchen there is a chest freezer where we go to stash our water; the incredible notion of ice. Inside there are carcasses, locked together, unmoving. They had better hope the electricity never fails.

The only place in Hanover that has any expanse of water is the hotel. We march in with our towels over our arms and are met graciously because we are white; we are allowed to walk anywhere on the musty red carpets, but not, hallelujah, on the water. We sink into it like fat mermaids with our tattoos and underarm hair. My breasts lose their heaviness in the water. Here everything floats unless we sink on purpose, like Midas's daughters.

Night comes; it always does in the desert. We search out a restaurant. Feed us, it is the end of the day. And of course there is one, but this is the thing; the manager is known to us, a refugee from Cape Town out here in the Karoo with his linen tablecloths and his smooth gay waiters. And outside, oh, outside is a high-walled garden, with long grass and fairy lights twining in the trees like well-behaved snakes. The wind chimes jangle with our footsteps as we walk towards our sets of silver cutlery, our waiting wineglasses; the clinks of other diners in this secret space attend us. At some point we will have to go out into the dust and the hardness. But not yet.

Giant's Castle

They make us go hiking and I drag along, hating the idea of uphill, hating to break a sweat. Everything in the Midlands is extreme and I have to close my irritable eyes against it; the sky is crayon-blue, the air is too humid, like putting your face in bath water and accidentally inhaling. Breathing is a conscious thing, a fight not to panic. The mountains are so green they are children's songs, *Green, green, green, the colour of my garments*, so bright they make my eyes water in defence and recognition, Enid Blyton throwback thoughts. So this is what she meant.

There is plenty of uphill; we are climbing into the sky. We walk down, too, through grass that whips against our legs, the prisoners of pirates. After two hours there is a rock pool, slippery and cold, and we strip off, pink and brown walking the plank. I am prudish and prune-faced, won't take off my bikini, which is not green. It is blue camouflage. I am a sky-soldier, an unco-operative hostage. My body has changed. I can't pull my stomach in. Last night I dreamed that I was sitting at a table with other people, and Gordon sat next to me, rubbing my back, rubbing my stomach, the warmth of his hands drawing out the ache.

Up ahead the sky falters and sulks, lowers itself. Clare makes us hurry down the mountain; we are skipping stones before the mist comes down, next to the silvery river winding beside us all the way. She says it's so cold it takes your breath away; she says that it's so dense the best thing to do is to sit down, just like that, because you are disoriented. We'd be a Barbara Woodhouse quintet.

We make it down. On the drive back there is the mist that makes you want a cardigan. The Midlands. Never comfortable; always too wet or too hot. Those poor settlers, growing orchids in their greenhouses and fungus in their armpits. Clare's father says that only one of the British generals wasn't sent back home in a box, and he is buried here. A hundred metres away a rubbish dump has sprung up and a woman bends over something salvageable. Dogs skip merrily over it on their bone-thin legs; they look like they have already been skinned. This is the law: however much we may not like it, the dead must give way to the needs of the living. I wonder how long it takes a healthy corpse to stop being a health hazard. Skull and crossbones.

A little way off there is another graveyard, much more recent. There are some headstones, but mostly only planks nailed together to identify the heaps. At the entrance there is a guard-house, empty, as if we should ask the ghosts permission before we trip in here to violate the dead with our tanned calves, with our Nikes.

It is, of course, a mostly Zulu cemetery, absolutely silent with its red soil and plastic flowers under their plastic domes. No one tends the plots. Pretty standard stuff; I'm not sure why we have been brought here, but then we read the dates on the wooden crosses, some carved, some only in ballpoint. All the people in this cemetery were born in the seventies and eighties. My generation. And some are babies, less than six months old. And now I understand. The plague is here; it's arrived, and there is no escaping. Clare's father says, 'They can't dig them quick enough. They have to use Caterpillars.' What if we have to flee and wall ourselves up together, only the clean allowed in? What if we will have to spend eternity listening to each other's stories?

On the news people walk in the streets waving placards with AZT slogans on them and the president mumbles about depravity and disease. He is the only person who doesn't blink, even as his fellow parliamentarians drop from unspecified long illnesses in their ranks beside him, a trail of tears. Pregnant women march. The hinges of my back twinge; my ovary twinges. I am lucky to have those.

Positive

Back home Karen-the-doctor is pressing her fingers against my stomach and ovaries. She says that she's never heard of one rotting, but that there's definitely a swelling. Actually, what she says is, 'Jesus, Diane! How long have you had this?' and it makes me wonder if this is her usual bedside manner. It had better not be; she works in an HIV clinic in Guguletu and panic is not received well there. She calls up another doctor friend and books me an appointment at Vincent Pallotti. It used to be run by nuns.

We are at Karen's house, having what Catherine terms a Guess-Who-Might-Be-A-Mom party. I'm very excited. I have the pregnancy testing kit with me. It is my second because the first one couldn't seem to make up its mind, perhaps because it had absorbed the disapproval of the bald little pharmacist who sold it to me. I had to lunge over the counter to grab it out of his hands.

I want women around me for this part. The problem with using a test kit is that your hands shake when you pee, and you miss the strip completely. I leave it alone in the bathroom, this little stretch of paper like a runway. In my head it is lit up in lights. I want to drink wine but it might damage the tadpole that has made my Levi's tight around the belly. How ridiculous to even think this; there is no way this child will ever be born.

It's positive when I go back, of course, of course. But at least I know now that I'm not mad, that the dreams were right, that the body knew.

Tadpole

I call Gordon. He is swimming against the deadline tide at work; because he is leaving there is more to do. He doesn't know what to say. He hates other people's children as much as I always have. This wasn't part of the plan.

In the waiting room of the doctor's office there are notice boards smothered in baby photos. The messages all say, Thank you. Thank you. I feel guilty at what we are about to do, just let go of something that thousands of other people cling on to. What if they're the ones who are right? Gordon alternates between squeezing my hand and fumbling with the work he's brought with him. For the first time I feel like we're grown-ups.

The gynaecologist talks gently; she doesn't want us to choose right away. In her other room she leaves me to put on the gown. It is brushed cotton tartan, the stuff of pyjamas; it reassures me. She does the routine inspection, on the hunt for lumps. And then it's the old swab story; check for major diseases. Your body may be a temple, but that also means that strangers pass through it.

She says she feels something, but will have to do a scan. We trek to the next room to attach me to machines. Steel. Flesh. K-Y Jelly. This I didn't know: if you're fewer than six weeks pregnant, a vaginal probe has to happen. Lucky me. She cheerfully whips out a condom and pops it over the probe. And there it is, on the screen, barely enough to cause all the heartache that it has; the tadpole nestled in the grey of my insides. The glee squeezes up from my hips to my throat and I laugh with the surprise of it. Gordon is dazed; he already has one foot out the door.

The aching ovary is something that some pregnant women experience for the full term. But I have a growth there as well.

I am pregnant because there was a breakthrough ovulation. This baby wants to be born.

In the car there isn't much to say; we both know that there is only the freedom option. He says, wondering, under his breath, We've mixed our DNA.

One Size Fits All

I am taking Misoprostol every twelve hours. In a perfect world, in a perfect womb, this ought to send out anti-invitations to anything lurking there, saying, You are not welcome. In a perfect world this causes cramping and the equivalent of a heavy period, and voila, bye bye baby. I am waiting for the end of the world, and I don't know how REM can be so flippant about it. I think about how if I'm going to be punished for anything then surely flushing a live thing into the sewage system will cost me a zillion cosmic points. Stories of township girls leaving their newborns in the sewage down the long-drops make less sense. I start seeing the word everywhere, hearing it bumble from the lips of men to their women, baby baby.

The sessions don't work. It's still too small, says the gynaecologist. She prescribes another round of drugs, but those don't work, either. I spend my holiday lying on my back with a kind of heartburn in my ovaries, wanting other people to go away. Light hurts my eyes, as if God is taking my photograph over and over again, storing it away somewhere in a grey cabinet. I am In Trouble. Gordon comes to lie next to me with his arm over his face. He is scratchy; he says he doesn't want to get rid of it. What he does want is for his friends to stop calling him Daddy.

We take ourselves back to the surgery. We walk quickly,

toddling like time-lapse in a *National Geographic* plant epic. My vegetable love. We are growing. We are songs about Shaka and poems about mushrooms. We know that we have to make a hospital appointment. We are in shock. We. Never. Thought. It. Would. Happen. To. Me. We have to go to the Milnerton Clinic, because Pallotti's ghost nuns purse their lips and cruise the corridors, well-scrubbed women carrying out the orders of the Ultimate Man. Thou shalt not kill.

They make me wait in the ghastly gown; they make me wait in paper panties that say, One size fits all. Ha. When I ask, Will this hurt? the nurses smile softly with their heads on one side like budgies. Not love birds; they twitter in the empty corridors where the only other signs of life are women wheeling squeaky carts full of cleaning products. The light is too flat for us to cast shadows; outside is the sea, unsmelled, unheard under the hum of disinfectant. I am too nervous to lie down so I do some yoga stretches on the carpet while Gordon paces and looks out of the window. They won't let him smoke, this magic dragon. I imagine steam coming out of his ears instead. I tell him to go back to work; there is so much to be done. Oh Mick Jagger, how could you ever trick us into thinking time was on our side?

The anaesthetist comes to get me. He is someone's dad, sandy and gentle. He is also in a gown, but less of him is exposed. His arms stick out like a puppet's. My gynaecologist arrives and I am giddy-glad to see someone I know. The needle jabs into my arm, pins down my vein and changes my circulation. They wheel me away, unsqueaky, to a waiting area where I know I'm never going to fall asleep. He leans over me and holds my hand; he says, Are you sure you want to do this? I don't think he knows that whatever is inside me now will never be what I want. I am Sigourney Weaver in *Alien*, but she at least had a gun. I am Allie-the-Mongol's mother when she watched him reach his first birthday, still as wobbly and moon-headed as the day he was born. My last chance happened two weeks ago. Amen, amen, it shall be so.

When I wake up I am still there and I think, Hasn't it happened yet? But then I realise that my panties are missing. I never thought I would want them back. When I go to the ward Gordon is there. He didn't go back to work; he only walked up and down the beach, measuring the minutes with his feet. He tracks sea sand into the ward, he brings in the outside. Our friend Christian says women always find Jesus after they've gone out with Gordon. 'Either they need absolution, or else it just doesn't get any better.'

The next day he makes me go back to the beach with him, even though I only want to lie still. The water is so cold it slaps the blood back into me, beats me into salt and sand shape. I find myself on all fours in the warm shallows, licked clean. The sea takes me back and I can see my own shadow under the sun.

PART SIX
DANDELION

To Get to the Other Side

I am a winter chicken waiting to cross the Liesbeek Parkway, with a parents' meeting but no punchline to get to. The cars are mean and streaming past with their spoilt driverfaces stretched behind glass and their tyres, turning, and they won't let me pass. On the other side the grass is uncut and acid green like a Saturday morning before you have your appointment with Peter the Haircutter. I know that the grass looks like it would feel good to roll in but up close it is wet and canal-rank with mattress stuffing and stolen handbags.

I am late and I run across in my grown-up clothes; I am sick of surprised parents saying, Oh, you're so young! as if I am a cannibal – interesting to look at, but you wouldn't want one too close to your child. I am in diamond earrings and boots with high heels, a brothel madam in a cowboy movie, or an English teacher early in the evening, working herself up into titter and simper and pass the Glen tea bags, please.

There is the building site crew, with their animal mouths and subcutaneous fat. Kss kss. Hoe lyk it, baby? Ek en djy, naked! Give us a smile. It's never the handsome or smart or rich ones, hanging out of Porsches, waving notes in high denominations. Always these, hanging off scaffolding and garbage trucks, language acrobats and legends in their own heads, except the only one in spangly tights is me.

The pavement pushes uphill and stony against my boot soles; everything is against a woman who has forgotten her teargas at home. Behind me there is a man who is walking too slowly even for African Swing Time, hunched into his pants or maybe just short. Tonight everything is ugly, like in the mirror in *The Snow Queen*. I am trying not to turn because I will not show him that I am afraid, but the truth is that one mugging spoils it for all the other rainbow-talkers and time-of-dayers in this land of plenty.

I am remembering how it feels to have a twelve-year-old wind his thin t-shirt arms around your neck because you're walking the one block home at ten o'clock, and yes, it's dark, and yes, maybe that was dumb, but this is Kimberley before 1994 and you are singing the Guinevere chorus from the *Camelot* rehearsal and swishing your costume along the ground, pointy shoes and all. No wallet, no discernible breasts. What could he possibly want? Maybe only to know that a penis still counts as a traditional weapon. And when you scream he lets go because he's realised that this is not his neighbourhood, and meaty white men will come to find him. They surely will, thudding across the lunar surface of the tar; his smell will give him away. And he runs as other people's doors open and shoes are found. My keys judder in the door and my mother's wintermelon face looks up from the news and she says, Why are you so late?

All this must be in my own face when I turn round, because Stalker Man sniggers closer. I stop and he stops, and I do all the tests of the paranoid pedestrian. Here is Kader Asmal's house, and here is the steeple, or at least the doors and Labradors of houses I will never own. Everyone has a chimney except me.

He loiters close and breathes at me, smug in his maleness and opportunism, sure of his scare value. And this makes me very angry. I stop again and look for a weapon because, goddamnit, if he's going to hurt me it's going to cost him in dried blood and equal rights. I am Just. On. My. Way. To. A. PTA. And I don't even want to be there. The hand that cradles the rock. Oh, and I just want to use it, have that shivery pleasure of beating in the brains of a man so that he won't move towards me again, like the junior school times I rolled with my brother, hating him so much I was sure I was going blind, yanking his hair out and punching his body in all its soft parts. But I know that I'd never be able to get them all. Maybe this is what it feels like to be a policeman.

He looks at my rock and the way it fits snug in my hand, and my knuckles are whiter than the rest of me, and I am whistling. He laughs out loud now but he walks away. And I go on, Puss in Boots in the street and Chicken Licken inside the school hall. 'Ha ha, yes. I've been working here for five years now. No, I don't think you need to worry about Nabeela. Make sure she structures her time properly. She just needs to read more novels.'

Second Coming / Bobby Shaftoe

And ye shall hear of wars, and rumours of wars: see that ye be not troubled: for all these things must come to pass, but the end is not yet.

For nation shall rise against nation, and kingdom against kingdom: and there shall be famines and pestilences and earthquakes, in divers places. All these are the beginning of sorrows.

People begin to understand that if they want to get rich they have to do it elsewhere. They take their useless white degrees and their new Nikes with them. They have done one-year courses in management and IT and they think their shoulders can carry their Cape Union Mart backpacks over the Alps like Hannibal. They shave their heads and give away their spanking new e-mail addresses to everyone they know, and a few more besides, Hare Hare Krishna Krishna, and queue at the airport with their shining blue eyes. They are breathless, and so are their mothers, who stand behind the barriers and cry down their own shirts while the ghost midwives cut those messy red apron strings.

Gordon says, *I went because you don't expect me to find a job on the strength of a BA, now, do you? I went because somebody else was paying, because I felt I needed to get out on my own more, grow a little. My friends were studying more. I wanted to get stoned on foreign soil, remove myself from the clutches of family, get lost.*

Or I went because I could, because it sounds good, because God is dead. Because it was free, other people were going, because male bonding and family bonding were mandatory at the time. Or to find surf.

Because if I had been born two hundred years ago I couldn't have done it without getting seasick.

The airport mothers go back to their houses, and dust and dust photographs of hikes and graduations and think of baby teeth falling out, and their own teeth following soon.

Wherefore if they shall say unto you: Behold, he is in the desert; go not forth: behold, he is in the secret chambers; believe it not.

They reach their thin strong mother arms down the telephone to their bartending sons on Sunday nights, thinking, He wouldn't even tidy his own room when he was at home. Thinking, I wonder if he's eating properly? They listen to the hum of the wires and the split second lapse that accentuates the distance between them. They say, When are you coming home? They buy more indigenous plants and make rockeries in the garden. They buy birdbaths to tempt back fluttering things.

Watch therefore: for ye know not what hour your Lord doth come.

And the boys live in tiny spaces with other South Africans, asking for Castle in every pub they go to, wanting the taste of heat and light and photosynthesis in a place where there are only plasticky daffodils in damp sacred spaces. Everywhere there are suspension bridges that let them walk on water without getting even the soles of their feet wet.

There is skiing in the Alps, and there are string puppets near Wenceslas Square and always there is dancing and drinking and drinking and dancing with people they will never see again. And no amount of panting sex with easy German girls and desperate American women with United Nations of STDs between their thighs will help them forget that pointlessness and loss.

The old girlfriends wait by the windows. For a few months we suck our thumbs and hope, instead of working, with our minds like bees, angry and sleepy at the same time because we are being smoked out and left behind as the hive moves on. Will we be able to find it again? Bad TV and the sounds of Saturday night, going on without us in the street. We are not virgins, but we are wise and foolish, just the same. We try to keep our lamps burning.

But eventually we must also go out again, because there are stinging margheritas and Afro-Cuban sounds at the Curve, and our throats and hips are stiff and dry with storage. We loosen them up again. We keep our condoms next to the bed, and the men we pick up are all gleaming teeth and CKOne, and they know where the clitoris is. And still there is that emptiness, that early Saturday morning feeling, where we turn to the warm shoulder beside us and it doesn't smell right, like hamsters who have been handled by humans and now their mothers won't take them back.

And strangely, we learn to say *I love you* over the telephone, like an afternoon at the doctor's – tongue depressor, lab coat – saying, Does it hurt here? And here, does it hurt? Dr Seuss and Strangelove, Mengele and Freud: we are here in our thousands, without medical aid. We listened to you and this is where it got us.

Correctional Services

The clinic is always depressing, like visiting East Germany in the eighties. Except that communists have some sense of colour, at least. Here everything is painted in two shades of government-sanctioned pink, prosthetic pink for the walls and cabinets, with their locks painted over and their secrets stored inside; binnepoespienk for the trimmings. That is the point – to damp down those unruly desires that led us here in the first place. You vill not be aroused, ja?

Women sit on the hard benches, guilty and sad-eyed in their uncomfortable shoes. They wait, docile as cows, for injections, pills, tests, smears. There is no foot and mouth, no Mad Cow disease, nothing as traumatic as burning carcasses or smelling ash on the wind. They are not accident victims. There is nothing to do but wait, as appointments are not an option yet. The hours, as kept by all vital government institutions, are designed to cause the maximum disruption to a working day as well as create the desire to chew through the stubby furniture with frustration.

The staff move like Esther Williams to and from the wire racks where the cards are kept. Slow motion, drugged with banality and introversion. This must be underwater love. The women read the notices: TB! IT'S CURABLE!!! Number of Sisters on Duty: 1. The Patient Inside Could Be You. Please Be Patient. You will wait an estimated twenty-three minutes before a health professional will see you. We replay the scenes of the Night Before, eyelids flickering in our skulls like the experimental group in a sleep deprivation lab. The sweat and the smells of damp humans between sheets, on floors, outside clubs, leaving their stains.

Men do not have to do this.

The nurses are always smooth-haired and whistling like

Tweety Bird in his swing; their small pieces of gold jewellery are embarrassing in their meanness. Always too few of them, always trying to care in the face of all this humanity; weeping, seeping women wanting ways out.

Outside there is the sound of high heels, clicking sloppy and snappy over the cement, carrying hoarse women into the waiting room. They won't wait at the reception window, and the security guard is too scared to stop them. They stink of meths and not enough sleep; their skirts are thigh-high, and their knees are bruised; three of them carry sticks. I am trying not to stare. My white neckskin beams like a lighthouse. Their voices really *are* hoarse, like gravel. Men must be dragged over it daily. And then I turn and stare. I can't help it, and the thing is, they're not women. But they are prostitutes. With their long brown teenager legs and false lashes, they are more desirable as mutants than one-gender women could be. The middle-class will never be any competition.

But of course. Where else would they go but here? They sweep through across the thin carpet, scooping up the free condoms and wanting to see the doctors. They won't whisper. Like anti-fairy godmothers, they will not give you grace and beauty. But there will be fingers pricked. Oh yes indeedy.

They sit behind me and I think I can feel their eyes burning into my hairline, but that can't be true. Their eyes are so bloodshot they are hardly open; being drunk in the middle of the day is such a luxury. Everyone knows who they are; no Jenny Joseph poems for these ladies. Their breath is putrid; they pant and wriggle on the hard seat behind me, and I feel my teacherliness shine out like a flare. I know that their blowjobs must be celestial. And then, praise Jesus, it's my turn to go into the pink warren in the back of the clinic, where no screams ever come out, and I can leave them with the calm nurse who has leaned in to hear what one of them is whispering. 'Oh no,' she says, 'you're going to have to go to the hospital for *that*.'

Scale, blood pressure, Triphasal. I ask about an HIV test. The sister blinks like a bad strobe at a tweener rave and hands me over to an affirmative action doctor. The dynamic is strained: one of them is experienced but the other has the constitution on her side. They smell different – old roses versus CKOne. A duel for the possession of the world. Columbus. Cortez.

The pre-test counselling is protracted, as the doctor takes me through transmission and safer sex yadda yadda. I am required to nod at intervals. Her fat orange braids fascinate me. This person, who is about to let me know the scariest thing I have ever wanted to know, has seen too many Li'l Kim videos.

I expect uphill. Somehow there is always a certain amount of self-righteous posturing whenever the government provides a service to its citizens, but there is none. The strained doctor-patient vibe disappears. She leans forward; her lips glisten with gloss. She says, 'I know. I always ask my boyfriend to use a condom if he's with another woman. I can't be there ALL the time.' She shrugs, accepting that this is okay and I am appalled. This is the twenty-first century. I know. There is no real need for monogamy in any moral sense. Sex is just sex. But still.

It makes me shift blame. It makes me want to hate men, and women, with their hypocrisy and selective morality. Women don't stand a chance against these mothers' sons, in their sharp suits and piercing aftershave, who stand blithely on the fingers of their girlfriends and daughters and sisters, the same fingers that prepare food from nothing and give handjobs and hand out bootleg medication and iron new shirts in thousands of kerosene kitchens. And more. The slow cycle of normality and dish-washing, a kind of resistance to governments that are happy to spend R50 billion on arms deals, maybe. They got the guns, but we got the numbers.

It makes me want to think that this isn't me, that at least I'm not stupid. That I won't keep going back. Neither of the above.

No laboratory here, no waiting with stubby nails or hunchbacked little men in *X-Files* gowns. The test works pretty much the way a pregnancy test does, and if you don't know what that's like, be grateful. A sharp pain from the needle stun gun and my blood won't flow, as if my body is drawing up into itself to crystallise around my heart. If they cut me open, they would find no thoroughfare for oxygen.

They say fifteen minutes and in that time there are rubberleg trips to the toilet and wide eyes in the waiting room. And in that time, I realise that I don't really care what the result is. Trauma is a kind of relief – at least you know where you stand, even if it's in the air over Chapman's Peak, even if your legs are a cartoon flurry because the ground isn't where it used to be. If it's positive, I'm earning enough to afford triple therapy. There are some advantages to not being previously disadvantaged.

Around me there are fat brown boybabies, stomping around their mothers' legs, dressed like mini jazz bandleaders, and smiling, always smiling now that my nightladies have gone.

Nena, not Nina Hagen, and Pliny the Younger

Est dolendi modus, non est timendi.
(Grief has limits, whereas apprehension has none.)
                                        Pliny the Younger

I have to tell my classes that I will be away for a day, and they want to know why.

I find that teenagers are more supportive than adults are. Maybe they understand because they are also travellers in a dark space, where the torch is dead and the maps were made by people who already have cars. One of them jumps down from her perch on the desk and grabs my hand. I almost pull back; we are taught never to touch them, *in affection or in anger*, but her grip is surprisingly strong. Her hand is small and mani-cured; hours of filing during English lessons have gone into this pointy prophetess. She says, 'We'll come with you. We'll stand next to the bed. We won't let them hurt you.' It is this more than anything else that makes me want to cry, the uselessness of all my childhood comforts. No number of hands being held or nightlights being left on or second helpings of vanilla ice cream will compensate. I settle for putting my head on the desk as the bell rings.

The doctor tries to talk me very gently through what is about to happen, but I don't care. I know this will hurt and I won't be able to see what's really happening, in a 1950s mental asylum kind of way, where they'll help you as long as you promise to be good. Apparently I have stage two cervical abnormalities. To stop this developing into full-blown cancer they have to chop bits out. 'The scarring is minimal,' she says. 'And most women don't struggle with natural childbirth after this procedure.'

The stirrups are faux white leather; I stick to them. There are clamps and four local injections in the cervix, burning like wasp stings, burning like martyrs. I keep hoping that this is a lobotomy; I won't have to think. I shout out once, when there is an incredible pinching pain. I wonder if the women in the waiting room can hear me, with their out-of-date magazines and patchwork leather handbags, if it makes them sympathy-shiver. I can smell flesh burning, and then it is over. What shocks me as I struggle off the table is the drop of my blood on the paper towel below. Surely that's a risk. Surely that's not supposed to happen. There isn't enough latex in the world to protect me from my new and visible ills.

After that the fear is gone, cut out along with the baddie cells and let loose like the ninety-nine poison balloons left over from an eighties music video. I wonder where they will come to earth, who will pick them up, unsuspecting, take on these rubber skins, attach them to their own lungs or throat or prostate gland, or whether the cells just die without their host. But I have nothing more to be afraid of.

For days my eyes are blue-ringed as a Saturday morning cartoon crook's. But that's not all, folks. I feel like Frankenstein's monster. I feel like Scully. I have been given this chance to rediscover my body, to take it back and familiarise myself with its smells and soft parts. Twisting or bending makes me leak. The panic of not knowing when this will happen forces me to appreciate when it doesn't. I have spent a fortune in broken hearts and panty liners.

People ask if I'm better now, as if this is a pesky case of flu, and I want to say, 'Better than what?' But that would be rude. Talking about my cervix has made me different, as if the boundaries have shifted. It's hard to talk about your insides without sincerity. And there is a captive audience for post-operative princesses. I have to walk carefully and wear dresses, and I realise that all those Victorian gynaecologist-butchers had something going there. For docility and humility, you can't beat the old stirrups and EST.

Anne Boleyn

I am sick; I sweat and sleep for a thousand days, always with a headache pushing my hairline back until I am sure I look like one of the wives of Henry the Eighth, with their impossible foreheads and eyes that were dead way before a man got near them with an axe. Except that they probably never slept with a roll of toilet paper at hand.

In my duvet cave I spend the June holidays, troglodyte and teary. I remember only Clare sliding in next to me at night and sleeping very still, and sliding out again the morning after with the smell of her hair left behind to pacify me. It mutates into a longing for my mother, even though I know there is nothing she can do to help. Clare excavates, hi ho, hi ho, under mountains of crusty dishes, tunnels behind pots that haven't seen sweet morning light for a week. Growing moss, they are trying to adapt to being underground.

Does she find gold? There are definitely rubies, because my cough hacks into the Aladdin's cave of my insides and I start bleeding and then it just won't stop. Open, Sesame, and the doors of skin can't hold it back and I am Modjadji the Rain Queen, raining blood bright like food colouring, Rock Star Red, on to the bathroom floor and then when the lumps of tissue come I don't know what to do with them. I throw them in the bath. They are exactly like the liver my mother used to cut up before it was fried and hidden under bacon. I am disintegrating, it's finally happening. Red on white, Christmas comes but once a year. I am tired of decking the halls so I scream for Clare and she comes to me, disappointingly calm.

She mops me up; women are used to blood. She calls Wendy to drive me to the hospital (oh, they must be tired of seeing me there) and we wait in the lounge. Having been sick for so long makes my feet feel funny when I try to wear shoes. Suddenly I understand how easy it is to turn into an Owl House puppet, to stiffen into a statue; this is how goat-girls end up on living room floors. They just forget how to be human.

I pinch up the lumps into a Tupperware; I want someone in a white coat to tell me what they are. It feels like I have had my insides rounded out with a melon scoop. Who will eat me now?

Outside there is the sound of a woman screaming curses, somebody getting mugged outside the Alma Supply Store again. Probably some poor mama with her pay stashed in her bra, getting it ripped off her. Doors open and there is a man shouting now, and the sound of feet slapping the cement under the streetlights. For this disturbance we have just one ear each; we are Van Goghs listening only for Wendy-car sounds and we will not involve ourselves in anything else. The screams persist. The mama has a *very* foul mouth on her.

We rouse ourselves from our whiteness and womanness and slap our own feet down to see, and there is Wendy, shaking, at the top of the stairs, with her red hair blazing and her eyes like flames. It was her screaming all along. Three schoolboys grabbed her handbag on the way up to save me, a Benetton of badness, coloured, black, coloured. One had a cup of wine in his hand; he didn't spill a drop.

We can't stop now; we race instead to the hospital, where we jerk into a slow-motion sequence, something with a soundtrack because the radio is on and all the computers are down. The security guard, who is also the reception clerk, tells me that my medical aid will not cover this trip to the Emergency Room. This is Fawlty Towers, with hypodermic needles instead of sharp tongues.

Behind the curtains we can see a small boy with his hair stuck to his wet forehead. He is moaning that he wants to go home. I know how it is. A sweaty white-coat man hauls his bulk in behind the curtains with me and jingles them closed on their rails. He has a beer gut but I don't think he's bringing me gifts. I feel like we are going to take a shower together. We both need to; my thighs are all sticky and his fingernails are filthy. When I tell him that my biopsy appears to be haemorrhaging he wrinkles even further and says, very slowly, that he doesn't think he ought to give me an internal right now, and he waddles off to phone my real doctor. I am relieved; the man had fingers like pork sausages.

While I am healing at the Emergency Room, the police are cruising the neighbourhood and hunting down the two smaller boys. At the station they tell Wendy not to press charges; they beat the boys with what seems to be the leg of the table instead. The older one, Mister Smarty Pants, has escaped. He has all her belongings. The younger ones refuse to tell on him. They also want to go home. They make their eyes big at the policemen and plead and gibber, and out of the corners of the eyes they look at Wendy, long and low and full of hate, like crocodiles. Crocodiles who are bleeding now and will be bruised inside tomorrow morning. They wouldn't make good handbags; you need a flawless hide for that.

My doctor tells the nurses to tell me that I'm not dying; the sweaty man has taken a look at the warm Tupperware and said the lumps were not my liver. They try to make me pay for antibiotics I don't need. They make me drink water and sit on one of the plastic chairs. The thin sounds of the radio trying to tune us on to a happier, un-hospital wavelength suddenly link hands into a pattern I know. It's REM come to save me again and it's this part of the evening that makes me cry. *This sugarcane, this lemonade, this hurricane, I'm not afraid.*

The Fat Cactus

On Sundays the faithful lie in their beds and hear the bells calling them; we go to the Fat Cactus every Tuesday. We trip alongside the traffic in our red sneakers until we reach the desert cult where there are sunset margheritas out of the soft serve machine.

They serve chillies that chop off the tongue like a slave in a story who has to keep his master's secret; if you are not used to it you will never speak again. They play the Cranberries and Louis Armstrong, and of course the tequila song, and you are reminded of all the things you have never done. At least in this space the dreadlocked waitresses always let you have your sticky booth by the window so that you can look down and out at the antpeople on their multiple ways home. They will not be having margheritas.

I feel safe here. I know where the bathroom is. John Wayne is for the boys, with his dust and boots and lop-sided smile; Raquel Welch is for the girls, yes, naked. Perhaps women have their weapons built in already. They let us watch *Big Brother* on DSTV. As we drink and talk and drink and talk the fleshy girls on the screen drink and talk over our real voices. I know that after this we will drag home, wobbly and as full of good things as Christmas stockings in June. Everything is known; this is where the swing is, in the park, and here is the SABS building, which has more fences and bars over its eyes each time we go by. They must be testing something very scary.

This Tuesday there are many people in the low-ceilinged restaurant – the sweating soccer boys and the balding man with his tight jeans who looks us over, hope and guilt – whom we know enough to nod to but not greet. Boundaries must be maintained. The animals belong behind the fence and the visitors are only passing through. At the outside tables there is a girl in a sweater that looks just like Gordon's. It is enough to make me weepy; I am not over this misspelled word, this lost limb, this coffee mug left behind. I peer at her through the smeary glass, at her narrow back, at her damp hair. The sweater does not sit well with her rusty Goth skirts; it suited him better. And then I understand with a lightning crack of silliness. It is Creeping Girl. I never thought she'd be up in the daylight; in my head she is only a trench coat, a smoking mouth, wet fungus on a fern. She is also drinking a margherita. Who would have thought that our insides were the same? My stomach contracts until it is bitter like the lemons and burning like tequila.

And I have to speak to her, tell her about my insides and make her get a check-up. Maybe all that has happened to me will also happen to her. I think in flashes of my mother and the Postmasburg secretary. The tequila makes me brave and sleepy, that strange flutter of feeling as you're standing on the starting block, waiting for the whistle before you make a clean dive into the chlorine and race out. Stroke, stroke, breathe.

My friend goes out, waits for me feet away on the pavement with his eyes taking up all of his face. I go to Creeping Girl (I will not creep), lean over the railing. I don't know how to say this without making a scene, without looking crazy. I am tempted to do that, bubble and bob like it is when you get to the centre of a Fizz Pop sucker, stop pretending that I'm sane and everything is all right, once and for all.

But I don't. I can't think of the right word so I ask her if she was *seeing* Gordon. I have to repeat this; maybe my tongue is lazy with booze, maybe she is leaning away from this beggar; her coat-hanger shoulders are pointing the way out through the sweater. She says, Yes, and I tell her against the silence of the other three at the table with their faces craning towards me like dead sunflowers, I tell her as politely as I can to go and get herself a Pap smear. She doesn't push me away or even look at me strangely. Her body shifts back into her seat and she looks down at her blue cheese hands. She says, Thank you, and I skip off as quickly as my legs will let me, through the traffic, on to the grass verge that will take me back home.

On Tuesdays we go to the Fat Cactus. We know everyone who is there. Boundaries must be observed.

PART SEVEN
SAGE

Hotel California

My mother calls to tell me that the men in Kimberley are dying. In their fifties their bodies are giving in after all the booze, the dawn stumblings and the screaming in the kitchen. Maybe my father knew what was coming for him; maybe he chose the shorter, messier route. The Kimberley men are dying of cancer. The lungs or oesophagus or stomach, mainly, their insides giving up. Sometimes it is purely cirrhosis, their hard livers finally made the same way as their hearts.

My mother tells me the story of the man she knew who bought three coffins that he found in an old hotel, from the digging days, when a man might suitably decide to go out one morning and not come home. He bought three because they were cheap, and because it was a joke. He said that they would be for himself and his two best friends. And it turns out, oh yes indeedy, that he was smarter than he thought. Or maybe he knew all along, had a presentiment of the weird gathering they would have one evening when they all went out for a birthday and they all turned up, leaning on their wives with wrinkled necks and worried hands. With their colostomy bags they came, with their canes and the holes in their throats they limped and wheezed and joked about sex and fishing, and how the two were not that far apart. They spoke of water. One of them, with the face so dissolved by the cancer that he could no longer eat, told them that all he craved was biltong. One day his daughter, tired of hearing his sighs, fed him some, and the salt and meat crawled over his tongue, spreading its soft wash of saliva, until he almost choked and she made him spit it out. It is a terrible thing, he said, always to feel empty.

And of course they died after that, a cosmic sum. Reduce, reduce, reduce, zero. Within weeks of each other, trying up until the last day to get their wives to make love to them. It was, they claimed, a sure way to get the ladies on top.

What it has to do with me is this: I feel that I have escaped, that when I die it will not have been because my body was rotting from the inside out in a weird inversion of its functions. Of course I do not know this. But Kimberley seems to have its way with you, keeping you close until it chooses a way out that will hurt, will make you sorry for all the days and nights you spent drinking there, trying to damp down the dust. And we will never be able to do that. The closest we have come is growing mushrooms in the old mineshafts, where it is dark and damp and not at all like being above ground. They are big enough to be a shelter for the fattest fairy, and frilled like a seventies dress shirt. If you eat more than one of them they will make you sick.

Putting on the Ritz

I have always wanted to be here, at the top of a world which is populated mostly by old men in cufflinks and cheeky coloured waitresses who can flambé anything you ask them to. They lean on one hip, demi-devils with the lighter fluid, and make casual sizzling miracles as we rotate in this restaurant through the Sea Point mist and lights. They say it takes an hour and three quarters for a full revolution; what this means in real terms is that you have to watch very carefully to see when you move. You open your eyes after a glass of wine and the landscape has changed. But this happens everywhere, yes?

At the table there are Kimberley people. We have got to the

point in the evening where we are telling stories about when we have seen each other naked. I cannot remember a time when I have not known these boys. Everything has always been clear, and in its place, even if that place was only ever in the Big Hole or out of it. The opposite of the Ritz.

This Christmas another man fell into the Hole. I don't know how that happens; there are thick fences all round and only one point of entry if you squeeze under the viewing platform. Perhaps he heard the voice below of the singing rock Ntunjambili that opens to receive hurt creatures; black people say that all sad hearts are mended there. Perhaps he heard Diamond Lil and could not resist.

How big is the Big Hole? So big that it has its own ecosystem. So big that you look down on clouds of birds as they whoop to the exposed water table. An inversion. How appropriate. And yes, it is collapsing, very slowly. When I was little I used to dread driving past with my mother because I knew that one day it would all suddenly rush towards the centre of the earth and we would all be sucked in. No one from the upper world would be able to find us but maybe the devil would. That sounds silly, but I hear they've just moved the bus stop that was on the pavement outside. It was condemned. I am safe here in Cape Town; I will not be a lemming to ugly things in the centre of the country with that huge dark belly button and all its cosmic lint. Born in the heart and living on the fringe.

'Ha,' I say, 'I have never got naked with *any* of you guys.' There is a pause. Pierre fills it. 'Actually,' he says, 'there was that one time.' I am shocked into silence. I know he is wrong. He says, 'It was at your house. You were hanging up the washing. But you were wearing a nightie. And underneath it you had no underwear on. Every time you lifted up your arms, the nightie rode up.' There is clapping and hooting and Pierre saying, 'That'll take her down a peg or two.'

The strange thing is that I cannot remember it at all. It sounds unlike me. I don't wear nighties. The maid did the washing. I cannot think why he would make that up, and I'm fairly sure that he didn't; in his head there is a memory of my naked backside. So there goes my theory, my careful idea of how much I've let people see. Perhaps I have not escaped; even though the geography is different, the landscape hasn't changed at all.

Lord of the Flies

And there is a strange energy in the air, like the smell of biscuits baking. The heat and the sweetness makes new shapes in the ovens of our heads, it burns through the wiring and short-circuits the safety switches. The Matrics take up more space than they used to because they are leaving; they aren't afraid of us any more. They look at each other carefully. Something is coming, but we don't know what it is yet. It gives us headaches and frazzles our nerves.

In the morning before school they rip up their uniforms and paint each other in glitter, Bond girls whose pores will suffocate them. They scrabble for lipstick and jabber. There is garlic water in their pistols and rubber animal masks appear on their heads. Four girls are transformed. New and hairy, they reverse Dietrich's *Blue Angel*. They aren't blue and they aren't angels, but they are, thank God, instantly lock-jawed with latex. They sit extra straight and look around proudly with their new eyes and I understand that Kahlil Gibran was dead right about our children.

At the ceremonies and dedications, drenched in the monsoon of girltears and hand-squeezing, I look up at the gallery and there are four dry spaces where students are missing. And I wonder if they are at a boys' school somewhere, taking Humpty Dumpty revenge for the harassment and sulphur we have to endure every year, each pack of furry Matric boys thinking itself funnier, more cunning, than the last in marking territory. And I think, Ha.

At the staff meeting afterwards there is also an empty place but no one notices until it's pointed out; we are stiff and stupid today, thick with avoiding puddles of water and farewell. *We are not strong*, especially in the rainy season. We want to avoid anything that will make our mascara run.

The headmistress in her tweedy disapproval says that four of our Matrics put on animal masks and went into this teacher's classroom at the other side of the school, that they tied her up in front of her class. That they hurt her. That she struggled and one of the ropes was around her neck. That she has whiplash. That she cried. That they tried to strangle her.

Much later they emerge from the office where their gangster fathers are huffing and their docile mothers are regretting marriages where the genes will out. The girls' shoulders touch; they are docile. They are without their masks but they have not cried. I think, Columbine High School. Back in the classroom, where there are strips of material splashed all over, where the floor is a scene at a car accident, I ask, 'Why did you do it?' and their tongues are slow with sulkiness and fright. 'In the corridors. Every time. She always looked at us funny.' And I realise why I have been thinking of bakeries all day, of blackened figures splayed on cooling racks. It wasn't anything you would ever want to eat. It was the smell of bridges, burning.

Waking for the Barbarians

Stanley Baldwin had a theory. He said that the bomber would always get through. Sometimes this happens with an explosion that rockets bits of us into the far corners of the room, but sometimes it is something else, something nearer to us that turns out not to be as we thought. Last week Manhattan was on fire, and our notions of safety were detonated with it. The Muslim girls at school are upset. In History lessons they slam their fists on the desks and say, 'We're not all like that. Even though this makes us want to be. This gives us cause.' People are paranoid; we look both ways when we cross in the corridors but the painters don't stop their maintenance. They tripple up and down their ladders in cartoon time; in their hospital overalls they scrape off mildew and try to stop the damp spreading. Scalpel. Suture. There are lots of cracks, as if something is trying to get in from the outside. It is nearly Valedictory and this is why we feel under siege – because we are. The Matrics are leaving, and the million refugee Renfields from the boys' schools, with their balaclavas and bad chemicals, like to jump over fences, come to hunt down what has bothered them throughout their careers.

We see them climb over the gates, protected by their stocking features and rich fathers. They spray-paint poorly-spelled graffiti on our new-painted walls, and throw eggs at cars so that the yolks slide down into the grooves of the windows and can never be cleaned. Getting into your car afterwards is approaching the entrance to hell; the inside smells of sulphur. Perhaps they are trying to obliterate what they always want and do not have – musk and girlness, the smell of Bjork and her Eskimo picnics.

At first they run in three-legged races, with their PT legs pumping in lieu of their hips, and the girls run, high with the terror of being chased. But then ligaments and uniforms are torn and it stops being cute and funny and something-that-boys-do, as their mothers insist, waving their fingers which are strangled with gold like the necks of Nigerian women. And so the girls turn one day and fight back with hard girlfists and their steel-toed shoes. From the windows of the high towers of the staff room we hear Rapunzels lashing out, and the princes screaming.

They come back at night, when there are no girls. With weed killer they draw huge penises on the manicured lawns in the dark. The next day the rude girls drag the benches over these cave paintings and sit down extra hard, laughing at their own size-counts jokes. So much for terror.

The difference between boys and girls is this: by the end of the evening, girls know if they're going to have sex. There is another difference too. They know when to hold hands.

One manless night it is time for the farewell to the Matrics in the hostel. The older girls are heavier. In their grown-up satin and high heels they touch each other's kindergarten fingers, puppy fat and homesickness at last melted away under the smooth hands of the candlelight and the shiny nails of the strobe.

The theme is heaven on earth and for these three hours this is true: the girls are angels; their happiness is helium balloons. The waitresses with their enormous wings bring us Appletisers and appetises. The sugarplum fairy guests have all the food that can fill their greedy little hearts, and still we all float. Like the candyfloss in its packets banked on the pathway, like the cotton wool they will use after midnight to remove the shadows of their eyes.

The black angels sing, with their eyes like glitter balls and their voices cracking. Not the music of the spheres, but the music of the seers. They are brushed and braided into their wings, kwaito angels snapping their tongues like the elastic under their arms. Keeping their wings on, keeping it real, enough to dazzle any Afghanistan shepherd with their visitation of hope and adolescence and fresh-shaven armpits.

We see only this tonight, not the sweeping up and taking down that must follow the day after a celebration or a catastrophe. Moving on. The painters do their painting, and the rescue workers do their panting in the rubble of our dreams.

Arrive Alive

My mother phones me. Whenever I hear her voice my first instinct is to brace myself, to press harder into the couch behind me because there is always something heavy coming, something that will crack my skeleton if I don't prop it up, make my bones brittle with the osteoporosis of dread. Her snuffling replaces my own inhalations and my heart hollows itself a place below my sternum, where it will stay for the next month. That it beats is a miracle; that I breathe at all with this weight on my lungs is proof of God in the daytime, and strange comfort for the terrors at night. How the body goes on, something all the title tracks from all the *Titanic* movies in the world will not erase. And on the outside, despite these repeated visits from the Four Horsemen, we do not look like mongols or drunkards. We look the same. Because in death we are in life, and not just the other way round, as the priests would have it.

My youngest brother, miracle baby, sugar-talker, bird-charmer and school drop-out, has finally gone and dropped out of being sixteen altogether. He has OD'd on lighter fluid in his bedroom and choked to death on his own vomit.

I have always known that she would bring me something terrible this way, and now that it has finally arrived I find that Barbara Kingsolver is right, and all griefs *are* bearable.

Travelling long roads to get home allows you to transform yourself back into something your mother will recognise, her mother nose sniffing out your familiar shape and your baby scent of longing and belonging. Sniff, sniff. The years fly off us like the calendar pages fluttering down from the wall in those old movies. We are five-year-olds with the steering wheel under our hands.

Or maybe the ageing happens in the opposite direction, turning me into one of those ladies who worries about having padkos for the car, the train, the plane, who fishes out sticky peppermints from the innards of her handbag.

Black cows in the wheatfields are placid and earthbound as orthopaedic shoes, which is probably why they never featured much for Van Gogh. Their white bathtubs lie in the veld, the memory of clean. All around us are the colours of TV, anthills–grass–sky in pixels that make up reality television. Big screen. Oh, anything could happen in the space before we have to get to the confines of our new childhoods. Family is family, because no matter how bad you are, they always have to take you back.

In the orange light of a scrubby plot an old priest comes out to look at us as we scatter stones with our twenty-first-century tyres; his thick white vestments flutter with our dust as he looks over the ant children poking at things on the ground we can't see, guarding them from people like us, with our screw-top Coca-Cola and funeral suits hung up so they won't wrinkle. Too late.

We stop when our legs get stiff, although our minds are stiffer with the loss that won't go away, even when we have a Whistle Stop breakfast with the biker gangs. The cafés are features in the faces of the mountains; they suck us in. Always kak coffee and a gang of Hell's Angels with their dirty fingernails and creaking knees. They eat quietly; we dribble at the thought of bacon, of piggy strips cut down to size. Pink and white, to match the insides of our mouths.

Even Hell's Angels have mothers. A woman gets up to pay for their meal at the till. With her man's fingers she takes the cash out of her man's wallet. On the back of her jacket there are studs that spell out S-a-n-d-y A-n-n-i-e. And she is sandy. There is even sand that falls softly from her curly mullet cut; it falls like witches' tears.

The road is twisty and smooth; we are rocked by cars that won't slow down. In the Hex River Valley a truck has overturned and we follow the dark streaks on the tar, tracing the tyre marks and joining the dots of blood. We need no dice and games of car cricket; we know how it is to gamble. We know how it is to be beyond the boundary. We creep towards the truck on its side with the slow motions of people who learn from the mistakes of others: we know what we will see at a fresh accident scene. We will see ourselves in the skins of others, like a Doors song, like the Bishop in his mitre laying his hand on your head.

On the road there are limp bodies, red and streaky. Our hearts beat up into our throats; they block our swallowing so that we can't take in anymore. There are people standing in the road in lemon yellow holiday shorts and cameras. With their peeling shoulders and their blank eyes they are staring; they are scratching their heads with their hands that can still move. They turn around blindly with no road safety rules to hold them; no learner's test will help them. The driver of the truck is trying to heave one of the splattered bodies out from behind the truck. Its doors hang off their hinges; they cannot hold back the 3D darkness humming from its insides. I'm glad that they are moving the bodies; no one wants to lie in the dust without a box to hide them.

As we cruise by, with all our limbs and our round heads intact, we strain back to get in a last glance. We need to familiarise ourselves with dead people; we are on our way to see another one. We need to be able to speak with our fingers and hold warm people in our arms. We need to know these signs of stillness and sleep. We must practise.

The carcass on the road looks peculiarly rubbed and raw, and in the last seconds before it is past we see that it is some animal, underbellied and overturned. The refrigerated truck mumbles a soundtrack to the inverted slogan on its side. We Deliver Peace of Mind.

Breakfast of Champions

The kids, who are really grown-ups now but will always be the lumpy teenagers sulking at the Sunday lunch table, gather for breakfast at a long table outside the new bookshop. We are grateful to be able to leave the house where my mother's voice is everywhere, thrilling along the telephone wires, sending her sorrow out in little letter bombs that will explode when the careful fingers of her friends open them up. Bang. We shift and squeak in our plastic chairs; with our plastic mouths we try to reach each other with words that aren't small talk. We know that later we will not be able to eat funeral food, sticky and limp with shredded lettuce and ham (it's important to be pink and fresh, just like at the mortuary). Oh Enid Blyton, why didn't the Famous Five ever do funerals? I don't know what to do. So we must eat muffins now while our stomachs can unclench in the sun that glitters through the branches, on to the new baby in his pram and the Appletisers that will make us clean on the inside; it doesn't care what we used to be like, it glitters on us all. My brothers and sisters smoke. They check to see that their valves and passages are still working, that their cilia can still be frazzled, that their noses are not out of joint.

Under the trees we are made new; my sister's pug eyes retreating into her skull with calm, with motherhood making her care about something outside herself. Everywhere there is the notion of babies, of new things, of starting over and making up, of new funeral clothes and new funeral fingers. We learn our lives different; we see each other with eyes we've not used yet. Around the table we are the survivors; we grin and grin at each other, cheeks tight with forgiveness, with our second-chance hearts.

Pillar of Strength

In my mother's house there are not many mansions; there are too many of us here and the walls are thin between members of split families who haven't seen each other in years. I sleep like a sack of oranges on the couch under my quilt. It is a reminder that I have another life, intact, somewhere else where the TV doesn't blare because the cricket is on, and there is not the constant gloom of cigarette smoke by day and the thick green smell of funeral flowers at night. They crawl towards me in the darkness with their stems wet and needy, and I wait for my dead brother also to come crawling to me from his room that still smells faintly of his vomit, with his blue eyes red and more power as a spirit than he ever had in his lifetime of blood and bone. At one o'clock the surrounding dogs start their howling, singing him away with a funeral tune that curls the toes. But after that I can sleep.

In the garden is my mother's old compost bin; when she moves house it goes with her, a way for her to categorise the world into organic and artificial, dead, undead. Its patient smell underlies all.

The day before the funeral we rush around, polishing and checking and arranging our living parts – doctor, hairdresser – while he is in the mortuary having much the same done, being sewn up to keep his insides in after the autopsy. I keep my insides in by not thinking. The doctor's offices squat under the sky like a duvet inner, low, muggy, stained with our effluvia. In the waiting room there is a New Testament and Psalms on the glass table. Oh, I look to the mountains. *I am poured out like water, and all my bones are out of joint: my heart is like wax; it is melted in the midst of my bowels. I may tell all my bones: they look and stare upon me. Deliver my soul from the sword; my darling from the power of the dog.*

Every person we know stops and talks to us; their eyes are big with imagined sorrow and I picture their nasty raspy tongues flicking out to lick the horror off us. They taste us like snakes. 'You've been such a pillar of strength for your mother.' I think of Lot's wife. Sometimes being a pillar dissolves you. Her phone rings incessantly. The tone is '99 Red Balloons' and I think of all the hopes my mother must be releasing, all that effort and love with each exhalation, blowing her youngest child away from her and into the sky. 'Yes,' says my mother, starting off matter of factly until her voice climbs away from her mouth, into the air, higher than the voice of the smallest boy in the Drakensberg Boys' Choir and she croaks and whistles from pain, 'He was inhaling butane. Lighter fluid. All the teenagers are doing it to get high these days. What? It's cheaper than dagga. Anyway, he passed out and vomited. Yes. It was an accident. I came in and he was blue. With my knowledge of CPR, you know, nothing, I turned him over and all the vomit came bubbling out. When I heard that sound I knew it. The death rattle.'

We have to go to the mortuary to view the body. Inside the car my mother's perfume is so thick I can see it around her like an aura. It is holding her up but it is also making me nauseous. It winds up into my brain, coating everything with its sweetness and glue, the same things we will have to draw on in a few hours' time. My sisters' eyes are red and so are mine. 99 Red Balloons. We are a family made only of eyes, green and blue and brown made red and equal for the first time. He was the link between us. From now on we will have to forge it ourselves.

His father, my stepfather, is there in his brown suit. The secretary he ran off with is beside him. She has grown taller while grief and gout have puffed him and shrunken him simultaneously. He looks like a Rice Krispie, and if he is breakfast cereal, then she must be the spoon, curved and shiny. I think, I was afraid of this? This is the man who frightened me so much I could hardly speak for ten years? We step up formally to greet him, one by one, in order of closeness. He keeps his dark glasses on. For each of us his lips move against our ears as he hugs us. What would you say if you had the chance to go back and say one sentence to each of the people you had ever hurt? The man's heart has imploded like a fizzball in the bath of his sadness. It keeps trying to froth out of his mouth. Perhaps each of us will find a way to take him back.

The mortuary keeps out rot with tiles and ribboned flowers; like our house it is a jungle of dead things to be negotiated. He is lying in the inside room, full-grown in a man's coffin with its glossy veneer and shiny, shiny handles. I am afraid to peer over the edge; only his head is showing. They've covered the mangled autopsy with a white lace coverlet. How embarrassed he would be if he could see this. His face is also white and his lips are bloodless; they have been joined together somehow, but the red-rimmed inside shows where they tried to resuscitate him at the emergency room. He is a sunken cherub, like those photographs they used to take of the dead cowboys in their coffins.

I need to touch him, to make sure he isn't joking. We file past him. My mother strokes his hair and says, 'My baby. Oh, my baby. You can go now,' until her knees buckle and she crouches over her insides spilling out, from her guts to her eyelids. She is zipped into her clothes but underneath them her insides slither. I touch his forehead and his skin is so cold that it burns my fingers. I feel stupid for not thinking about the fridges (of course! In Kimberley the birds would start circling in the heat above the building. They always know.) and also so scared that I want to pass out. How terrible it is to understand that clichés are true. My stepsister steps up behind me and puts her warm hands on my hips. I am shocked; we never touch each other. There are distances that cannot be bridged with only the fingers. I lay my hands over hers and she cries her hot tears against my back. I am more grateful for that than I could ever tell her. She thawed me. Outside the birds are circling.

Tin-Tin in Kimberley

My mother has to go through all my brother's stuff. We trace his secret footsteps and are shocked because we think we know each other and have found that we do not. The dog had been vomiting every day for months. When my mother took him to the vet he wagged his Mickey Mouse tail but said nothing. The vet also could not say what it was. My mother reads an article in a women's magazine on the corruption of the modern teenager or some such rubbish, and decides that the dog's vomiting must be connected with whatever my brother had been inhaling. 'Petrol', she says, 'you don't just breathe in. You breathe the fumes out again. I always wondered why the dog didn't want to go into his room for the night. We had to lock him in there.'

She looks down at the dog. He grins up at her, healthy and lonely, a Snowy without a Tin-Tin. He won't sleep in the room with me. What adventures did they have together in that room at night? Lotus-eaters.

My brother's frightened friends tell my mother about his trips when she asks. They will only admit to dope. They thought he was funny. They tell her stories of the scrollwork on the burglar gate turning into tiny figures with their arms linked, which danced around him as he sat, blasted, in the back garden at two in the morning. 'Mom,' I try to tell her, 'that wasn't grass.' What I want to say is that it's Kimberley that catches up with you and makes you hate things, or makes you bored, or both. But it won't come out in a way that that will sound reasonable. So now she just tells people that I hate coming home. They laugh awkwardly and secretly think that I am ungrateful. And oh, it may be true.

People come by to ask for my brother's particulars; they want to keep his smell. In our forays into his room we find tiny g-strings and used condoms. My mother is not shocked; she says, grimly, 'At least he tasted *that* before he died.' Grief is strange and heavy; she carries it with her like bricks in a satchel. Afraid to hold on, afraid to let go. She says, 'I've learned to cry in supermarkets.' She has developed a strange growth on the left side of her neck; maybe the devil on her shoulder has burrowed under the skin. He says, You should have, You shouldn't have. The x-rays show it up as muscle. She has broad shoulders.

People come to the house with their own grief satchels; they unpack them on our lounge floor, their tales of lost sisters and car crashes, of sons decapitated (never stand up on the back of a moving bakkie) and retarded daughters who must be taught not to open the front door. Or they stand with their sad eyes like sacred cows, watching her move about the room. She has a problem staying still. Eventually my mother milks them. She draws out of them all these things, a milkmaid with her glass and a half of misery, a speaking Jesus with their flaming hearts on her sleeve. I can't possibly know what you're going through. Let me tell you what happened to me.

As they talk she thinks back to her wedding days, where she always wore pearls, and pearls, as everyone knows, are for sadness. In the evenings when they have gone she takes the kitchen scissors and snips off the rose bush tips; she calls them deadheads. She has no mercy. She watches them in their cycles and says, 'My period is a week late.' She laughs, and then cries. 'What if they just stopped from now on?'

Oral Hygiene

We cling to the shade of the jacaranda trees outside the church. Black is too hot. The purple blossoms drop to the grass, too tired to stay up. Inside them there are their bee buddies; you never grab at jacaranda blossoms. That beauty and terror. All the pall-bearing men are gathered away from us in their thick suits under the sun, not caring about being burned. Their ties have pictures of springboks on them, drinking ties, not dying ties, and that is the only thing they have in common apart from my brother. Two fathers, two brothers, two friends to carry him into the church where he refused to serve as an altar boy after he lost his God. These pall-bearers never thought they would have to do this; they could be gathered together for no other reason. The older men are swollen out like raisins in the hot water of their sorrow, fat with tears. Others are taller and shrunken, their flesh reduced in the fever of their sadnesses, evaporating off their bones under the kettles of their insides.

With my stiff knees and my stiff neck I pray to a God who's

moved away and left no forwarding address. My mother's preoccupation with going to a better place has always pissed me off, with the irritability of those with nothing to look forward to. She says, 'Ah, he's safe now. Nothing bad can happen to him any more.' I keep thinking, They raised him on Coke, that's what it was. Rotten with sugar. It made him a charmer but he didn't stand a chance. I am trying to find hooks to hang reasons on so that I can look out for them and not be caught. I will be vigilant. I sweat. The hooks I have found are not strong enough to support the weight of blame.

The priest drips sweat, too. How can he not? He talks about farmers and harvests, about how we do not receive full yields from the crops we plant, for all the careful love in the world. Oh, he smells of grief and sweat afterwards when he hugs me. It is bitter as fynbos, kept green by sorrow and hand-holding.

In the sober sandwich hall afterwards we stand and (*deliver*) receive the Sorries and I-can't-imagines and Your-poor-mother-ings. A chubby teenager with bits of bread in her braces bounces up to me and says, sunnily, 'I'm so sorry.' She says that she's my brother's girlfriend. It's strange. She doesn't look like the girl in the pornographic drawings we've found in his room. I ask her if his other girlfriend knows about her, and says, 'Oh yes, he broke up with her. I was the last one with him. She's been SMSing me to stay away from him.' Her braces glint proudly silver and black in the afternoon light. I want to mash her wet little lips against them.

At home his other girlfriend phones my mother five times a day. She lives in Pretoria, and her parents won't let her near us. She says he's been coming to her at night. She says that her posters rattle on the walls, and her cellphone falls off the night-stand. She feels a warmth in her chest when she talks to him, and it rises up around her mouth and all the places he touched her with his skin fingers. I stop myself saying that her crotch must be a goddamn *fire hazard*. She is waiting for him to call her and she wants to hear his voice. My mother wails into the receiver, 'Let him go! Please! Don't keep him here!' And I begin to understand that I will never pick up the receiver to hear his voice with its sixteen-year-old shyness and husk, saying, Hello, my sister, ever again.

White Wedding

And in the midst of this other people's lives go on, and I don't understand how, like that Carpenters' song. So why *does* the sun go on shining? Back in Cape Town, I have to be a bridesmaid for my best friend's wedding. In the weeks before there is the usual panic and the late-night phone calls to Lily Marsh, the florist whose name would be Marsh Lily if there was any justice in the world. There is talk of frangipanis.

In the afternoons her mother pins me again and again into a shimmery blue dress that dampens with my sweat. They want me to wear shoes with heels. I will teeter down the aisle with her, and God help her if she feels faint, because I won't be able to hold her up. We will subside slowly into the carpet, digging our heels in. Cold feet. I have been to weddings before, but never for someone I cared about. She is going away from me, to share a bed with a man and never be alone again. And the wedding tank rolls forward, smooth and loud, crushing the fingers of anyone who will be stupid enough to take advantage of the silence in the service to say, Yes, I object.

The rehearsal is also hot because the fans in the church are off. The priest stands there in his shorts and Jesus sandals that say, I am in God, and dress sense doesn't matter. I wish I could be like that. He makes me think of the tap in the middle of nowhere, on a farm in Schmidtsdrift, that produces water so cool and sweet-smelling that grown men who only drink beer will drive a hundred kilometres when the need comes upon them, with their tongues swollen beyond language, thick in their mouths. Kombuistaal. Perhaps the water is this way because this is the place where the army cordoned off the Bushmen until they needed to use them for trackers. Perhaps if you live in a tent your whole life walls don't make sense any more. Perhaps your sorrows seep underground to the water table. You learn to sniff out the wet places; you learn to swell your cells into fat shapes that will sustain you.

In the pews the two raggedy families sit in their summer clothes, saying, 'When do we walk out? Must we hold our hands like this?' and I want to cry because in the air between the two lovers there is a thickness, a memory of water, a halo of tenderness that bypasses grumpiness and nausea, a love that clings to the legs and won't let you out the door.

Eskimo Kiss

In the hot actual morning everything clicks into wedding-place and Barbie-time – bodice, hair, make-up, so that there is a space for her to swish down the corridor of her old house with her skirts in her hands, singing loudly and nervously, 'Here comes the bride, all fat and wide,' while our childhood expectations and adult realities bump noses in an Eskimo kiss and everyone else scrabbles for their corsages and waits for the bathroom.

In the living room there is a chest-high arrangement of white flowers (oh, for weddings and funerals we send them like animals into the ark, as protection, as preservation); they are proud and perfect and smell of money. They are from the maid.

In the church they've put the fans on at last; they sweep out our last-year lusts. In my hands there are frangipani flowers bound tightly into their sticky green suits. They smell of weddings in the southern hemisphere, saying, I do, I do, to Capricorn and wet armpits. Down the aisle in kitten heels. We pace ourselves; we can only go forward. There is father handing off, there are vows remembered, and there it is. And this is no Eskimo kiss. This is full lip and future promise. Full body contact.

All through the afternoon there is the familiar wedding miracle of water into tears, into champagne; it flows for clarity, it flows for relief. It fizzes in our faces, it washes people down the driveway and into their cars where they will drive, unsteady, to their homes as the sun goes down. They will be grateful for their children. They will remember how their husbands looked on their wedding day.

Upstairs in the hotel room the new husband and wife are in shorts; they sit, dazed in their pale flesh; they sit in the middle of the wrapping paper because no man is an island. It is their Hallmark cocoon. What will they be when they emerge from it all? We sit also, best man and bridesmaid, and he lets me curl my toes against his chest. Underneath his muscles are slick and warm, like one of those anatomy books where the pages are transparent and each one reveals a new organ, a different layer. And I know what will be underneath even that. I let him give me a lift home though I know we will not end up there.

He drives, fast and numb, up to the cable car station in the dark. Even the policemen, smooth and greasy as bricks of medium-fat margarine in their vans, do not come up here, where the lights of the houses and sports fields blink sleepily below and the sea blows its fish breath in through the windows. It is a water world, and their tyres won't grip. God, how beautiful would it be if all the dry bones of the telephone poles burst into blossom right here? Callmore time. Time to heal, desire time. Reach out and touch someone.

We twist round and round and up and up, like a stick of rock candy or the road to the Tower of Babel. Perhaps he will teach me to speak in tongues. Other cars are parked along the way, and there is never any movement; they may as well be empty but we all know what's inside, we can count the breaths because we take our air the same way.

We are out of the car, talking of rape and beating, as we always do in a hurt country, as we always do when we don't want to be afraid of what is waiting for us in the bushes, cracking its knuckles. If we say it then maybe it won't happen.

The engine is warm under the bonnet, ticking like a suicide bomber loitering outside his building, ticking under my legs. And then he has pulled me around to his mouth, oh yes, and then our shirts are off and I am not afraid. Under the dead stars we face each other, and I understand that our warm bodies go on and we need to be there with them, we need to be in them properly to know how it feels to be me. I don't know what this means in the long-term. What this means now is that I am grateful that he has a mouth like a litchi and lateral muscles that spread into wings; what I am grateful for is that I can get out of my damp blue dress.

Place of Doves

I am home for the holidays, where for the first time in my life I will be an only child. My mother is taking care of me in a way she never used to; she is tending me like a plant. I hope I will not turn out to be a Venus Flytrap. In the mornings she wakes me by rubbing my back; I am learning to touch people, too. She wants us to go to the cemetery and look at the crematorium. She wants to see where they burned him, but I do not. I think of that teenage flesh blackening like pork rind as we bump over the ruts in the red cemetery ground, some of it fresh-turned and sown with dragons' teeth. There are separate plots for the N. G. Kerk and the Baptists. *Só ken God se kinders mekaar / aan die reuk van ons truie / aan die weemoed in ons oë.*

And of course there are no billows of smoke above, like the skirts of some Victorian monster, bustle and crinoline roiling in the sky to cover up what is happening inside; no clouds of smoke to alert the villagers on the other side of the fence that all is not as it may initially have seemed at Auschwitz. It is long and low and rectangular, a Lego brick ready for other bricks to be attached to it as more people die faster of their long illnesses than before and there are more bodies to burn, even though they are thinner than they should otherwise be. A man who burns bodies for a living will soon have money to burn, too. So the building lies quiet and pink, a Turkish Delight with extractor fans, powdery and cloying in the distance behind its razor wire. Quiet. Who would possibly want to get in?

In the middle of the Jewish graveyard there is an anteroom. If you peer through the wrought iron of the doors the air inside is blue with the light shining down through the glass; it is the only cool spot in a burnt space. It is quiet, as it should be, and spades lean against the wall and rust and rust to themselves in the stillness. This room is the colour of heaven and you cannot go inside. Outside the old man bends and creaks to pull up weeds from between the licorice paving stones. Even the dead need to floss.

My disappointed mother drives me to the church. She wants me to see my brother's ashes. 'He's up there,' she says, and points to the columbarium. He has a window all to himself. We plead for the key and make our dusty way up the spiral staircase. The ropes for the bells dangle down, hairy and thick with their own importance, and they make me want to jump and hang on to them like Tarzan used to do and jingle and jangle the high tunes of our ears right out of our heads so there will be no listening any more to the scales of my mother's constant sorrow in the afternoons.

But instead we go up. I tuck my dress into my panties. I am still alive. Like a Pearl Jam song. Like a cockroach the day after the bomb. My mother says, 'These stairs killed his two fathers when they came to settle him in.' She says, 'His father groaned his way up, and the next day he was flat on his back. The doctor had to come and give him an injection just so he could walk.' He has to have a hip replacement. We are both quiet, thinking of why a man in his fifties would need one of those, thinking of his secretary, and all those women on the road. 'It was your brother's revenge,' she says and laughs at herself.

We are left alone, bricked in with the other collections of bone and ash. I expect to see skin lampshades, or bars of soap, but there is only this pink brick room, still raw even though the cathedral must be a hundred by now, still raw, which is right for a womb tomb as this is. The late sun lights up my mother as she paces; like a giant pair of rose-tinted lenses it shades every name she reads, exclaiming at the ones she recognises. She says hello to the dead and I pick up my brother in the mini coffin.

Some of the others even have teeny silver handles. If Jesus was a carpenter, this isn't going to impress him. The casket is heavy with wood, but not with what is inside. Dust only, so that a golem could be reconstituted if there was a rabbi foolish enough to make one, come to eat ghetto children or at least the ones who have to sleep in their dead brother's room.

The ashes shift when I shake him, but there is no rattling. They must throw away the bits that won't burn; he was always stubborn. And there is no tricking me. I know all about how they save the bodies up because it's not worth stoking the fires

240

for just one, and of course they are all mixed, so at the end all you have is dry mulch. Bone is good for gardens. My mother looks at me and she says, 'Ah, sweetie, it really doesn't matter. What we're left with isn't him.' And I feel silly, because I know that she is right. I am not used to this, but she is. My mother has started over again and again; with her trowel and her wheel-barrow she makes something out of nothing. And she understands that everything is useful. Especially compost.

She leans against the bricks, glowing pink like she is inside a rose quartz (for healing, they say, for proximity to angels) and stares out of his window, to where the high altar is inside the church, while I look for live things in the columbarium. There is nothing. Even the fish moths are dead. The alley of ashes, the anti-garden. My stepfather was horrified at the neglect, at the bird shit and dust, but my mother thinks that the columbarium should be left to wildness and ruin. The place of doves.

She sends her own Noah messages out on her cellphone; she needs to make contact, and his girlfriend SMSs back. It's a month today, she says. My mother looks slapped. 'I haven't been counting,' she tells me, and then subsides. 'You know it was too late for the last rites. I didn't want him out there wandering in the darkness. But then I think about what they said.' And I remember what that was. We do not worship a god of time.

The Importance

The driving instructor takes me to a tarmac parking lot. 'I can't drive,' I tell him. He says he knows, and this is precisely why he has brought me here. Ernest explains the logistics of it. It seems easy enough, the bits about plates rubbing together; I can do tectonics. It's the gearbox I can't negotiate. 'You can feel it,' he says, and tries to show me how to change gears with only the soft webbing of my thumb or else the very tip of my middle finger. I understand how it is *supposed* to work; it's just that I can't concentrate on all the things you have to do at the same time. We cruise up and down the tar until I am sure I have worn a groove in it like a Scalextric car but when I look back there is nothing.

The next lesson is in Pinelands, a kind of Mini Town where everything that they have in real-life traffic situations is there, only quieter. The drivers have better manners, or perhaps it is only the idea that road rage can happen that keeps them in their seats behind my tortoise crawl at the stop signs. I think of my mother who always tried to tell us that the clutch and the accelerator worked in conjunction with each other. 'Smooth,' she said, 'like a seesaw. Your father taught me that.' These things I must remember: mirror, indicate, gear, blind spot. If only Meatloaf hadn't made these into a godawful song already, they might be part of the framework for the next world religion. And that would make Ernest the high priest. He has a metal plate in his skull, he says. He worked for the Traffic Department for twenty years.

It does get easier. You have to concentrate but eventually these things become muscle memories, like a swimming stroke or a piece for the piano, part of you if you do it often enough. And Ernest says that I am a smooth starter.

Epitaph

This is where we are now: I still live away from my home because everything there is a slow smothering and I cannot go back. My mother has chosen to live on there, holding the pillow over her own face. We both still cry into them sometimes. The uglinesses and the proud scars are a topography of a kind; our bodies show us what our choices have meant, how well we are in the mornings – see, here there was an excavation, look, just like Doubting Thomas, put your fingers in the spaces that are still warm (like that poster they used to have up on the wall at the Star of the West, of the naked woman whose body was also a golf course. On the curves and dips of the She Gulliver the little cartoon men stood; with their pencil golf clubs and knobby knees, with all the traditional weapons in the world they could not ever hope to be as whole as she was).

But we don't ask just anyone to feel us up, to wade through our waters and emerge dripping like the seals that follow Gordon when he surfs. And this is where you come in. Think of yourself as having felt up my family, as having skinny-dipped under our surfaces.

Alice Walker said that one day all the people who were alone as she was would gather at the river. And there, in the darkness, perhaps we would know the truth. It's a nice idea but don't just believe her, either. Remember that in our bathroom cabinets there is more truth than anything writers can put on their outside faces. Ah, and now, it's time for a home-base happy ending, isn't it? A miracle cure, a snake-oil surprise, where we rise up from our emotional wheelchairs like Christopher Reeve. Over the tarmac at the airport, maybe, Gordon will come to me, with his arms wide open and the sky in his eyes. That used to be my starlight-starbright wish, but now I'm not sure. What if he turns out to be only human? And what happens when his travelling shoes start tap-dancing under his bed again, pittering and pattering into the Pinelands night?

So I will wish instead for my mother to stop longing for the infinite and to understand that there is no tea or tablet that will give her second wind or second sight. I wish for her to continue to bend down in her evening garden. She will say as she always does, 'There is nitrogen in hail. If your plants survive, it's really good for them.' Even though her knees will start to stiffen, her heart will not. And while I'm here I should probably wish for these things for myself, too.

And this is where we are now: I am sitting in this armchair, changing. I can feel it zing up like a relaxation exercise, from the bottoms of my feet to my stomach where it curls around and around like a dog making a soft place in the weeds, trampling my intestines, all the way up to the elevator of my forehead, and it will burst out of me like Halley's Comet, trailing faint stars as small children in their sleeping-bags look up and go, 'Where is it? Is it here yet?' Or maybe it feels like this to me, but it's really just a faint glow – I won't hide my light under a bushel – that can be seen even in the daylight, like a nightlight left on so that I never have to be afraid of anything ever again.

This is what I hope will happen.

This is what will happen: every morning we will make our beds. Every evening we will lie in them. Under the covers we will hold our breath and wait for the sound of hoofbeats. The Four Horsemen will soon be here again. It's nearly time.

Or perhaps I have been wrong all along; it's hard to see how many of them there are here in this light. They could just as easily be the Three Wise Men. They will be surprised to see a man of spectacles and suspenders instead of an evening star, but that's only because we've traded constellations for satellites, and it's true. Knowledge is King.

Glossary

bakkie – light delivery van or small rugged-terrain vehicle, used mainly by farmers

bakore – protruding ears, typical of Dutch descendants

bankie – a small plastic bag of the sort used for coins

biltong – dried spiced game meat, usually springbok, equivalent to beef jerky

binnepoespienk (vulg.) – a deep pink colour, literally the kind of the inside of the vagina

boep – beer gut

boeremeisies – (Afr., lit. 'farmers' girls') indicating rural and hence unsophisticated background

braai – barbecue

broekies – literally from the brand Brooks; knickers

dagga – marijuana

doek – headkerchief, worn by domestic workers but also old Voortrekker types and coloured people in South Africa

dolosse – triangular Escher-like cement structures used to break waves at beachfront or docks; urban legend (but not a certain reviewer, darling) has them taking the name of their inventor

dooswyn (vulg.) – means 'cunt' but also 'box'; cheap wine in a cardboard box in this context

duiker – small antelope

fynbos – Cape wildflowers and scrub

jammerlappie – damp cloth used to absorb spills at table

kaffir takkies – canvas high tops, usually North Stars. Cheap in the eighties, now required skater/hip-hop wear

kiff – (Moroccan Arabic slang, lit. refers to marijuana) as an exclamation has come to mean 'good' or 'cool' in South Africa

Klipdrift – brandy drunk by farmer types

knobkierie – sceptre-shaped club

Koeëlskoot (kop) – bullet wound (head)

kombi – minibus

kombuistaal – used in this context as a pun. Literally, Afrikaans is a 'kitchen language', used by servants

kwaito – African rap/hip-hop blend, from Afrikaans word 'kwaai', meaning angry or dangerous

Langneus – (Afr., lit. 'long nose') racial characteristic used to insult white people

mielies – maize

moffies – male homosexuals, usually camp

okes – slang for 'men'

opsitkerse – (Afr., lit. 'courting/sitting up candles') used by Afrikaner fathers before electricity to regulate time spent by potential suitors who came courting their daughters. The young men were allowed to remain in the house (usually the kitchen) until the candle burnt itself out.

oudoos (vulg.) – (Afr., lit. 'old cunt') old-fashioned, dowdy

padkos – (Afr., lit. 'road food') snacks bought for travelling plaas – farm

poes (vulg.) – cunt

pula – Botswana currency denominaton; literally means 'rain'

sjambok – whip

slaan-my-vrou – (Afr., lit. 'beat my wife') brandy and Coca-Cola. This macabre nickname refers to the aggression this drink engenders; formerly drunk by white trash who have now defected to Red Bull

soek[ing] 'n man – look[ing] for a man, on the prowl

sonbesies – cicadas

spanspek – rough-skinned, sweet melon

stoep – porch, veranda

swartoog – (Afr., lit. 'black eyes') intimate, sexually loaded comment on eyes

takkies – trainers, sneakers

Tassies – red table wine made from the dregs of more reputable wines. Surprisingly palatable.

toyi-toyi – group African dance, used on ceremonial occasions and in protest demonstrations; has come to indicate celebration as well as defiance

vingertaal – (Afr., lit. 'sign language') also used lewdly, 'finger-speaking'

windgat – (Afr., lit. 'windy arsehole') show-off, braggart

witblits – (Afr., lit. 'white lightning') moonshine, illegally brewed domestic alcohol, usually about 80 per cent proof